THE SERPENTS
OF
HARBLEDOWN

Also by Edward Marston

In the Domesday Book series

The Lions of the North
The Wolves of Savernake
The Ravens of Blackwater
The Dragons of Archenfield

In the Nicholas Bracewell series

The Queen's Head
The Merry Devils
The Trip to Jerusalem
The Nine Giants
The Mad Courtesan
The Silent Woman
The Roaring Boy
The Laughing Hangman
The Fair Maid of Bohemia

THE SERPENTS
OF
HARBLEDOWN

A NOVEL BY
EDWARD MARSTON

VOLUME V OF
THE DOMESDAY BOOKS

ST. MARTIN'S PRESS ❧ NEW YORK

Map © 1998, Mark Stein Studios

Library of Congress Cataloging-in-Publication Data

Marston, Edward.
    The serpents of Harbledown : a novel / by Edward Marston.
       p.   cm.
    "Vol. V of the Domesday books."
    ISBN 0-312-18021-7
    1. Great Britain—History—William I, 1066–1087—Fiction. 2. Delchard, Ralph (Fictitious character)—Fiction. 3. Bret, Gervase (Fictitious character)—Fiction. 4. Middle Ages—Fiction. I. Title. II. Series: Marston, Edward. Domesday books ; v. 5. PR6063.A695S47   1998
823'.914—dc21   97-34838
                                         CIP

First Edition: June 1998

10 9 8 7 6 5 4 3 2 1

To
Elizabeth Peters
Scholar, scribe and friend
Fellow toiler in the scriptorium of history

. . . the way of a serpent upon a rock; the way of a ship in the midst of the sea; and the way of a man with a maid.

PROVERBS 30.19

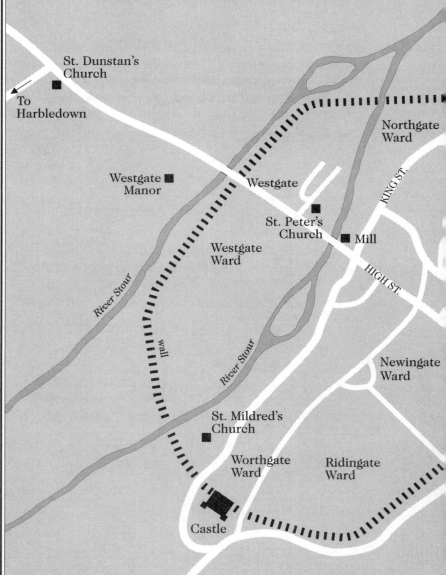

DOMESDAY CANTERBURY

St. Dunstan's
Church

To
Harbledown

Northgate
Ward

Westgate
Manor

Westgate

KING ST.

St. Peter's
Church

Mill

Westgate
Ward

River Stour

HIGH ST.

wall

River Stour

Newingate
Ward

St. Mildred's
Church

Worthgate
Ward

Ridingate
Ward

Castle

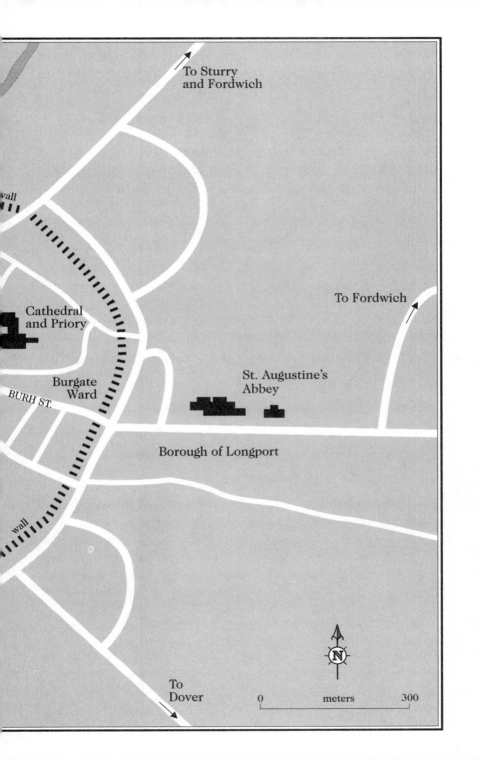

✒ PROLOGUE

THE SEARCH BEGAN at dawn. It was led by Alwin, the distraught father of the missing girl, a big, brawny man with a dark beard fringing his weathered face. No sleep had relieved his anxiety that night. He simply stood at the open shutters and gazed up at the heavens in mute supplication. Alwin was an experienced sailor. He had endured hostile elements a hundred times in his small vessel and shown the routine bravery of his occupation. But he also had the strange fatalism of the seafaring man.

"She is gone, Brother Martin. I know it."

"Do not believe that," said the monk with a consoling hand on his arm. "Have faith, Alwin. We will find her."

"Alive or dead?"

"Alive—God willing!"

"Why did she not come home last night?"

"We will chide her with that very question."

"It can only be that she was prevented by force."

"No, my son."

"Bertha met with some terrible accident. I sense it."

"Be calm. There may yet be another explanation for her disappearance. The girl is young and sometimes headstrong. Adventure may have directed her feet farther than she intended to go. Finding herself lost, Bertha sheltered for the night and is even now taking her bearings."

Alwin was beyond comfort. "She is gone," he said with a shudder of resignation. "My daughter is dead."

They left Canterbury as the first faint beams of light were being heralded by cockcrow. Alwin strode purposefully along but the ancient monk kept pace without difficulty. Time had robbed Brother Martin of many things but it had left his vigour untouched. Beneath the black cowl of the Benedictine Order, his sinewy legs had a tireless rhythm. It was in the wrinkled benevolence of his face that sixty years had scrawled a larger signature.

He sought in vain to soothe his companion with words. "She may have spent the night with friends."

"Bertha made no mention of it to me," grunted Alwin.

"What if she met someone on her way home?"

"That is my fear, Brother Martin."

"Someone she *knew*," said the monk. "A chance encounter with a close acquaintance. They fell into conversation, time raced by, the friend's house was nearer than yours . . ."

"No," insisted Alwin. "Bertha would have sent word."

"Has she stayed out before?"

"Only once."

"With whom, pray?"

"Her aunt. In Faversham."

"Then that is where she is now," decided Martin with a surge of hope. "Instead of returning to Canterbury, she first went on to visit her aunt. Bertha is in Faversham. Even for legs as brisk as hers, it is a tidy walk and left her no time to get home before dark. Is this not possible, Alwin?"

"Possible," conceded the other. "But unlikely."

"Why?"

The question hung unanswered in the air. Alwin's gaze had been distracted by a group of figures conjured out of the gloom. They were waiting at the base of the hill and stiffened at the approach of the two men. A voice rang out.

"We are ready, Brother Martin."

"God bless you, Bartholomew!"

"Tell us what we must do."

"First, we will offer up a prayer."

"Who are they?" whispered Alwin, looking around the faces that now took on shape and character.

"Friends," said Martin.

"But I do not recognise any of them. Do they know Bertha?"

"They know that she has gone astray. It is enough."

Alwin was touched. There were over a dozen of them. Three monks, two novices, a priest, a woodcutter, a shepherd, a couple of yawning boys, a blacksmith and three men with vacant grins, whose distinctive garb and pungent smell identified them as swineherds. All had heard and all had come to help in the search, asking for no reward beyond that of finding the girl safe and well.

Brother Martin led them in a short prayer. Brother Bartholomew, a square-jawed monk in his thirties, gave Alwin an encouraging smile.

"Take heart, my friend," he said. "We are with you."

"I thank you all."

"Brother Martin will teach us where to look but you must lend some guidance. We know your daughter by name but not by sight. Describe her to us that we may recognise Bertha, if and when we find her."

"As assuredly we will," added Martin. "Alwin?"

They waited a full minute as the tormented father wrestled with his tongue. It was ironic. In the midst of biting rain and howling tempest, Alwin never lacked voice. When his boat was tossed helplessly on the waves, he would rant and curse for hours on end. Put his own life in danger and his defiance was ear-splitting. Yet now that his daughter was at risk, now that he was caught up in another crisis, now that he had equal cause to hurl profanities at a malign twist of destiny, he was numbed into silence. Shrugging his shoulders, he threw a helpless glance at Brother Martin and the monk came to his aid.

"Bertha is seventeen," he explained. "Tall, fair and as comely as any young maid. Dressed in a blue that matches her eyes and a white wimple. Thus it stands. Bertha gathered herbs for me yesterday and brought them to the hospital of St. Nicholas, as she had done many times before. She talked with me then lingered to speak to my charges, for she is the soul of compassion and her very presence is a medicine to the minds of our poor guests." He took a deep breath. "At what time she left Harbledown, we do not know but one thing is certain. She did not return to Canterbury by nightfall."

"We searched," said Alwin, finding his voice at last and eager to dispel any suspicion of lack of paternal concern. "Brother Martin and I searched in the darkness with a torch but it was hopeless. We need daylight."

"You have it," noted Bartholomew, as the sky slowly cleared above them. "And you have several pairs of eyes to make best use of it. Let us begin."

Alwin nodded with gratitude. "Spread out," he urged. "Move forward together. And I beg of you, search thoroughly."

They fanned out in a line that covered well over a hundred yards then ascended the hill with careful footsteps. Most of them used a stick or a staff to push back the brambles or prod among the bushes. One of the swineherds had brought a mattock and he sang tunelessly to himself as he hacked a way through thick undergrowth. A long iron poker was pressed into service by the blacksmith.

Alwin and Brother Martin were at the centre of the search party, moving upward either side of the track which Bertha habitually used on her way home from Harbledown. Trees and shrubs offered countless hiding places but none disclosed any trace of the girl. Progress was slow and painstaking. A shout of alarm from one of the novices brought them all running but Bertha had not been found. The boy had simply stumbled on the half-eaten remains of a dead dog. When the line formed again, they picked their way steadily on.

Morning dew glistened as the sun took its first full look at the day. Birdsong covered the hillside. Far below them, Canterbury had come noisily to life and carts trundled into the city with produce for the market. Alwin searched on with mounting desperation, his fear now mixed with a scalding guilt. As they got nearer to the crest of the hill, he felt as if his heart were about to burst asunder.

His mind was a furnace of recrimination. Pain forced him to drop down on one knee. Brother Martin came across to the stricken father at once.

"What ails you, my son?" he asked.

"Nothing."

"Is the sorrow too heavy to bear?"

"I am well now," said Alwin, struggling upright again.

"Rest here awhile and leave the search to us."

"No, Brother Martin. She is my daughter. I must be there."

The old monk saw the haunted eyes in the grim face.

"Is there something you have not told me?" he said.

Alwin winced then shook his head firmly in denial. He could not share his thoughts even with the kindly Brother Martin. Remorse was stifled. Using his staff to ease back some bushes, Alwin continued the search.

Appropriately, it was the leper who found her. Nobody had even noticed him, emerging from the trees like a ghost to join the end of the line. He was a tall, stooping figure in a leper's cloak with his wooden begging bowl and clapper dangling from the cord at his waist. His head was enveloped by the hood and his face shrouded by a veil. The sound that came from his throat was high and piercing, like that of an animal caught in a snare.

Pointing with horror, the leper was standing beside a clump of holly. His withered hand seemed to feel no pain as it pushed through the sharp leaves. He let out another cry before shuffling away in the direction of the hospital. By the time they reached the holly, the leper had vanished.

Bertha was there. Lying on her back in the moist grass, she looked at first as if she were sleeping peacefully. Her apparel was slightly torn and soiled but there were no marks of violence upon her. The ring of faces watched as Alwin pushed his way through to her. Torn between hope and despair, he crouched beside his beloved daughter.

"Bertha," he called softly. "Wake up, Bertha."

He reached out to shake her arm but a sudden movement in the grass made him draw quickly back. Gasps went up from the watching group. A long, thick, gleaming snake darted from the shadow behind the girl's head to make a bid for freedom. One savage blow from the mattock killed it instantly but its venom had already claimed a victim.

The telltale marks of fangs showed on Bertha's exposed

neck, dark spots of doom on white alabaster innocence. Alwin collapsed in tears beside his daughter. Her young life had been snatched away by one of the serpents of Harbledown.

⤴ CHAPTER ONE

MARRIAGE HAD DEFINITELY mellowed him. There was no outward difference in Ralph Delchard but his attitudes subtly changed, his manner softened perceptibly and he even became acquainted with such virtues as patience and consideration for others. A quiet wedding had suited them both. He and Golde exchanged their vows in the tiny chapel at his manor house in Hampshire. Gervase Bret and Aelgar, the bride's younger sister, were among the handful of witnesses, though a service of holy matrimony before a large congregation at a cathedral could not have bound the couple more indissolubly together. Ralph and Golde found an even deeper contentment. Only one shadow lay across their happiness.

"I am eternally sorry, my love," sighed Ralph.

"You have been saying that since we left Winchester."

"Had my wishes prevailed, we would never have stirred out of Hampshire. Nor out of the bedchamber. The delights of marriage are there to be savoured to the full."

"They will be."

"Not while we are riding across three counties."

"The King's orders must be obeyed," said Golde.

"Even when they countermand our pleasure?"

"Being with you is pleasure enough, Ralph."

She held out a hand and he squeezed it affectionately.

They were on the last stage of their journey into Kent, riding at the rear of the little cavalcade as it wended its way between trees in full leaf, hedgerows in their summer radiance and wildflowers in colourful abundance. Sheep and cattle grazed on rich pastures. Orchards blossomed. The warm air clung to them like familiar garments.

Golde looked around her with wonder and approval.

"Kent is one huge garden," she observed.

"That is why we have been sent here," he said sourly. "To pluck up weeds. To cut back brambles. To clear away stones. I yearn to be a lusty bridegroom and am instead employed as a royal gardner."

"I will wait."

"You will have to, my love. So will I. The King's acres must be tended." They rode on in companionable silence for a few minutes, then his shoulder accidentally brushed hers. He turned to smile down at her. "Are you happy?"

A deliberate pause. "I think so," she teased.

"You only *think*? You do not feel it in your bones?"

"It will take time to grow accustomed to the shock."

"Shock!" he exclaimed. "Becoming my wife was a kind of shock to you? Is that what you are saying?"

"I never expected to marry a Norman lord."

"No more did I look to wed a Saxon brewer."

"Then we have each surprised the other."

"That is certainly true," he agreed cheerily. "We are a portent of the future. Enemies blending into friendship. The conqueror reconciled with the conquered. The wolf lying down with the lamb." He gave a wry chuckle. "When time and the call of duty permit him that joy."

They were seventeen in number. Apart from the newly-weds, there were twelve men-at-arms from Ralph's own retinue, a vital escort through open country where bands of robbers and masterless men lurked in wait for prey. The sight of so many helms and hauberks, moving in disciplined formation, would deter any attack and lend status to the embassy when it reached its destination. Sumpter horses were pulled along on lead reins, though most of the provisions they carried had already been eaten on the previous day.

Ralph usually rode at the head of the column to set the pace, lead the way and attest his status. Pride of place on this occasion had been yielded to Canon Hubert, face aglow with missionary zeal, voluminous body overflowing and all but concealing the little donkey who toiled so gallantly beneath its holy burden. Behind Hubert was Gervase Bret, the shrewd young lawyer, riding beside the gaunt figure of Brother Simon, who sat astride a horse almost as frail and emaciated as himself. Plucked from the cloister against his will and suffering extreme embarrassment whenever he was thrust into lay company, Simon had nevertheless proved himself a loyal and efficient scribe to the commissioners.

Though a wedding ceremony had absolved Ralph and Golde of the sin of cohabitation, and made their love acceptable in the eyes of God, the monk still found the mere presence of a woman unnerving and he preferred to travel in the wake of the huge undulating buttocks of Canon Hubert rather than risk any contact with the gracious lady behind him. Simon also drew strength from the friendship of Gervase Bret, whose intelligent conversation was a blessed relief after the robust mockery to which Ralph Delchard often subjected the monk.

Hubert goaded a steady trot out of the hapless beast beneath him. Ordinarily, the canon was a reluctant traveller who punctuated even the shortest excursion with a series of harsh complaints but he was now beaming with satisfaction and making light of any bodily discomfort. He tossed words of explanation over his shoulder.

"Canterbury is not far away now," he said excitedly. "I long to meet my old friend and mentor. Archbishop Lanfranc will be pleased to see me again."

"He holds you in high regard," said the admiring Simon. "And with good reason, Canon Hubert."

"I was his sub-prior when he held sway at Bec."

A memory nudged Gervase. "Was not Abbot Herluin the father of the house in your time?"

"He was indeed," confirmed Hubert, "and held the office worthily. But he was much troubled by sickness. Abbot Herluin was the first to admit that it was Prior Lanfranc who gave the house its spiritual lustre and its scholastic reputation. That is what drew me to Bec as it attracted so many others." A fond smile danced around his lips. "I revere the man. He is an example to us all. A saint in human guise."

Scattered copses thickened into woodland before giving way to pasture and stream. Canon Hubert pointed with almost childlike glee at the hill which came into view in the middle distance. It rose sharply toward a straggle of thatched cottages. Nestled cosily into the hillside, like a cat in a basket, was a small stone church with a steep roof and windows with rounded arches. Wattle huts were clustered below it in a crude semicircle.

"Harbledown!" announced Hubert. "That must be the

leper hospital of St. Nicholas, built by the archbishop to care for the diseased and the dying."

"A truly Christian deed," remarked Simon.

"Poor wretches!" murmured Gervase.

"They are all God's creatures," said Hubert with brusque compassion. "Lanfranc has opened his arms wide to embrace them."

He feasted his eyes on the scene. Buttered by the sun and stroked by the soft fingers of a light breeze, Harbledown looked tranquil and innocuous. The little church with its makeshift dwellings was a private world, a self-contained community with a charitable purpose. The hospital of St. Nicholas seemed completely at ease with itself. As they rode up the incline, the newcomers had no idea of the sorrow and the turbulence within it.

Alwin was inconsolable. As he lay facedown in the nave, he twitched violently and beat his forehead hard against the stone-flagged floor. It was all that Brother Martin and Brother Bartholomew could do to prevent him from dashing out his brains. They clung to the tortured body as it threshed about with renewed wildness. Alwin would not be subdued.

"Peace, peace, my son!" urged Martin. "Desist!"

"Remember where you are," added Bartholomew sternly. "This is the house of God. Show due reverence."

"Bertha would not have wanted this, Alwin."

"Think of your daughter, man."

"Put her needs first."

"Spare yourself this rude assault."

"It will not bring her back."

"Hold, Alwin!"

The grieving father suddenly went limp in their arms. They rolled him over on his back and saw the blood streaming down his face from the self-inflicted wounds on his brow. At first, they thought he might have expired, and frantically sought to revive him, but he was only gathering his strength for a long, loud, heartrending howl of anguish.

"BERTHA!"

The cry brought him up into a sitting position and he saw his daughter not five yards away. It set him off into a fresh paroxysm and the two monks wrestled with him once more. The dead girl lay beneath a shroud on the cold and unforgiving stone. Rough hands had carried her into the church with astonishing gentleness. A boy had been sent to the nearest farm to beg the loan of a cart so that Bertha might make the grisly journey down to Canterbury with a modicum of comfort and dignity.

The search party had dispersed and gone its separate ways. There were souls to cure and pigs to herd. Only Brother Martin and Brother Bartholomew remained to struggle with Alwin. Both monks were now panting stertorously.

"In God's name, I beg you—stop!" gasped Martin.

"Mourn your child with decency!" said Bartholomew.

"This is unseemly, Alwin!"

"Madness!"

"Calm down, my son."

"I want to die," hissed Alwin. "Leave me be."

"No!"

"I have nothing to live for, Brother Martin."

"But you have."

"Let me go. Let me follow my daughter."

"We will not!"

"No," added Bartholomew, tightening his grip. "To take one's own life is a sin. To commit such a sin before the altar is an act of blasphemy. You will not follow Bertha this way. While she has a Christian burial, you will lie in unconsecrated ground. While she soars to heaven, you will sink into the pit of Hell. You will spend eternity apart from her."

"Is that what you want?" challenged Martin.

"Think, Alwin. *Think.*"

Alwin stopped trying to fling them off. Gleaming with sweat and dripping with blood, he sat on the floor and took the measure of their words. The impulse of self-destruction which had overwhelmed him now weakened beneath the power of reason and the fear of consequences. What would be gained? What purpose would be served? Would his gruesome death really be a suitable epitaph for his daughter?

He allowed himself to be soothed by their kindness and persuaded by their argument. When Brother Martin fetched water to bathe his wounds, Alwin did not complain. When Brother Bartholomew helped him to stand up, he did not resist. The fire in his veins had burned itself out and a cold dread had settled upon him.

Alwin looked down sadly at the body of his daughter. The shroud concealed her but the marks of doom on her neck were a vivid memory. She had left the world in agony.

"This is a judgement upon me," he said.

"No," insisted Martin. "This was not your doing. Bertha was called to God. Only He knows why."

The father made his simple confession before the altar.

"I killed her," he affirmed. "In a sense I killed my own daughter."

The weary travellers conspired in their own deception. They were so relieved to see their destination at last that they invested it with qualities that were largely illusory. Viewed from the hilltop, Canterbury appeared to them to be a golden city, its great cathedral of white stone dominating the prospect with massive towers at the west end, topped by gilded pinnacles, and a central tower at the junction of nave and choir that was surmounted by a shimmering seraph. The adjoining priory, with the same arresting style and the same generous proportions, reinforced the sense of magnificence and authority commensurate with the headquarters of the English Church.

Shops, houses and civic buildings clutched at the hem of the cathedral precinct like children around their mother's skirt. Small churches served the outer wards. On the glistening back of the River Stour, mills had been built to make use of its swift passage through the city. A high wall enclosed the whole community with solid reassurance. Outside the ramparts, the newly built rotunda of St. Augustine's Abbey displayed a gleaming whiteness. Canterbury seemed to throb with religiosity.

Canon Hubert was transfigured. His bulbous heels kicked more life into the donkey and it went scurrying down the hill with its precarious cargo. The rest of the cavalcade followed at a more sedate pace. After passing the church of St. Dunstan, they rode on to Westgate, went under the cross above it and entered Canterbury. Disenchantment set in at once.

Its rowdy populace encumbered them, its haphazard streets confused them, its filth disgusted them and its stench invaded their nostrils with a suddenness that took them unawares. They quickly understood why Lanfranc had broken with archiepiscopal tradition and built his home outside the city in the cleaner air of Harbledown.

Canterbury was a dirty, smelly, boisterous place which made few concessions to order and tidiness. Luxury was cheek by jowl with squalor. Fine new houses stood beside the charred remains of old ones. The neat little church of St. Peter was surrounded by beggars. The bridge at the

King's Mill was littered with offal. Knights and their ladies wore bright apparel among the dull homespun of most citizens. Market stalls were laden with food while skeletal urchins searched the ground for scraps.

Ralph Delchard observed it all with a mixture of curiosity and disappointment. There was a pervasive air of neglect and decay. The majestic cathedral was a pounding heart in a rotting body. Gazing at its stark contrasts, Ralph was struck by the thought that Canterbury had not yet fully accepted the Conquest. After twenty years, it still reflected an uneasy and unconsummated marriage between Norman power and Saxon resentment. The thought made Ralph slip an involuntary arm around Golde's waist.

Disillusion made no impact on Canon Hubert. Alone of the company, he was inspired by what he saw and bestowed a beaming condescension on all around him.

"We have reached the Promised Land!" he declared.

"Yes," said Brother Simon meekly. "But I had hoped to find more milk and honey awaiting us."

"There is food for the soul," chided the other, adjusting his paunch with a flabby hand. "That is true nourishment. Look inward and praise God for his goodness."

Ralph trotted to the head of the column and called a halt. It was time to separate. During their stay in the city, Hubert and Simon would be guests at the priory. The men-at-arms were lodging at the timber castle which stood outside the wall. Had not Golde been with them, Ralph and Gervase would have joined the soldiers, but his wife had such unhappy memories of staying in a similar motte-and-bailey structure in York, during their last assignment, that Ralph sought alternative accommodation.

He, Golde and Gervase made their way to the home of Osbern the Reeve. It was a long, low, timber-framed house in Burgate Ward, occupying a corner site which gave it greater space and significance while exposing it to the passing tumult on two sides. Ralph had severe reservations about taking up residence in a Saxon household but most of them vanished when he met his host.

"Welcome!" said the reeve, answering the door in person and bowing politely. "I am Osbern and it is a privilege to offer you the hospitality of our humble abode. Step inside, pray. A servant will stable your horses and fetch your belongings."

The visitors were conducted into the solar and introduced to Eadgyth, the reeve's wife, a plump but attractive young woman with a shy smile and a submissive manner. Osbern himself was fifteen years older, a short, neat, compact individual with a well-groomed beard. His tunic and cap gave him a touch of elegance and Ralph admired the precision of his movements. The reeve exuded a quiet confidence. He would be helpful without being obsequious.

What really appealed to Ralph was the fact that Osbern spoke in Norman French to him, revealing an easy command of the language of his masters. Refreshment was at hand and Eadgyth went off into the kitchen to supervise it. Her husband took the opportunity to show his guests to their chambers on the floor above. Gervase Bret was tactful. Conscious of their need for privacy, he took his host aside so that Ralph and Golde could have a moment alone together.

The chamber was small but spotlessly clean and the bed was invitingly soft. Ralph held her in his arms to place a first long kiss on her lips.

"At last!" he said.

"Are you glad that I came with you?"

"I am in a state of delirium, my love."

"You must not let me become a distraction."

"That is exactly what I hope you will be."

"You have obligations as a royal commissioner," reminded Golde. "They must be fulfilled."

"Even royal commissioners are allowed to sleep."

"Then I will do my best not to keep you awake."

He grinned happily and reached for her again but the hubbub from the street below came in through the open window. Ralph closed the shutters to lock out the disturbance. He embraced Golde in the half-dark and kissed her with the ardour of a bridegroom. She responded with equal passion and they moved closer to the bed. Before they could tumble into it, however, a booming sound rocked the building and reverberated around the chamber. The bell for Tierce was chiming in the nearby cathedral.

The sudden noise made them leap guiltily apart. Golde recovered at once and burst out laughing. Ralph did not share in the amusement.

"The Church has come between us," he said bitterly.

It was an omen.

ᘓ CHAPTER TWO

GERVASE BRET MADE good use of his time alone with his host. He plied him with questions and garnered an immense amount of valuable intelligence about the city. Born and brought up in Canterbury, the reeve had an intimate knowledge of its people and its administration. He volunteered information freely and was clearly impressed that Gervase was able to speak the Saxon tongue so fluently. Osbern would be a key figure in the work of the commissioners, summoning witnesses before them, giving advice on local customs and generally supervising their activities in such a way as to make their visit at once pleasant and productive.

The two men came back downstairs to the solar.

"Our first dispute concerns land in Fordwich," said Gervase. "It sets cathedral against abbey."

"Then you must brace yourself," warned the other.

"Why?"

"Passions run high between them."

"Indeed? With two such intelligent parties, I hoped for a fierce legal debate but one conducted in moderate tones."

"There will be no moderation, Master Bret."

"Oh?"

"Cathedral and abbey are already locked in combat. A property dispute will only add to the ferocity of that combat. Take care that you are not caught between the two warring factions."

"What is the nature of their quarrel?"

"The election of the new abbot," explained Osbern. "St. Augustine's Abbey was a place of holy zeal and contentment under the late Abbot Scotland."

"Tales of his enterprise reached us in Winchester."

"Then you will know how selflessly he dedicated himself to his mission. When he came here, the abbey itself was in a sorry state and many of its monks were wayward. By the time of his death, Abbot Scotland had rebuilt and refurbished the house and imposed the Rule of St. Benedict strictly upon it. He was deeply loved by all and they mourn him still."

"I see the problem," guessed Gervase. "The new abbot is a lesser man than his predecessor."

"That is inevitable, Master Bret. They would never find another Abbot Scotland. The monks were resigned to that."

"Then what is their complaint?"

"The successor, Abbot Guy, is being forced upon them."

"By whom?"

"Archbishop Lanfranc."

"That is his prerogative."

"They are challenging it."

"In what way?"

"Every way at their disposal," said Osbern. "The abbey is in turmoil, as you will soon discover."

"Why is Guy so unacceptable to them?"

"I do not know, Master Bret."

"You must have heard the gossip."

"It is too wild to be taken seriously," said the other with a noncommittal smile. "In the heat of the moment, even monks will use intemperate language."

"Yes," agreed Gervase ruefully. "I was once destined for the cowl myself. I know that holy brothers can bicker every bit as violently as simple laymen. But how will this argument be resolved?"

"Who can say?"

"What is your own opinion?"

"I take no sides," said Osbern cautiously. "It is not my place to be drawn into this battle. All I wish to do is to forewarn you of its existence."

"We are most grateful."

"It will add heat to your deliberations."

Gervase smiled. "That may be no bad thing."

Golde came back into the solar with Ralph Delchard. She was still wearing her travelling clothes but he had removed his hauberk and now wore a long tunic. Osbern waved them to seats, then called to his wife in the kitchen. Eadgyth brought in refreshments on a wooden tray and the guests were soon enjoying warm honey cakes with a cup of tolerable wine.

In the relaxed atmosphere, Ralph casually interrogated the reeve to find out exactly what manner of man he was and how much they could rely on him. Ralph was pleased to have his earlier good impression of Osbern confirmed. Their host was clearly honest, conscientious and discreet. They were qualities not always to be found among town officials.

While the three men conversed, Golde sat in a corner with Eadgyth and tried to dispel her shyness with a show of friendship. Eadgyth was slowly won over. When she realized how much she and Golde had in common, her defences were gradually lowered. She was an attentive hostess but she excused herself from time to time to slip away into another part of the house, only to return with a smile of relief. Golde eventually divined the reason for her disappearances.

"How old is your baby?" she asked.

"Barely six months," said Eadgyth with a faint blush.

"A boy or a girl?"

"A boy, my lady. Named after his father."

"You must both be very proud of him."

"We are," she admitted, throwing a fond glance at Osbern. "But my husband has warned me that we must not let our son disturb you in any way. You are important guests and must not be bothered by our family matters."

"That may be true for Ralph and Gervase," said Golde. "They are here on royal business which claims their full attention. But I insist on seeing this wonderful baby."

"You shall, my lady."

"I want to see, hold and rock him in my arms."

"Do you have children of your own?"

"Alas, no."

"There is still time."

"We shall see."

Golde looked wistfully across at Ralph but she was not allowed to dwell on her thoughts. A servant appeared at the door and beckoned Osbern with some urgency, indicating that Eadgyth should also hear the news. The couple excused themselves and followed the man into the next room. A muttered conversation was heard through the door, then Eadgyth let out such a cry of grief that the three guests jumped to their feet in concern.

When Osbern came back in, his face was ashen.

"Bad tidings?" surmised Ralph.

"I fear so, my lord. The death of a close friend."

"We are sorry to hear it."

"My wife bears the heavier loss. She and Bertha spent much time together. The girl was almost one of our family."

"Girl?" repeated Golde.

"She was but seventeen, my lady."

"So young."

"What cruel disease carried her off?" said Ralph.

"It was no sickness, my lord. Bertha was here in this house not twenty-four hours ago, as fit and healthy as any of us. No," said Osbern with a sigh, "it seems that she was bitten by a snake while gathering herbs in Harbledown."

"Harbledown?" echoed Gervase. "That place on the hill? We rode through it on our way here."

"Then you must have passed the spot where her dead body was found. Poor Bertha! I would not wish such a fate on anyone, but least of all on such a gentle creature as her."

"Where is the girl now?" said Ralph.

"According to our report, they are bringing her down from the hospital of St Nicholas." He looked up as they heard the front door of the house open and shut. "Please excuse Eadgyth's rude departure."

"No excuse is needed, Osbern."

"My wife feels that she must be there."

"We understand."

"She can help to comfort the girl's father."

"Father?"

"Yes, my lord. Alwin. He will be utterly destroyed."

It took them a long time to persuade him. Alwin sat motionless beside the dead body of his daughter and refused to let anyone touch her. Whenever they tried to move the corpse, he crouched protectively over it and let out a strange keening sound. Brother Martin and Brother Bartholomew were patient. Relieved that Alwin's suicidal rage had spent itself, they now waited until he was ready to surrender his daughter to their care. A horse and cart stood outside. The lepers kept a silent vigil in the shadows.

Brother Martin crouched beside the suffering father.

"Bertha may not stay here, Alwin," he whispered.

"I know."

"Then let us carry her to a fitter place."

"In time, Brother Martin. In time."

"We leave the decision to you."

Alwin looked disconsolately around the dank nave.

"Bertha loved this hospital," he murmured.

"She was an angel of mercy," said Martin. "She had an affinity with the piteous wretches who lodge here. It is such a brutal irony. Their hold on life is so tenuous and so painful yet it is Bertha who has gone to her Maker first. She will be sadly missed by all the friends she has here."

"And what of me?"

"You, Alwin?"

"They have only lost a friend."

"A friend and a benefactor."

"I have lost everything."

Alwin fell into a kind of trance. Oblivious to his surroundings, he stared unseeing at one of the stone pillars, his body slack, his mind empty, his mouth open. When they tried to speak to him, he did not hear a word.

Brother Martin decided that their moment had finally come. He signalled to Bartholomew before crossing to open the heavy oak door. Sunlight flooded in. The two monks moved gingerly into position so that they could lift the body between them but Alwin came out of his reverie at once. Pushing them firmly away, he knelt beside his daughter in order to slip his arms under her, then he lifted her without effort and took her slowly out through the church door.

The waiting congregation of lepers at first stepped back with a gasp of horror. Realising that Bertha was now beyond reach of their contagion, they then moved in closer to take a final look at her, one of them, an old lady, putting out a flaking hand to touch the flimsy shroud as it fluttered past. Another fell to his knees to offer up a prayer for the soul of the departed. The cart was rough-hewn and covered in mud but someone had flung an old woollen blanket over it to hide the worst of its defects and kill some of its noisome stink.

Alwin laid the body in the back of the cart with great reverence before turning to survey the watching lepers. Their cloaks and hoods gave them a fearful anonymity and he could not even discern the male from the female victims, but he accorded each in turn a mute farewell. After glancing back at the corpse, he made a forlorn gesture of apology to everyone.

Brother Martin gave the order and the boy led the horse away from the church. Alwin walked behind it with the monks at his heels, chanting in unison. The little cortege crested the hill and began the long, bumpy downhill journey. As it passed the clump of holly where Bertha had been discovered, a tall, stooping figure seemed to materialise out of the trees. Face still hidden behind the veil, the leper who had found her waited until the cart trundled on out of sight.

Then he took something out of the fold of his sleeve and held it on the palm of his hand to examine it with an almost tentative affection. He felt its smoothness and held it up for the sun to polish its dull sheen. After placing a dry-lipped kiss on it, he opened his sleeve and put the object safely back in its hiding place.

It was his memento.

Ralph Delchard was in such a genial mood that even his protests had a chuckling mildness to them. They were the token complaints of a husband who can deny his wife nothing.

"We will be bored to death!" he said dramatically. "Who on earth could wish to look at a cathedral?"

"I could," said Golde.

"But you have seen cathedrals before, my love."

"Not this one."

"Since you met me, you have visited Winchester, Lincoln and York Minster. They are enough to glut any appetite. When you lived in Hereford, you saw a cathedral every day."

"Canterbury is different."

"Why?"

"It is the best."

"Yet not the biggest."

"None can match its importance."

"York Minster would try."

"And fail. Look, Ralph!" she said, pointing a finger at the looming splendour before them. "From this cathedral, the whole of the English Church is ruled."

"It is ruled by the whims of King William."

"This is the spiritual centre of the country."

"Dear God!" he said in mock alarm. "Have I married a devout Christian? Am I matched with a holy nun? Do I lay with a bride of Christ? Why did you keep this hideous truth from me?"

"I thought to convert you by stealth," she teased.

"Horror of horrors!"

They shared a laugh and he embraced her warmly. The commission would begin its investigations on the next day and Ralph would be caught up in its activities. This was the only time when they might view the city together and they snatched eagerly at the chance. It was only a short walk from Osbern's house to the cathedral precinct. While Ralph blustered amiably, she marvelled at what she saw.

"The place had such a sense of power," she said.

"All I can see is a pretty pile of Caen stone."

"Are you blind to the beauty before your eyes?"

"No, my love," he said, holding her face between gentle hands. "It is what drew me to you in the first place."

"I talk of the cathedral."

"A finer edifice stands before me."

"Be serious, Ralph."

"I am. Never more so."

It was difficult to have a private moment in such a public place. Dozens of people were going past in both directions and others were idling in corners. Golde was conscious that curious eyes were upon them but that did not hold her back from broaching a delicate subject. Ralph was her husband now and she had never felt closer to him than at that precise second.

"Did you know that Eadgyth has a baby?" she said.

"It does not surprise me."

"She asked me if we had children."

"What did you tell her?"

"The truth. We do not."

"Yet."

She held his gaze, wanting reassurance, hoping for a sign of commitment, searching for a need in him as deep as her own.

"I am somewhat older than Eadgyth," she warned.

"I am somewhat younger than Osbern."

"A child never came with my first husband."

"Perhaps it rebelled against your choice of a father."

"Do not jest about it, Ralph."

"It was no jest."

"This weighs heavily with me."

"Then so it does with me," he promised, squeezing her shoulder. "Whatever touches your heart finds it way straight to mine. Is that plain enough for you?"

She nodded. "We have never talked about this before."

"I took it for granted."

"It is not as simple as that."

"You will have to teach me the way," he said with a grin.

"If a child comes . . ."

"It would give me such joy and pride, Golde."

"But if it does not . . . ?"

He winced slightly as a distant memory jabbed at him. With an arm around her, he looked up at the cathedral.

"Come, my love," he said. "It is time to go inside."

When Osbern decided to visit the bereaved man, Gervase Bret immediately offered to bear him company. It would not only allow him to explore part of the city and to glean further information from the reeve on the way, it would help to assuage his keen interest in the circumstances of the girl's death. The bare facts of the case intrigued and puzzled him.

"She was killed by the venom of a snake?" he said.

"That is my understanding."

"When? How?"

"I have no details beyond those I have given you," said Osbern as they strode along. "And they may prove to be wrong. News changes in the telling. I do not know how many hands the report of this tragedy passed through before it reached us, but I would guess at several."

"Your wife was distressed at the tidings."

"She had cause, Master Bret. They have known each other many years. Before she wed me, Eadgyth was a near neighbour of Bertha and her father."

"No mother?"

"She died some years ago."

"What is the father's occupation?"

"Alwin is a sailor. The captain of a small boat which brings stone from Normandy for building work. You have seen how much reconstruction there is in Canterbury. Alwin's vessel has been in constant demand."

"Tell me about his daughter."

"The one delight in Alwin's life. A fair maid in every sense. Bright, lively, dutiful yet not without an independent spirit. A true friend to Eadgyth. Kindness itself."

"Why would she be gathering herbs?"

"For the leper hospital of St. Nicholas. Bertha was given to charitable impulse. She was a regular visitor to Harbledown. The lepers came to know and trust her."

"So young and yet so caring toward others?"

"Her goodness may have cost Bertha her life."

Alwin the Sailor lived in Worthgate Ward and so the body of his daughter was taken to the tiny morgue at the parish church of St. Mildred. When he saw her bestowed there, he was led back to his home by Eadgyth and by Brother Martin. Both were still trying to comfort him when the visitors arrived. Profoundly moved by Alwin's plight, but concerned as well about the intensity of his wife's grief, the considerate Osbern went into the house to lend support to both of them.

Gervase did not wish to intrude. He stayed outside and pondered further on the girl's demise. It was a long wait but it brought an unexpected reward. Brother Martin came out alone and fell into conversation with him. The duty of helping Alwin through his pain had given the monk little time to express his own sadness. When he left the house of mourning, he was able to confront the enormity of the loss. It made him go weak at the knees. Seeing his distress, Gervase steadied him then eased him down onto the hearthstone.

"Rest here awhile," he counselled.

"Thank you, my son. Sorrow has taken all my strength."

"You knew the girl?"

"Knew her well and loved her dearly."

"Have you heard how she was found?"

"I was there."

Gervase gave him time to recover before introducing himself to the monk. His bearing and his gentle manner enabled him to win Brother Martin's confidence and the latter was soon giving a full account of what had happened. Gervase listened with rapt attention as the old man relived the ordeal. Only when Brother Martin had completed his tale did Gervase raise a few queries.

"How long had Bertha been coming to the hospital?"

"A few years or more," said Brother Martin.

"So she would know Harbledown well?"

"Every tree, bush and blade of grass."

"And every hazard, too, I think," said Gervase.

"Hazard?"

"Wild animals or snakes."

"Bertha knew how to look after herself, Master Bret."

"Until yesterday, it seems. You mentioned holly."

"That is where she lay when we stumbled upon her. She was surrounded by it. Caught in a holly wreath, as it were."

"What herbs would she find there?"

"None that I know of, my friend."

"Then why subject herself to the scratch of holly?"

"It is a question I have asked myself," confided the monk. "And it is matched with others that arouse suspicion."

"Suspicion?"

"That wound upon her. Bertha would have had to be on her back for a snake to sink its fangs into her neck. Why would the girl risk lying down in a place of danger?"

"Perhaps she tripped and fell," said Gervase.

"She was too strong and sure-footed."

"How, then, do you explain the mark upon her neck?"

"I cannot," admitted the monk. "There are poisonous snakes in Harbledown and Bertha would not be their first victim. I have treated others who have met with the same misfortune. Treated them, Master Bret, and saved them."

"What are you telling me?"

"When venom gets into the blood, it can kill as surely as a sword or an arrow. But nowhere near as quickly. Bertha was young and healthy. Had she been bitten by a snake, why did she not run for help before the poison took full effect?"

"Have you raised these matters with anyone else?"

"No, my friend. I dare not."

"Why?"

"Because I have no proof."

"Your evidence is sound enough to me."

"It is only an old man's foolish instinct," said Brother Martin. "And I do not wish to go where it leads me."

"What do you mean?"

The monk looked around to make sure that they were not overheard, then pulled his companion closer. Gervase saw the watery apprehension in his eyes.

"Bertha may not have died from the snakebite."

"But you saw the marks upon her neck."

"The girl was bitten," confirmed the monk. "No doubt about that. There was poison in her veins. The signs were clear. I begin to think that they were too clear."

Gervase's interest quickened. "Are you suggesting that she was killed by other means and bitten by the snake when she was already dead?"

"It is possible. Bertha may have been murdered."

❧ Chapter Three

CANON HUBERT WAS in his element. The visit to Canterbury was both a duty and a form of pilgrimage and it never occurred to him that these might be in any way contradictory. His status as a royal commissioner gave him a thrusting self-importance while his presence in Christ Church Priory brought out an ostentatious humility. Within the safety and sanctity of the cloister, Brother Simon was able to accommodate both aspects of his colleague with relative ease.

"Seven years!" boomed Hubert.

"A miracle in stone."

"Seven years. When Archbishop Lanfranc first came here from Caen, he found the cathedral in ruins and this priory in disarray. Behold what seven years of prayer and planning and ceaseless labour can achieve."

"It is a monument to the archbishop's genius."

"It is an inspiration, Brother Simon!"

"Yes, Canon Hubert."

"I see the hand of the blessed Lanfranc everywhere."

"You would recognise its character."

"That is why I am so grateful that my work has at last brought me to Canterbury," said Hubert, looking around with a proprietary air. "This is truly uplifting. I *belong.*"

Simon was also experiencing a sense of joyous kinship but he was too mild-mannered even to mention it. When Hubert was in such a state of spiritual replenishment, his buoyancy left no room for the thoughts and feelings of others. Simon did not complain. At the heart of the community, the priory was yet gloriously isolated from it, high walls and a protective austerity allowing its monks to serve God without any worldly distraction. No woman could ever penetrate the enclave. Brother Simon was at home.

Christ Church Priory was built on a scale which showed vision and high aspiration. As they perambulated around the spacious cloister garth, the visitors noted the large chapter house, the sizeable refectory and a dorter range capable of housing a hundred and fifty monks. Particular care had been lavished on the scriptorium so that it could in time become a centre of learning unrivalled in England. Canon Hubert might dream of high office within this monastic community but Brother Simon's ambition stretched no further than the wish to be shackled in perpetuity to a desk in the scriptorium like one of the great chained Bibles.

The two men were still luxuriating in their respective fantasies when they were joined by a fresh-faced young monk with a message for Hubert. Abandoning his companion without a word, the canon followed his guide to the prior's lodging.

"Welcome to Canterbury!"

"Thank you," said Hubert deferentially. "This visit is the fulfillment of a long-held wish."

"I trust that you will enjoy and benefit from your time here in the city."

"That is a foregone conclusion."

"You might be wiser to reserve your judgement."

"There is no need."

"There is always need for caution."

Prior Henry was a striking man of medium height and middle years. The slim, intelligent face had a swarthy complexion which showed his Italian ancestry and the remains of a handsomeness which was at odds with his tight-lipped asceticism. Dark eyes probed from beneath black eyebrows and the high forehead had a quizzical frown. It was almost as if he were assessing the strengths of a possible adversary.

They were in his private parlour, the chamber from which the whole monastic community was administered. Henry sat behind a table which was covered with letters, documents and accounts. Hubert was irresistibly reminded of his time at the famous abbey of Bec when a conference with the prior was a daily event. Across just such a table, he and Lanfranc had discussed every aspect of monastic business in exhaustive detail. Those memories were cherished afresh now.

Prior Henry read his thoughts. Indicating a chair so that his guest might sit down, he sounded an apologetic note.

"Archbishop Lanfranc sends his greetings to you and regrets that he is not able to meet you in person."

"I understand," said Hubert, lowering his bulk onto the carved oak chair. "The archbishop is extremely busy. When he has the affairs of the entire Church of England to conduct, he cannot easily break off to see an old friend."

"Indeed not," agreed the other. "If he did that, he would never begin to address the huge volume of work that confronts him. He has rather too many old friends, I fear."

Hubert was momentarily stung. Feeling that he was being both rebuked and patronised, he displayed his credentials at once.

"I was sub-prior at Bec under Prior Lanfranc."

"I am aware of your brief tenure of that office."

"He and I worked closely and harmoniously together."

"That was over a quarter of a century ago."

"It gave us a deep and lasting mutual respect. Prior Lanfranc, as he then was, paid me the highest compliment when he left to be abbot of Caen."

"Not quite, Canon Hubert."

"His praise was unstinting."

"Yet it still fell short of the highest accolade," said Henry coolly. "That would have been to take you with him to Caen to occupy a higher station. As it was, you did not even succeed him as prior of Bec. That honour fell to Anselm."

"I approved wholeheartedly."

"You had no choice."

Hubert was even more annoyed. There was no enmity or malice in Henry's voice. It was his cold statement of facts which discomfited his guest. Hubert had indeed never risen above the position of sub-prior at Bec. Having leapfrogged over him, Anselm had gone on to become abbot of the house.

"There is another reason," continued Henry.

"For what?"

"The archbishop's reluctance to give you an audience."

"Reluctance? He has a personal objection?"

"No, Canon Hubert. He spoke well of you. But he is also mindful of the role in which you have come back to him."

"I do not follow."

"You are part of a royal commission. One of the disputes to come before you concerns Archbishop Lanfranc. He does not wish to meet you beforehand in case the renewed ties of friendship might influence your judgement."

"I would be wholly impartial," asserted Hubert.

"You must also be *seen* to be impartial," emphasized the other, "and that would not be possible if it were known that you had a private audience with the archbishop. When your work is complete—and the cathedral no longer implicated—the situation will be different. Archbishop Lanfranc may well be able to create some small space in his day for you."

Prior Henry rose to his feet with a dismissive smile to signal that the interview was at an end. Bristling with dissatisfaction, Hubert struggled out of his chair. Contact with his revered friend would only be through the agency of Prior Henry and he sensed that the latter would be an obstructive interlocutor. Hubert eyed him warily.

"I may, then, still hope to meet the archbishop?"

"When this issue is resolved."

"Even if the judgement goes against him?"

"There is no chance of that, Canon Hubert," said Prior Henry, briskly. He forced a thin smile. "Is there?"

"Why did you not raise these doubts earlier?" asked Gervase.

"I had no chance, my son," said Brother Martin. "And I must stress that they still are lingering doubts rather than firm convictions. I did not examine the body closely."

"Why not?"

"Her father would not permit it. Alwin is a powerful man. He was in no mood to be resisted. All I saw of Bertha was the glimpse I had when we first discovered her."

"But that was enough to feed your suspicion?"

"To plant a tiny seed of doubt, Master Bret."

"More than that, I think."

Brother Martin was in a quandary. Having confided his worries to Gervase, he was now deeply troubled by regret and uncertainty, wondering if he should have spoken so openly to a complete stranger and questioning the suppositions he had made about Bertha's untimely death. He felt that he needed far more evidence before he made accusations of foul play.

Gervase persuaded him to go in search of that evidence and the two of them were now walking towards the parish church of St. Mildred. When it came into view, the hesitant monk stopped in his tracks and shook his head.

"We should not be doing this," he complained.

"Would you let Bertha's murderer go unpunished?"

"I am not at all sure that she was murdered."

"Inspect the body and you will satisfy yourself on that score," argued Gervase. "If you then decide that she was killed by the venom of a snake, you can let the burial take place and no harm will have been done. If, however, you detect any signs of foul play, we can take appropriate action."

"I am not happy about this, Master Bret."

"You owe it to Bertha to find out the truth."

"Do I?"

"Of course. And you owe it to her father."

"Alwin concerns me the most," sighed Martin. "He was so crazed by the death of his daughter that he sought to kill himself in a fit of grief. Brother Bartholomew and I had to fight to keep him alive. I still bear the bruises about me. Think how much more violently he will react if he is told that Bertha was slain by a human hand."

"It would be a sin to keep that intelligence from him."

Brother Martin thought long and hard before coming to his decision. The image of Bertha, assisting him at the hospital, was at the forefront of his mind throughout. Drawing himself up, he set his jaw and nodded.

"You are right," he said firmly. "Truth is paramount here. I must know if my old eyes deceived me or if those lingering doubts of mine are justified."

"Let us go."

St. Mildred's Church stood in the southwest of the city near the town wall. A Saxon foundation, it was built of flint and local stone and comprised a long, narrow, aisleless nave, a small vestry and an even smaller morgue. When they let themselves into the church, they found Reinbald the Priest kneeling before the altar in an attitude of submission. They waited for some minutes until he rose, genuflected, then turned toward them.

"Brother Martin," he said, recognising the familiar face. "What brings you back to St. Mildred's?"

"I came to pay my respects to Bertha."

"But you delivered her up to me only an hour ago."

"I would value a moment alone with her," said the monk. "When I came earlier, her father's grief was my main concern. I fear I have neglected the girl herself."

"She lies in the morgue. You know the way."

Brother Martin first introduced Gervase to the priest, then slipped quietly away. Reinbald came slowly down the nave toward the stranger, regarding him with trepidation. Gervase spoke in Saxon to put him at his ease.

"Where do the bones of St. Mildred lie?" he asked.

Reinbald was surprised. "You have *heard* of St. Mildred?"

"Indeed I have. She was the abbess of Minster-in-Thanet, not far from Canterbury. Her mother, as I recall, was Princess of Kent. Ermenburga. Am I correct?"

"You already know more than my parishioners."

"Mildred was a virtuous lady. Her charity toward widows and children was legendary. When she died, her tomb became a place of pilgrimage. Her relics were translated to St. Augustine's Abbey."

"That is true. Some fifty years ago."

"A portion of those relics was sent to Holland. Is that not so, Father Reinbald?" The priest nodded. "How, then, did Archbishop Lanfranc come to bestow her relics at the hospital of St. Gregory, here in the city?"

"That is a vexed question, Master Bret."

"Hospital, abbey or foreign shrine? Which, if any, holds the true bones of St. Mildred?"

"Nobody can be certain."

"The archbishop is. So, I understand, is the abbey."

"It is a source of friction between them," lamented the other. "I hesitate to call it a bone of contention." He repented of his levity at once. "Forgive me. That was unseemly. Our thoughts should be with that poor girl in the mortuary. God rest her soul!"

Reinbald the Priest was young, earnest and open-faced. He had the look of someone who had found his desired place in life and who would serve his flock with diligence for the rest of his days. There was a slightly defensive air about him but Gervase put that down to his own presence. Being the servant of the King always created unease and distrust among the Saxon populace.

"To answer your question honestly," said Reinbald with quiet dignity. "Wherever her relics lie, we believe that the spirit of St. Mildred is here in the church which bears her name. We celebrate her Feast Day with great joy." He cocked his head to one side and studied his guest. "How do you come to know Brother Martin? Is he an old friend?"

"A new acquaintance," said Gervase. "We met outside the home of Alwin the Sailor. I was taken there by Osbern the Reeve with whom we are lodging while in Canterbury."

"You have a fine host. Osbern is a good man."

"So I have noticed."

"His wife, Eadgyth, was very close to Bertha. She was here when the body was brought in from Harbledown. Then she helped to convey Alwin back to his house."

"Has anyone else been here since?"

"Been here?"

"To view the body."

"None save Brother Martin. And Helto, of course."

"Helto?"

"The doctor. He came to verify the cause of death. He examined the girl with great care before he pronounced."

"And what was his verdict?"

"Snakebite."

"Is he sure?"

"He was absolutely certain."

Gervase found himself curiously disappointed but he was ready to accept the diagnosis of a doctor. Their visit to the church had been in vain. Brother Martin's reappearance seemed to confirm this. His head was low, his face expressionless and his gait unhurried. After a nod of farewell to the priest, he led Gervase back out into the street. They were several yards away before the monk stopped.

"I owe a debt of gratitude to you," he said softly.

"Why?"

"Your voice compelled me to go back to the mortuary."

"Unnecessarily, Brother Martin."

"Not so."

"The girl died from snakebite."

"Who told you that?"

"It is medical opinion," said Gervase. "Bertha was examined by one Helto the Doctor. He was adamant that she had been killed by the venom of a snake."

Martin was outraged. "Is that what Helto *said*?"

"Apparently."

"Then he was lying."

Ralph Delchard was peeved. When he dispatched Canon
Hubert into the cathedral precinct that morning, he
thought he had seen the last of him for that day. Since his
colleague had sung the praises of Lanfranc all the way
from Winchester, it was a reasonable assumption that he
would not stir from the proximity of the archbishop until
it was unavoidable. Yet there he was, red with indignation,
banging on the door of Osbern's house and interrupting
what had been for Ralph and Golde an idyllic few hours.

Having seen the sights of Canterbury, they returned to
Burgate Ward to find that the baby had just awoken. A servant girl was rocking the child in his crib but Golde swiftly
took over the duties of surrogate mother. With Ralph
watching fondly over her shoulder, she cooed and hummed
the baby slowly back to sleep. It was then that the unwel-
come Hubert arrived. He was shown into the solar.

"Whatever are you doing here?" demanded Ralph.

"I need something."

"Could it not wait until morning?"

"No, my lord."

"Why not?"

"Because it concerns tomorrow's deliberations."

"The property in Fordwich?"

"Even so," said Hubert. "The relevant documents are in
Gervase's satchel. I wish to study them with care before we
sit in judgement on the case."

"For what reason?"

"I need to be well prepared."

"Then why did you not ask Gervase for those documents
at an earlier stage? You have had many opportunities."

"I want them now, my lord. That is all that matters."

"But it is not, Hubert," countered the other. "You go into the priory without the slightest interest in that case. Then you come charging out in search of material relating to it. What brought about this sudden conversion?"

"Please hand the documents over. It is all I ask."

"They are in Gervase's possession and he alone can pass them on to you. Like me, I am sure, he will first want to dig below the surface of your request."

"What do you mean?"

"May I speak bluntly?"

"You have always done so before," said Hubert ruefully.

"Who is going to read these confidential documents?"

"I am, my lord."

"No other eyes?"

"Brother Simon might usefully peruse them as well."

"So might someone else," said Ralph, standing close to bark his accusation in the other's face. "Someone in rather higher authority than our humble scribe. Have you been sent here on an errand by Archbishop Lanfranc?"

Hubert turned puce. "No, my lord!" he exclaimed.

"Doing a favour for an old friend? Serving the head of the English Church? Sniffing your way to preferment?"

"These are gross calumnies!"

"Are they?" pressed Ralph. "The cathedral lays claim to land that is held by the abbey. It would advantage Lanfranc greatly to have sight of the evidence we have collected and the questions we have agreed to put to him. I'll not stand by and condone such vile injustice."

"The vileness lies in your charges against me."

"Then defend yourself."

"I hoped that my record would to that for me," said Hubert with quivering indignation. "Impartiality has been my touchstone throughout. We have sat in commission together in Wiltshire, in Essex, in Herefordshire and in Yorkshire. Have you ever seen one hint of prejudice in me, my lord? Can you recall one instance when I did not embrace and embody judicial independence?"

"No," admitted Ralph. "Not one."

"Then why insult me with such an accusation now?"

"Because a new element exists. Friendship with one of the claimants. By rights, you should not act as judge in this case. You should declare an interest and withdraw."

Hubert struck a dignified pose. "My only interest is in securing a just and fair settlement," he said. "Were my own mother to appear before us, I would not yield to promptings of affection. It is so with Archbishop Lanfranc. Heaven forfend! Even if I *did* try to assist his case, I could not materially influence the outcome. Mine is but one voice. You and Gervase together can shout me down."

It was a sound argument. Ralph scratched his head and moved away for a moment to ponder. When he came back to Hubert, his tone was more conciliatory.

"I may have spoken too hastily," he conceded.

"Hastily and hurtfully, my lord."

"We have to be on guard at all times."

"From *me*? Your fellow commissioner?"

"Perhaps not." An awkward pause. "What did he say?"

"Who?"

"Archbishop Lanfranc. Was he pleased to see you?"

"I was not given an audience with him."

"An old friend like you?"

"The archbishop is a busy man," said Hubert sadly. His ire rekindled. "And he knew that he would not get me to divulge one syllable about our work in Canterbury."

"He did consider asking you, then?"

"No, my lord. He is above such things. This is a minor dispute to him and hardly merits his attention. When he was first made archbishop, he discovered that a vast amount of church property had been seized by no less a person than Odo, the King's own half-brother, Bishop of Bayeux, and then Earl of Kent. Do you know what Archbishop Lanfranc did?"

"He brought a lawsuit against Odo."

"He took on one of the most powerful men in the kingdom in a trial that lasted three days. Lanfranc won. Everything that was purloined is now restored to the church." He wagged an admonitory finger. "We are talking about one of the finest jurists in Europe. He does not *need* my help."

Ralph smarted under the reprimand but felt that he deserved it. Hubert's outbursts usually amused him but this one earned his respect. The request could not be denied.

"You may have the documents when Gervase returns."

"And when will that be?"

"Soon."

Canon Hubert clasped his hands in his lap and settled down in a chair like a hen brooding on some eggs. He did not have long to wait before he heard the latch lifting on the front door.

"That may be Gervase now," said Ralph.

"At least *he* will not hurl wild accusations at me," said the other, excavating himself from the chair. "Gervase appreciates my true merit."

"I will send him in to you."

Ralph went out of the room to be met by a worried Osbern.

"I have brought Eadgyth home," he said sadly. "You will have to forgive my wife if she is not able to attend to your needs. She is heartbroken at Bertha's death. I think it best if she keeps to our bedchamber."

"Of course," approved Ralph. "But this tragedy makes our own presence here a burden to you. We will find some other lodging and leave you to mourn in peace."

"That would distress Eadgyth even more, my lord. And it would certainly disappoint me. You are our honoured guests. We have servants enough to look after you." The sound of weeping came from upstairs. "Eadgyth needs me. I must go." He paused on the first step. "Oh, I almost forgot. I have a message for you. It is from Master Bret."

"Where is Gervase? We need him here."

"You may have to wait, my lord."

"Why?"

"He has gone to Harbledown."

❧ CHAPTER FOUR

t

THE EFFORTS AND agonies of a long morning had taken their toll of Brother Martin. His vigour had waned, the spring in his step had gone and he leaned more heavily on his staff. Fatigue and sorrow had also clouded his mind. When he and Gervase Bret climbed up the hill, the monk had some difficulty finding the exact spot where Bertha had been found and he became increasingly frustrated. It was with a sigh of relief that he finally located the clump of holly.

"Here it is!" he promised.

"Take your time," said Gervase tolerantly. "There is no rush. I want you to be quite sure, Brother Martin."

"This is the place. I would swear to it."

"Then let us take a closer look."

The holly bushes grew in wild profusion around a slight depression in the earth. Someone lying in the hollow would be invisible to anyone passing by. It was hardly a place to search for herbs, still less one where a girl would choose to lie down and rest. Twigs, stones and some exposed roots would have made it an uncomfortable bed. Flies buzzed inhospitably. The scratch of holly was an added deterrent.

"Where was she lying?" said Gervase.

"Right here."

"On her face, her back or her side?"

"Her back."

"Which way were her feet pointing?"

"Down the hill, I think," said the monk, ransacking his brain. "No, wait. That was not it. Bertha was stretched out the other way. Or was she? How strange! My memory is playing tricks on me again." He looked at Gervase. "Is it important for you to know?"

"It could be."

"Then I will try harder."

Using his staff, he pushed back the holly and stepped down into the hollow. Prickly leaves attacked his hands and ankles but he was inured to such routine pain. He searched the tufted grass and flicked away the sharpest of the stones with his sandalled foot before lowering himself gently to the ground. Gervase watched as the old man lay on his back and experimented with various positions, changing his angle each time. He eventually made up his mind.

"This is how she was, Master Bret."

"Feet pointing this way?"

"I am certain of it."

"Then she must have been dragged backward into her hiding place," observed Gervase, running his eyes over the bushes. "You can see where some of the leaves have been snapped off. Unless you caused this damage when you reclaimed her body earlier."

"No," said Martin. "We eased her out on the other side with all due care. Bertha had suffered indignities enough.

We did not want to add to them by pulling her roughly out like a dead cat. Brother Bartholomew and I inflicted no further damage on her or her apparel."

"Her apparel?"

"Yes, Master Bret. It was torn and soiled."

"Then there may be a thread or two caught on the leaves," said Gervase, searching in vain. "What colour was her kirtle?"

"Blue."

Brother Martin groaned as he forced himself upright.

"Are you hurt?"

"My old bones do not like this mean bed."

"Let me help you up."

"Stay there and I will teach you how."

Holding his staff in both hands, Martin extended it toward Gervase so that the latter could grasp it and haul his companion to his feet. The monk shouldered his way through the bushes and collected a few vengeful leaves in his cowl. A sudden thought made him swing round to stare back into the hollow.

"It is gone," he said. "I knew something was missing."

"Missing?"

"The snake. The adder curled up beside Bertha."

"You told me that the swineherd killed it."

"He did. And left it in two parts on the ground. There is no sign of it now. Where can it have gone?"

They got their answer within moments. The delighted screams of children hit their ears and they walked quickly past the bushes to witness an impromptu game. Two small boys were running around in happy terror, pursued by a third with the carcase of the snake in his hand, whirling it like a whip as he tried to strike his friends. When he failed to catch them, he instead hurled the severed head of the creature after them, hitting one boy on the side of the face and producing howls of ghoulish glee.

Brother Martin shook his head philosophically.

"The young show no respect for the dead," he said without rancour. "It was ever thus. When I was their age, I found a human skull in a field. No thought of who he or she might have been or what form of death they had endured. It was a plaything to me. I kicked the skull along the ground for sport until it fell into a stream." He gave a mirthless chuckle. "I often wonder if I became a monk by way of penance for my childhood sin."

"It was only the sin of ignorance, Brother Martin."

"That is no excuse."

Gervase stopped to watch the three boys, haring down the hill together before vanishing out of sight among the trees. They had lost interest in the snake and it had been hurled with cruel indifference into the bracken. Excited laughter showed that they had found a new game.

"What now?" asked Brother Martin.

"I would like to speak to the man who found the body."

"But he is a leper."

"That will make no difference."

"It would to most people." He regarded Gervase with a mixture of admiration and curiosity. "You are an unusual man. When you have pressing business of your own, you give time and energy to something that is of no real concern to you. Why?"

"Because of the girl."

"You have never met Bertha."

"No, Brother Martin, but I have seen her through the eyes of those who did. She was deeply loved by all who knew her. Osbern the Reeve told me much about Bertha. He fed my interest."

"What did he say?"

"That she was an exceptional person. Young, fair, full of sweetness, generous toward others." He became wistful. "I have someone like that in my own life. We are betrothed and she waits for me even now in Winchester. When the reeve talked about Bertha, he might almost have been describing my beloved Alys." He put a palm on his chest. "I am here to help. Make what use of me you see fit."

"I am most grateful to you."

"Let us go on." The monk fell in beside him and they continued on up the hill. "We passed your hospital on our way here and offered up a prayer for the souls within."

"Leprosy is a dreadful affliction. Its victims deserve the utmost sympathy and yet their very condition provokes disgust. Many turn away in horror."

"Bertha did not."

"No more do I. The lepers are my flock."

"Which one of them discovered the body?"

"His name is Alain."

"French?"

"Of mixed blood."

"Then he and I will have something in common."

"It will be the only thing, I fear."

"What do you mean?"

"Be warned, Master Bret. He is an odd fellow. Withdrawn and often unfriendly. Even I cannot reach him at times. Alain is not liked by the others. Talk to him, if you must."

"He may have seen something that nobody else noticed."

"He may, indeed," said Martin. "But will he tell you what it was? That is the question. Alain is very stubborn. The likelihood is that he will refuse to say a single word."

Golde was saddened by the turn of events and anxious to do all she could to relieve the distress. She sat at Eadgyth's bedside to console her, she helped to tend the baby, she took charge of the servants and she shouldered the household cares as if they were her own. Osbern the Reeve was struck by her maternal warmth and loving kindness. Ralph looked on with proud approval. Canon Hubert, finding the house too full and too preoccupied, returned to the prior after asking that Gervase should send the requested documents after him in due course.

Eadgyth was patently unwell. When the first shock of the tragedy had worn off, it was replaced by a deep and agonising sense of loss. The effort of comforting Bertha's father had also told on her. She was pale, distracted and very queasy. It was after she had been sick for the third time that her anxious husband sent for the doctor.

"How is she?" asked Ralph.

"As well as can be expected."

"Have you given her physic?"

"I have prepared a sleeping draught for her. Eadgyth needs rest. Grief is a form of illness. It taxes the mind and debilitates the body. Sleep is the only cure."

Helto the Doctor was a tall, thin, angular man with a peremptory manner which did nothing to recommend him to Ralph. The doctor was used to talking to patients who were too unwell to answer back and too weak to resist any medicine he prescribed or any course of treatment he advocated. Five minutes alone with Eadgyth had been followed by some clipped orders to Osbern. Intercepting him as he was about to leave, Ralph was less inclined to defer to him or to tolerate his professional brusqueness.

"Is there no more you can do for her?" he demanded.

"No, my lord."

"Could you not at least show the woman some sympathy?"

"I do," said Helto, bridling at the implied criticism. "I have the greatest sympathy for Eadgyth and by far the most understanding of her condition. She has been a patient of mine for many years and it was I who helped to bring her child into the world."

"I am sure you are an able midwife," said Ralph.

"Do I detect a note of sarcasm, my lord?"

"You hear only a slight irritation."

"With me? What is the cause?"

"Your haste, for one thing. The lady of the house lies in obvious distress yet you do little more than look at her before you are rushing out of the house again."

Helto was checked. There was an authority and firmness of purpose about Ralph that he did not care to challenge. A Norman lord who was the guest of the town reeve had to be a person of some consequence. The doctor rubbed his palms and swiftly adopted a more respectful tone.

"I am sorry, my lord," he said. "My haste must not be taken as indifference. There are facts about the patient that you do not know and cannot be expected to know. Eadgyth is not in robust health," he confided. "She may look plump and rosy-cheeked to you but she is still sickening. When the baby was born, there were . . . complications. I can say no more than that. Childbirth is always an ordeal. I thank God that I was able to save both mother and son."

Ralph felt a sharp twinge of remorse. His own wife had died in childbirth and their son had followed his mother to the grave soon after. It had been a devastating experience. He was thankful that it had not been visited on Osbern.

"Eadgyth is fragile," continued Helto. "A blow like this has reminded us how far her recovery still has to go. Now you will understand why I did not need to spend an hour in her bedchamber to determine what was ailing her. I am a frequent caller at this house. One look at her is enough."

Ralph warmed to the man. There was a genuine concern in his voice. Helto the Doctor must have spent at least twenty years in his profession and he was well-regarded enough to be the physician of the town reeve's wife. It was wrong to doubt his ability or to question his methods.

"I have done all that is needful here," said Helto. "If I was speeding away, it is because I have to call on someone else who has been laid low by this melancholy event."

"Oh?"

"The dead girl's father. Alwin the Sailor."

"Eadgyth went to offer him solace."

"Yes, my lord. And she is now in need of it herself. I begin to wonder where they will end."

" 'They'?"

"These ever-widening circles of grief," explained the doctor. "Bertha's death is like a stone dropped into a pool. Her father is distraught. In comforting him, Eadgyth is crushed by the weight of a double suffering. Osbern is anxious about her and the lady Golde is troubled by his evident distress. You, in turn, are no doubt worried that your wife will take on too great a burden."

"She did that when she married me," said Ralph easily. "But I take your point. One stone. Endless circles."

"That snake has poisoned the lives of many people."

"Is that how the girl died?"

"It is, my lord."

"Has that been confirmed?"

"I examined the body myself at St. Mildred's Church. The fatal marks were upon her neck."

"Her neck?" said Ralph in surprise. "How so? The snake

could surely not have dropped down on her from a tree. And she would hardly have lain on the ground to offer it so enticing a target."

"She may have done so. Unintentionally."

"Explain."

"Come, my lord," said Helto with a knowing smile. "We have both been young. The summer sun has warmed our blood. Bertha was a comely girl. When she lay down on the grass yesterday, it is possible that she was not alone."

"A lover?"

"She had many admirers."

Ralph tensed. "Then why did the rogue not come to her aid when the snake bit the girl? Why did he not carry her at once to a doctor? What sort of lover abandons his mistress like that?"

"He may already have left her."

"Would she stay on the ground alone?"

"Why not?" argued Helto. "Musing on her lover. Or even falling into a light sleep that left her off guard. I am not saying that it did happen that way but it *could* have. It would certainly account for the wound upon her neck."

Ralph was unconvinced. "Other girls might have come to grief that way but not this one. Bertha was by report devout and caring. Look at the work she did at the leper hospital. That was a martyrdom. Here was no normal, carefree, amorous girl."

"That is true."

"Bertha had all the attributes of a nun."

Helto the Doctor whispered a discreet contradiction.

"Not all, my lord. I do assure you."

When they reached the leper hospital, Brother Martin first showed him around the little church. He drew particular attention to the medicine cupboard, which was filled with oils, lotions and ointments. Bound by cord, various herbs were hanging from hooks to dry or lying in jars to be ground and mixed. The monk did not only care for the souls of his tiny community. He was its father, its teacher, its cook, its doctor and its link with the outside world.

Gervase Bret was deeply impressed by his dedication.

"What sorts of herbs did Bertha bring you?" he said.

"Whatever was in season. Rosemary, rue, mint, figwort. I use them all. Parsley, lavender, thyme, sage, mustard seed and a dozen more besides. A lotion of pellitory will soothe the skin. Crushed lavender will sweeten the air. A mustard poultice will draw the sting of an ulcer. And so on. Bertha knew them and their properties as well as I."

"How will you manage without her?"

"We will not."

"Can nobody else take on her office?"

"I may scrounge a boy from the Master of the Novices for one day a week but what use will he be? It would take me an age to teach him which herbs to pick and where to find them. And what boy could match the medicine that Bertha brought?"

"Medicine?"

"Herself, Master Bret," said the monk, closing the door of his cupboard. "Leprosy is not simply a foul disease. It is a steep and twisting staircase into the grave. Its victims know that. There is no escape. Their hope is eaten away just as mercilessly as their bodies." He led Gervase outside. "Bertha could not arrest their decay but she was a salve to their minds. She offered friendship and understanding to wretches who have seen little of either."

He pointed to the wattle huts, primitive dwellings into which the lepers crawled at night like dogs into their kennels. Their fetid lodgings might provide shelter from the elements but scant comfort and only the most meagre decoration. Some of the occupants were asleep in their huts, others were sitting outside the door, others again were talking in a somnolent group. The whole place was still dazed by the shock of Bertha's death.

Alain was not at the hospital and it took some while to track him down. They found him propped up against the trunk of an elm, brooding in the shade of its foliage. When he saw them approaching, he pulled his hood even further forward and sank back defensively into his cloak.

"You have a visitor, Alain," said Brother Martin softly. "His name is Master Bret and he is eager to meet you."

"Good day," said Gervase, stopping a few yards away.

"He wishes to ask you about Bertha."

Alain turned to scrutinise the stranger through his veil and Gervase felt the hostility of his glare. The visitor was at a disadvantage. Unable to see anything of the leper's face or body, he had no idea of the age, character and build of the man sitting before him and he could not decide if the concealment was a weapon used against him or an essential mask over hideously corrupted flesh.

"I was sorry to hear the sad tidings about Bertha," he began. "Brother Martin has told me how important and loved a figure she was at the hospital." There was no response. "I believe that you were the person who found her body."

"Is that not so, Alain?" prompted the monk.

"We have just been examining the spot ourselves."

"Please help us."

"We are acting on Bertha's behalf."

Alain gave no indication that he had even heard them. He remained deep in his hooded cloak like a snail in its shell, watchful against danger, looking no further than its own immediate needs. Brother Martin turned to Gervase and arched his eyebrows in apology, gesturing that they might as well withdraw from the uncommunicative leper. Gervase held his ground and instead politely waved the monk away.

When he was left on his own with Alain, he first took a step nearer to him, then squatted on the ground. Since most of the lepers were native Saxons, theirs was the tongue used at the hospital of St. Nicholas. Gervase now spoke in French in an attempt to prise something out of the dumb and resentful figure before him.

"Where were you born, Alain?" A strained silence ensued. "Brother Martin tells me you are of mixed parentage. My mother was a Saxon but my father hailed from Brittany. I grew up with a foot in both camps." The leper was in no mood for personal reminiscence. Gervase plunged straight in. "We do not believe that Bertha died from snakebite. Do you?"

A faint, hesitant, parched voice eventually emerged.

"Who are you?" asked Alain.

"My name is Gervase Bret. I am a Chancery clerk in the royal household at Winchester. I have come to Canterbury on business."

"Then go your way and discharge your duty."

"I have vowed to help Brother Martin."

"This is nothing to do with you."

"It is. I can help."

"Bertha was our friend. Not yours."

"That is true."

"Leave us alone."

"But I care."

"And leave Bertha alone."

He lapsed back into silence but Gervase stayed his ground. Folding his arms, he waited for several minutes in a patient and unthreatening way. When the leper spoke again, a distant curiosity lay behind his contemptuous question.

"What can *you* do for her?"

"Find out the truth."

"Only Brother Martin could do that."

"He needs support."

"Why are you here?"

"Because of Bertha."

"She was bitten by a snake."

"Afterward."

"I found her. I know."

"Brother Martin examined the body."

"It had marks of poison upon it."

"Yes, Alain," said Gervase quietly. "But it also had bruising on the throat. Bertha was not killed by a snake."

"Stop using her name!" snarled the other with sudden fury. "You never knew Bertha as we did. You never could."

"I accept that."

"We do not want your help."

"You do, Alain."

"Let us mourn her in peace."

"I will," agreed Gervase. "When we have caught her killer. Until then, I will not rest and she will not lie easy in her grave." He leaned forward. "Can you hear what I am telling you? Bertha was murdered. Brother Martin has looked on death too often to be deluded. Someone strangled the life out of the poor girl."

Alain took time to absorb the news then he began to shake and moan. Convulsed with fury, he lashed out impotently with both fists but his energy was soon sapped. Gervase stayed calmly out of his reach and waited until he had subsided.

"Bertha was part of your little family here. Someone stole her away from you, Alain. Does that not make you want to answer a few simple questions for me?"

"No!"

"Do you not believe in justice?"

"Justice!"

Alain let out a hiss of anger and reached up to pluck away his veil, flinging back his hood at the same time and lifting his chin defiantly. Gervase was shocked but did his best not to flinch. The voice had deceived him. Expecting a middle-aged man, he was amazed to see someone who was younger than himself, no more than twenty, perhaps even less. Alain had a full head of dark hair and eyes of an even blacker hue. One side of his face was only partially affected by the disease and Gervase could see something of the olive complexion and the regular features.

But it was the other side of Alain's face which transfixed any onlooker. The skin was white, puffy and visibly crumbling away, the nose was half-eaten and the eyebrow was no more than a commemorative white slit. The lips were like an open wound. Leprosy had so disfigured the face, tearing the one eye down an inch below its companion, that Gervase felt as if he were staring at a rotting corpse.

"Do not talk to me of justice!" cried Alain, pointing a trembling finger at his face. "Where is the justice in *this*!"

"There is none," said Gervase simply.

The leper's frenzy faded and a sense of shame returned. Hood and veil were soon replaced and he withdrew into himself again. Nothing could be gained by pressing him for help. Rising to his feet, Gervase lifted a hand in farewell then walked quickly away in the direction of the hospital.

Long after his visitor had departed, Alain took the memento out from his sleeve and placed it in his lap. When he looked down at it, he saw the prone figure of Bertha lying dead among the holly with marks upon her white neck. She would never again come to Harbledown to talk alone with him.

The first hot tear trickled down the ravaged cheek.

~ CHAPTER FIVE

INACTIVITY MADE RALPH Delchard extremely restive. With everyone else in the house engaged either in soothing Eadgyth, nursing the baby, preparing the food or doing the many other chores, he felt both neglected and in the way. Sensing his discomfort, Golde urged him to take himself out.

"You will not object, my love?" he asked.

"Why should I?"

"For deserting you like this."

"I will hardly notice that you are gone," she said. "Eadgyth's need takes precedence over all else at this moment. She is in pain. I cannot stand by and watch her torment without doing something. I must help."

"Then so will I, Golde. You can best help by staying here, and I, by getting out from under your feet."

"Where will you go?"

"In search of Gervase."

"It might be a kindness to keep him away for an hour or

so at least. Explain the situation and he will understand."

"We will stay away all night," he teased. "If you wish."

"I would only come looking for you."

"That would be my hope."

She kissed him lightly on the lips and went back upstairs to continue with her self-appointed duties. There was stabling at the rear of the house, reached from the street by a narrow, rutted lane. When a servant had saddled his horse for him, Ralph went trotting back toward the crowded High Street.

His first visit was to the castle to see if his men were safely lodged and to give them their orders for the morrow. Finding them well-fed, flushed by wine and in noisy good humour, he treated them to a burst of vituperation in order to remind them that marriage had not entirely blunted the edge of his temper. Having asserted his authority, he felt able to go in pursuit of his friend. His horse moved off at a steady canter toward the rural peace of Harbledown.

Gervase Bret was halfway down the hill when he caught sight of Ralph. The pounding hooves soon closed the gap between them. Ralph reined in his mount beside Gervase.

"Where the devil have you been?" he demanded.

"To the hospital of St. Nicholas."

"Consorting with foul lepers when the city is full of comely wenches? Speak to my men. They only arrived at the castle this morning and already they know the whereabouts of every brothel in the city. Seek pleasure for once."

"I have other things on my mind, Ralph."

"What is more important than a warm woman in a soft bed?"

"Solving a cruel murder."

Ralph was jolted. "Murder?"

"The girl they found dead. Bertha."

"But she was killed by a poisonous snake."

"It was made to *look* as if she had been, Ralph."

"The cause of death has been confirmed. I talked with the doctor myself. He examined the girl's body and spoke with assurance on the matter."

"You have met Helto the Doctor?"

"Yes," said Ralph. "He was called to the house when Eadgyth's grief was too much for her to bear. His visit calmed her. Helto was going on to perform a like service for Bertha's father. He, too, is suffering the agonies of the bereaved."

"How would you describe this doctor?"

"Helto?" Ralph inhaled deeply before giving his judgement. "Difficult to like but just as difficult not to respect. A sound physician, certainly, and with more compassion than first meets the eye. Osbern the Reeve could not speak too highly of him."

"An honest man?"

"Honest and straightforward."

"Capable of dissembling?"

"On my short acquaintance, I think not. Why do you ask?"

"We came to the conclusion that Helto was lying. It may just be that his postmortem examination was careless."

"I would doubt that."

"It is the only way to explain his mistake, Ralph."

"What mistake?"

"Bertha was strangled to death."

"Who says so?"

"Brother Martin of the hospital of St. Nicholas."

"On what evidence?"

"Let me show you some of it."

Ralph dismounted and Gervase took him back up the hill to the clump of holly, recounting on the way how he and the old monk had first begun to question the apparent cause of the girl's demise. Tethering his horse, Ralph pushed his way down into the hollow to take a close look for himself. Gervase slowly built up the web of detail for him.

"We have another case to judge," commented Ralph.

"Case?"

"Monk versus doctor. Whom do you favour?"

"Brother Martin. You have heard my reasons."

"I warrant that Helto is the truer physician."

"Even the finest doctor can err at times."

"If that is what he did, Gervase."

"Rule out dishonesty and it is all that is left. Who knows? Helto may have been too lax or perfunctory in his work. And the morgue at St. Mildred's may be partly to blame."

"In what way?"

"I am told it is a small chamber with no window. Perhaps the candle threw inadequate light for Helto. That was why he did not discern the bruising on the throat."

"Brother Martin worked by the same flame."

"True."

"Helto's eyes are keener than those of an old monk."

"Instinct comes into it as well, Ralph."

"What does yours tell you?"

"There has been foul play."

Ralph nodded. He remembered what Helto the Doctor had said about a stone hurled into a pool. Bertha's death had already caused violent ripples to spread. If the girl was indeed the victim of a murder, those ripples would become huge waves and they would wash through the very house where Golde and the two commissioners were staying. It would not advantage their work in Canterbury.

That was a secondary consideration in Ralph's view. Now

that the crime had been brought to light, it had to be reported and investigated. Someone needed to be called to account for what appeared to be a calculated murder.

"The sheriff must be informed, Gervase."

"I was on my way to do exactly that when we met."

"Let us go together," suggested Ralph. "But when you have reported your findings, you must hand over the inquiry to the proper authority."

"I am bound to retain a keen interest."

"Your interest must be concentrated on the problems we were sent here to resolve. They will keep us busy for a week or more before we can quit the city. Forget the girl."

"How can I?"

"You are not involved."

"I must be, Ralph. He is depending on me."

"Who is?"

"Brother Martin. He is the crucial figure here and he is ready to speak up before the sheriff and to challenge the opinion of Helto the Doctor. That will place Brother Martin under great strain. He is old and no longer as clear-minded as he would wish to be. I can support him. Encourage him. Buttress his evidence with my own observations."

"Not while you are sitting in commission with me."

"I will contrive to help somehow."

"Gervase—"

"I am sorry," interrupted the other, "but I cannot turn my back on this crime. There are things that I might learn which would be beyond the reach of the sheriff's officers."

"Give me an instance."

"Alain's testimony."

"Who is Alain?"

"The leper who found the girl. I am sure that he knows

something which may provide a vital clue. I sensed it when I spoke to him. He was holding something back from me."

"Let the sheriff shake it out of him."

"He would not dare to go within ten yards of Alain."

"That sounds like a wise precaution to me."

"I could do it," said Gervase. "If I can win Alain's confidence, I am sure I can draw the truth out of him."

"And what is happening to affairs of state while you are running off to Harbledown to befriend lepers?"

"You will not find me shirking my duties."

Ralph held him by the shoulders. "The girl is not your problem, Gervase. Let her go. You did not even know Bertha."

"I feel as if I have got very close to her in the last few hours. For someone so young and innocent, she had a profound effect on others. Brother Martin talked at length about her and I saw for myself what she meant to the lepers at the hospital. They looked upon her as a kind of saint."

"You must speak to Helto the Doctor."

"Why?"

"He examined the girl's body at the morgue."

"And?"

"In one respect, Bertha fell short of sainthood."

Osbern the Reeve was too responsible a man to allow any domestic problems to interfere with his official duties. Everything was in readiness for the commissioners on the following morning. The shire hall had been cleaned, a table and four chairs had been set out, and benches had been put in position for the various disputants and witnesses who would come forward. Mindful of the wearying length to which such deliberations could go, Osbern had even organised some interim refreshments for the visitors.

While the reeve was absent, Golde took over the care of his wife. The sleeping draught had allowed Eadgyth to pass the night in restorative slumber and she awoke in a far less agitated mood. Rumours of an inquiry into the alleged murder of Bertha were buzzing around the city but Eadgyth was protected from them at this stage, allowing her to mourn the death of a dear friend without the terrifying knowledge of how that death might have been brought about.

The shire hall was a long, shapeless, timber-framed building with low beams and undulating flagstones worn smooth by the regular passage of feet. Canon Hubert and Brother Simon were the first to arrive, the former pleased to see everything conspicuously in order and the latter weighed down by a leather satchel stuffed with documents, rolls of fresh parchment and writing materials.

Ralph Delchard arrived with his men-at-arms, six of whom were left outside as sentries while their fellows took up their station inside the shire hall. Gervase Bret followed them in, carrying his own large satchel of letters and documents. As leader of the commission, Ralph took the chair at the centre of the table with Gervase and Hubert on either side of him. Simon was at a right angle to them, perched at the end of the table so that he could watch them to receive direction while at the same time keeping an eye on those who occupied the benches.

"Are we all ready?" asked Ralph, glancing around and collecting general assent. "Good. We have all studied the material relating to the first dispute. Let us begin."

Ralph gave a signal and three figures were soon being conducted into the room. Prior Henry was accompanied by two monks who walked deferentially behind him. Their entry coincided with the strident clang of the cathedral bell as it announced Tierce.

"I am glad to see that you are punctual," said Henry.

"We are punctual and punctilious," warned Ralph.

"I would expect no less, my lord. I am Prior Henry and I speak for Archbishop Lanfranc. May I know whom I face?"

Ralph introduced himself and his colleagues. The prior's eyes appraised them each in turn, showing no flicker of recognition when they rested on Canon Hubert. Lowering himself on to the front bench, Prior Henry held out a bony hand. One of the monks handed him a sheaf of letters from his satchel, then sat, with his colleague, on the bench behind the prior. Their role was purely supportive.

"We do not wish this dispute to continue," said Ralph. "It has already dragged on for far too long."

"I could not agree with you more," said Henry. "It is my hope—and the archbishop's fervent desire—that we may reach some sort of resolution by the end of the day."

"It lies within your power to reach it immediately."

"Does it, my lord?"

"Surrender your claim and the matter is ended."

"I see that you mean to draw some amusement from this case," said Henry, drily. "Do you have any more jests to make before we address this dispute with requisite solemnity?"

"My suggestion was quite serious, Prior Henry."

"Then make it to the Abbey of St. Augustine. Persuade them to abandon their folly and cede the property to its rightful owner, the Archbishop of Canterbury."

"King William owns the land," corrected Canon Hubert with terse pedantry. "His subjects only hold it from him as tenants."

"A pointless quibble."

"Not to royal officials, Prior Henry."

Hubert sat back complacently, feeling that he had just repaid the prior for some of the slights he believed he had suffered at the man's hands, and grateful to have been given an early opportunity to demonstrate to Ralph Delchard that he showed no favour toward the cathedral. Prior Henry seemed quite unperturbed. Any irritation or discomfort was carefully hidden behind an inscrutable expression and a voice of measured calm.

"Why do you offer such preposterous counsel, my lord?" he asked. "I presume that you have some sort of reason."

"The desire for a swift and just solution."

"Swift, it would certainly be—but hardly just."

"A pointless quibble," echoed Ralph with irony.

"I see that you are no lawyer, my lord."

"Gervase fulfills that role," said Ralph, turning to his colleague. "He will refresh our minds on this issue."

Gervase glanced down at the parchment in front of him and translated the Latin abbreviations with practised ease.

"This is the entry for Fordwich Hundred. 'A small borough which is called Fordwich. King Edward gave two parts of this borough to St. Augustine's; but the Bishop of Bayeux, with King William's assent, also assigned to St. Augustine's the third part, which had belonged to Earl Godwin. It answers for 1 yoke. There were 100 measures of land less 4 there which paid 13 shillings. Now there are 73 dwellings which pay as much. Value before 1066 and later 100 shillings; now £11,2 shillings. There are also 24 acres of land which St. Augustine's always had, where there were and are six burgesses who pay 22 shillings.' "

Ralph smirked. "Note how often the name of St. Augustine's Abbey is mentioned."

"There is more," said Henry. "Allow him to finish."

"Gervase?"

"One last entry, my lord. 'In this Borough Archbishop Lanfranc holds seven measures of land which served St.

Augustine's before 1066; now the Archbishop takes their service from it.' That is a full extract from the returns."

"There it stands," said Ralph. "Such are the facts as elicited by our predecessors when they came into Kent to collect all the information germane to the Great Survey. They were exceedingly thorough."

"They were," said Prior Henry equably. "Thorough and conscientious. They worked to the best of their limited abilities. I look for no less of their successors."

Ralph was jangled. " 'Limited abilities'?"

"That is not meant as a criticism."

"It does not have the ring of praise about it."

"Let me explain," said the prior easily. "The first commissioners were trusted laymen of high rank, sent into this county to assess the value of its property and to determine its ownership. Or," he added, flicking a glance at Canon Hubert, "if that word offends you, to determine which of his tenant-in-chiefs held the land of the King. But your predecessors worked under two huge constraints."

"Constraints?" said Hubert.

"They were not well versed in the laws of property and they were ordered to collect their evidence quickly and send their returns to the Exchequer. Ignorance and haste are the enemies of fair judgement. You see both reflected in the extract which Master Bret read out to us just now." He aimed a polite smile at Gervase. "On which subject, may I say that I would have preferred to hear the original Latin so that I could place my own interpretation upon it. Certain words always pale in translation."

"I am starting to pale under your strictures," said Ralph in exasperation. "May I remind you that we are here by royal warrant, Prior Henry, and that entitles us to your respect? We sit in judgement on you and will not have our own work, or that of our predecessors, put on trial. You are not in the chapter-house now, talking down to a flock of monastic sheep, too frightened even to bleat in protest. If the meek are set to inherit the earth, you will not find any landholders sitting at this table." He heard the squeak from the shocked Brother Simon. "Except, perhaps, our scribe."

Canon Hubert goggled and the two monks from Christ Church Priory were so scandalised that they began to gibber. Gervase smiled inwardly. But the outburst had no discernible effect on Prior Henry. He remained calm and poised. It only served to annoy Ralph even more.

"Let us proceed to the crux of the matter," he said.

"I am listening, my lord."

"In the survey of this county, Fordwich is listed as part of the land held by St. Augustine's Abbey. There is documentary evidence to support this. You have none."

"The charters were destroyed by fire."

"What proof do we have that they ever existed?"

"Letters and depositions from some of the brothers who were at the priory before it was caught in the blaze."

"Saxon monks?" said Hubert.

"Naturally."

"You accept their word?"

"Without reservation."

"Then your memory betrays you, Prior Henry," said the canon with relish. "When Archbishop Lanfranc first came to Canterbury in the year of our Lord, 1070, he was appalled by what he found. The monks had dwindled in number and strayed disastrously from the Rule. They hunted, fished, bloated themselves on rich food and often drank themselves into a stupor. Some—I am ashamed to recall this—were given to carnal pleasure with women."

"God protect us!" gasped Brother Simon.

"Duty and reverence were forgotten. They were a stain upon the reputation of the Benedictine Order."

"All this is true," confessed Henry. "The archbishop moved swiftly and sternly to remedy this disgrace. Those who stayed within the enclave are truly contrite."

"I find it difficult to trust them wholeheartedly."

"Because they are Saxon?" The prior clicked his tongue. "I am disappointed in you, Canon Hubert. The cowl makes us all equal. Saxon, Norman, Welsh, Irish, Breton, Flemish or Spanish, monks are brothers who make no distinction about nationality. Archbishop Lanfranc is an Italian. So am I. So, of course, is Anselm of Bec, who became prior there when you felt that you were destined for that office."

Hubert smouldered. The reproof was all the more wounding for being delivered in such an even-tempered way. Prior Henry's mild tongue had the power of a lash. It had been painful enough when they were alone together but this public humiliation was far worse.

"Our hopes of a speedy end to this dispute have been dashed," sighed Ralph. "You clearly mean to contest this case."

"What is the alternative, my lord?"

"A sensible compromise."

"Victory is the only compromise we will accept."

"That will mean a long and bitter battle."

"So be it. The abbey is grievously at fault here."

"Not only here," intervened Gervase. "I believe that cathedral and abbey have other differences to settle."

"Other differences?"

"The election of their new abbot."

"He has already been appointed."

"Without their endorsement."

"Abbot Guy is the archbishop's nominated choice."

"Why does St. Augustine's resist it so strongly?"

"Their obstinacy is no concern of yours," said Henry with his equanimity intact. "It is an internal matter and has no bearing whatsoever on the business in hand."

"Unless it provides a motive," added Ralph.

"Motive?"

"Abbey and cathedral are at each other's throat. The cowl may make you equal brothers but that does not stop you squabbling like fishwives." Ralph stared him in the eye. "I have heard of this wrangling over the new abbot. Is that why you lay claim to St. Augustine's property? Is the archbishop punishing them for daring to defy him? Tell him this, Prior Henry. We will not be used as a stick to beat the abbey into submission."

"I will report all that has passed between us," said the other, quite unruffled. "What more can be done now?"

"Nothing, until we have studied your documents."

"Then I will leave them in your safekeeping." He rose to his feet and the two monks leaped up obediently, hanging on his command. "When will I be required again?"

"When we send for you, Prior Henry."

"We must hear from the abbey first," said Hubert with a placatory note, fearing what might be said about him to the archbishop. "Prior Gregory is on his way here now."

"Yes," said Ralph pointedly. "Had you been more amenable, we might have saved him the journey. But your mind is plainly set on joining battle."

Prior Henry looked along the table with a quiet smile.

"We mean to fight," he vowed. "Tooth and nail."

Golde sat with her beside the crib and gazed down at the sleeping baby. He looked peaceful and contented. Eadgyth had been well enough to feed him and her love had surged when she saw her son guzzling happily at the breast. The

needs of the child had pushed her grief aside and concentrated her mind. Golde sought other ways to deflect
her from a brooding sadness. In the brief time they had
known each other, she had grown fond of the young
mother. Studying her now, Golde found it hard to believe
that someone who looked so robust could really be so delicate.

"You are blessed in your husband," said Golde.

"I know," agreed the other, "and I am never likely to forget it. Osbern is a wonderful man. He is so tolerant of my
weaknesses and so uncomplaining about my follies."

"He is a lucky man to have such a beautiful wife."

"That is what he tells me."

"How did you meet him?"

"By chance, Golde. It was in the market. I had been sent
to buy some fish. When I looked up from the stall, I saw
him not five yards away. Osbern was arguing with one of
the stallholders. It was about payment of rent, he later told
me. Osbern suddenly caught my eye and gave me such a
sweet smile that I carried the memory of it around with me
for days."

"Did you not speak to him?"

"I did not dare, Golde."

"Nothing else passed between you?"

"Just the look. And the smile. They were enough."

"When did you see him again?"

"Not for a week or more," said Eadgyth. "I thought he
had forgotten me. Or left Canterbury altogether. For all I
knew, he was just a visitor to the city. I had no idea that he
was so important. The town reeve, no less." She gave a
girlish laugh. "It seemed impossible. I was so young and
silly. Osbern was so mature and serious."

"But it happened."

"Yes, Golde! He came looking for me."

"And all because you went to buy some fish!"

They exchanged a laugh and Eadgyth's face lit up with joy. She looked at her son, remembered the loving husband whose name he bore and she basked for a moment in her good fortune. The clouds soon came. A frown distorted her brow and her lip began to quiver. Golde embraced her and rocked her gently to and fro.

"It is a sin to be so happy," sobbed Eadgyth.

"No, it is not."

"Bertha lies dead and I am boasting about my husband."

"He will help you through your bereavement."

"I cannot believe I will never see her again."

"Fate can be very cruel."

"Bertha was so kind to me. She took such a pleasure in my joy. At our wedding, Bertha was the first person to rush up to kiss me. She was delighted that I found Osbern. She loved to see me happy. Bertha was never jealous."

"That is true friendship, Eadgyth. To look on the joy of others and feel no envy. You and she were so close. When you married Osbern and committed yourself to him, there must have been a sense of loss for her."

"Bertha never complained. She understood."

"Understood?"

"Yes," said Eadgyth dreamily. "It happened for her, too. Bertha knew what it was to love a man so completely. She told me about him." She clutched at Golde as the sobbing started again. "Bertha is dead. He has lost her forever."

"Who has?"

"Her friend."

♘ CHAPTER SIX

THE CONFRONTATION TOOK place in the parish church of St. Mildred's. Reinbald the Priest was there with two of the sheriff's officers but they were largely silent witnesses. Monk and doctor went into the morgue together with a candle apiece. Earnest discussion was heard in the cramped chamber where the girl's body lay under its shroud. When the two finally emerged into the nave, each was firmly convinced that he was in the right.

"Will you agree with me now?" asked Brother Martin.

"Indeed I will not," said Helto the Doctor. "My initial diagnosis was correct. Bertha was bitten by a snake."

"After she was dead."

"That is an absurd suggestion, Brother Martin."

"All the evidence points to it."

"Only in your mind. And that, with respect, is befuddled by the natural grief you feel at this terrible loss. You knew Bertha as a dear friend and a loyal assistant at the hospital. Her death is bound to affect you deeply."

"Her murder affects me even more."

"The girl was killed by snakebite."

"Then how do you explain the bruising on her neck?"

"The result of the poison."

"The throat would not be so discoloured."

"Strange things happen to a body after death. They can be very misleading to the untutored eye. I see nothing here to indicate foul play."

"Then you are badly mistaken!" insisted the old man.

"And you are very confused!"

The priest stepped in. "Do not raise your voices in the house of the Lord," he chided. "If you want an argument, take it outside into the street."

"It is no argument, Father Reinbald," said Helto. "It is just an honest difference of opinion. Brother Martin and I have viewed the body together. He sees one thing, I see another."

"Who is right?" asked one of the officers.

"I am," said the doctor peremptorily.

"No, *I* am," argued the monk. "Helto the Doctor may know more about medicine than I do. I accept that. He looks on corpses in this city every week and recognises death in its various guises. His reputation is high."

"Then why do you challenge him?" asked Reinbald.

"Because he is mistaken for once."

"Impossible!"

"You are wrong, Helto!"

"Not so, Brother Martin!"

"It is! I would take an oath on it!"

"Who is the physician here!"

"Peace, sirs!" implored Reinbald, moving between them to push them gently apart. "Remember the poor creature who lies not ten yards away from us. She is entitled to respect."

"Respect and reverence," added the monk sadly. "We are justly rebuked, Father Reinbald. I beg your forgiveness."

"We are both to blame here," said Helto, regaining his composure. "Nothing is served by altercation. Let us take this discussion out into the fresh air where it belongs." He led the way to the door. "I am sorry if I spoke harshly, Brother Martin. It was unpardonable. I am simply not used to having my opinion questioned."

"I can see that," murmured the old man.

Reinbald and the two officers followed them out. They found it difficult to decide whose word to trust. Helto spoke with more authority but Brother Martin's cowl, his longer experience and his luminous honesty were powerful factors. The onlookers waited for the debate to start once more.

Helto the Doctor tried to seize the initiative at once.

"Let us begin afresh," he suggested calmly. "We know where we differ. What are the points on which we actually agree?"

Martin shrugged. "The girl is dead. Everybody can agree on that. Beyond that fact, we have no common ground."

"That is not so, Brother Martin," mollified the other. "Will you accept that she was bitten by a snake?"

"Bitten by it, yes. But not killed."

"Will you confirm that the creature was poisonous?"

"Yes. We saw it curled up beside her."

"And had you not seen it?" pressed Helto. "How could you tell whether or not it had been venomous?"

"From the nature of the bite. Two small puncture marks on the neck where the fangs went in. If Bertha had been bitten by a harmless grass snake, she would have had a set of tooth-marks in the shape of a crescent moon."

"Correct."

"I have suffered such a wound on my own hand."

"What are the symptoms of a fatal snakebite?"

"A swelling near the fang-marks and some bruising around the affected area."

"And the more sensitive that area—the soft and delicate white skin of a girl, for example—the worse the bruising is likely to be. Will you concede that as well?"

"Gladly."

"We are making progress at last."

"Hardly," said Brother Martin. "Instead of talking about the body, you must first look at the circumstances in which it was found. Hidden away behind a clump of holly. Bertha had no reason to be in such a place."

"Except the obvious one, perhaps?"

"What is that, Helto?"

The doctor spoke discreetly. "Even a lovely young girl like Bertha had to satisfy the wants of nature."

"Lying down?"

The two officers laughed coarsely but checked their mirth when Reinbald reproached them with a glance. They turned to Helto for his reply but the doctor sighed wearily and shook his head.

"We will never come to composition here," he decided. "It is a waste of breath. If you insist on believing that she was murdered, I will try to dissuade you no longer. Let the sheriff and his men search for this phantom killer. When they find him, they can ask him a question from me."

"What is that?" wondered Reinbald.

"Harbledown is full of places where a dead body could be concealed and never found. The earth is soft at this time of year. It would not take long to bury her." His voice took on a sarcastic edge. "Ask the murderer this on my behalf. When he killed Bertha—from motives I could not even guess at—why was he foolish enough to leave the body where a search was bound to discover it?"

Helto the Doctor turned on his heel and marched away. It was a dramatic exit and it had the desired effect. Both Reinbald and the two officers tilted toward an acceptance of the physician's medical opinion. There was an unassailable confidence about him which gave his words the ring of truth.

Brother Martin was completely unabashed.

"She was strangled," he said. "I'd stake my life on it."

In character and appearance, Prior Gregory was very different from his counterpart at Christ Church Priory. He had none of Henry's studied poise and cold spirituality. His face was no impassive mask. The prior of St. Augustine's Abbey was instead a short, sturdy, bustling man with hands toughened by early years of manual labour and shoulders rounded by long hours of study over a desk. The bulbous nose and the rubicund cheeks were the salient features of a large, round, mobile countenance. Concealment was an art which he had never cultivated. Whatever his mind thought or his heart felt showed in his expression.

Ralph liked him on sight. He usually treated anyone from a monastic community with an amiable irreverence but Prior Gregory somehow appealed to him. There was a refreshing openness about the man and a total lack of pomposity. Here was a combative Christian who had to be admired.

When greetings were exchanged, Prior Gregory sank down onto the bench vacated by his adversary. Bearing a satchel of charters, a young monk sat beside him. The prior did not need to bolster his importance by relegating his companion to an inferior position behind him.

"We come to Canterbury at an awkward time," said Ralph. "It seems that relations between abbey and cathedral are somewhat strained at the moment."

"That situation is not, alas, an unusual one," explained Prior Gregory. "We pray daily for deliverance."

"From what?"

"The dilemma that confronts us."

"This row over the new abbot?"

"That is certainly one part of the problem."

"What are the others?"

"We are met here to address the main issue. The abbey holds the borough of Fordwich yet the archbishop claims that much of the property rightfully belongs to him."

"Why does he do that, Prior Gregory?"

"Ask him."

"I would prefer to hear your assessment."

"May I speak freely, my lord?"

"Of course," encouraged Ralph. "You have my personal assurance that nothing you say will be repeated outside these four walls."

"Very well," said the prior forcefully. "You ask me why Archbishop Lanfranc contests this land when he already holds vast amounts of property in Canterbury and elsewhere. I will tell you in one word. Pique."

"That is a serious charge to level," said Canon Hubert.

"It is justified."

"Pique is alien to his character."

"Judge for yourself." He turned to his companion and extracted a roll of parchment from the satchel. "With your permission," he said, standing up, "I would like to show you a map I have drawn. It is very crude but it may explain things which are not clear from mere description."

He unrolled the map on the table and Ralph placed a

cup and a heavy hand on it to hold it flat. Prior Gregory had poor skill as an artist but they could recognise the rough outline of Canterbury and the oblong shape with a cross inside it, which represented St. Augustine's Abbey, outside the eastern wall of the city.

"Here is Fordwich," explained the prior, using a stubby finger to point to a blob of ink in the far corner. "It is our port. This thick line on which it stands is the River Stour. The port is never idle. Apart from coastal trade, it handles regular imports of stone from Normandy. Canterbury not only gained its archbishop from Caen but huge quantities of building materials as well."

Gervase thought of Alwin the Sailor, steering his little vessel across the Channel and returning with a full load of Caen stone. Cathedral, abbey and churches had benefitted from the industry of Alwin and his kind. Fordwich had thrived.

"After the Conquest," continued their guide, jabbing his finger at another portion of the map, "Bishop Odo of Bayeux seized property in and around the city, including two sulungs above Fordwich, where he cut out a deer park."

"Sulungs?" said Ralph. "Why do you not measure your land in hides like most other counties? Two sulungs, you say?"

"It amounts to over three hundred acres," said Gervase. "Odo was always fond of hunting."

"Thanks to Abbot Scotland," said the prior, "we reclaimed the property, and other land in the area of Fordwich, for the abbey. Nobody disputed our holding until now. Until Archbishop Lanfranc turned on us in a fit of pique."

"Because you resist his choice of abbot?" said Ralph.

"Chiefly for that reason."

"Are holy relics also a factor here?" said Gervase. "I spoke with Reinbald the Priest on that matter. He tells me that the archbishop found the bones of St. Mildred."

"The abbey houses the true relics," asserted the prior. "Some were sent abroad but we retain the better part of them. But you are right, Master Bret. It is another source of friction between cathedral and abbey. There are more besides and all help to ignite the archbishop's enmity."

Canon Hubert erupted. "I cannot let these aspersions go unchallenged," he said. "Archbishop Lanfranc is too noble a man to allow any pettiness to creep into his dealings. You say that Abbot Scotland reclaimed that land for you?"

"He did," consented the prior.

"On whose advice?"

"Archbishop Lanfranc's."

"And who brought the good abbot from Mont St. Michel?"

"Archbishop Lanfranc."

"Who consecrated him?"

"Archbishop Lanfranc."

"Who directed him to rebuild the abbey and restore the full rigour of the Benedictine Rule within it?"

"Archbishop Lanfranc."

"And who worked so closely and effectively over the years with Abbot Scotland?"

"The answer is the same, Canon Hubert."

"But the person is not," retorted the other. "I have just talked about one Archbishop Lanfranc but you have told us about something completely different. Are there *two*?"

"Why not?" said Ralph mischievously. "We have two matching skeletons of St. Mildred here. Why not a pair of identical archbishops?"

"Canon Hubert raises a valid point," said Gervase. "If a

man is to be judged by his deeds, then the archbishop must be venerated for his great vision and holy endeavour. He has been an exemplary primate of the English Church. It is difficult to believe him capable of vengeful behaviour."

"We are all subject to human frailty," said the prior.

Hubert still chafed. "The archbishop must be absolved of acting out of pique."

"What else would make him lay claim to that land?"

"A legitimate right."

"We have brought the abbey's charters with us."

"Prior Henry will contest their validity."

"Let him do so."

"It will be a bloody battle," warned Ralph.

"We are ready, my lord," said Prior Gregory with a note of fierce pride. "The abbey has been bullied and intimidated by the cathedral. On many issues, we have been forced to yield. Not on this one." He snatched up the map and held it high. "We will not cede one square inch of our land. The archbishop has chosen this fight, not the abbey. Let him come on. We will give no quarter."

Alwin the Sailor was so stunned by the death of his daughter that he did not stir out of his house. A sleeping draught prescribed by Helto the Doctor had given him rest but it did not ease the agony of loss. When he awoke, the searing pain was still embedded in him like a knife in his chest. A neighbour called to offer help and comfort but he waved her away. When a second knock came on his door, Alwin did not even answer it. Head in hands, he sat on a wooden stool and brooded on the misery of his future.

The visitor eventually let himself into the house.

"How are you, my son?" asked Brother Martin softly.

"Go away," murmured the other.

"I wanted to see how you are. Did you manage to sleep last night? Have you eaten today? Is someone looking after you?"

"I want to be left alone."

"I know, Alwin," said the priest, putting a hand on his shoulder. "And I promise that I will not stay long. But I felt that it was my duty to come. I am sure that you would rather hear it from me than from one of the sheriff's officers. They would be more blunt with the tidings."

Alwin looked up. "What tidings?"

"Something I can hardly bring myself to tell you. But it is your right as her father to know it."

"Something to do with Bertha?"

"I fear so."

"What? Tell me, Brother Martin."

"It is grim news. Prepare yourself."

"Why?"

"You will soon see." He took a deep breath but the words would not come. He shook his head in despair. "God help me! I do not like this office. Truly, I do not. I feel as if I am hitting a man who has already had blows enough."

"What do you mean?" said Alwin, rising to his feet in concern. "If you have any news about Bertha, I must know it instantly. She was my daughter. Tell me, man!"

"Be brave, Alwin."

"Tell me!"

He grabbed the old monk and shook him hard but stopped when he saw the tears forming in his eyes. Brother Martin was suffering enough on his own account. It had clearly cost him an enormous effort to come to the house. His whole body was limp with despair.

"I must know!" pleaded Alwin with quiet intensity.

"Bertha was murdered."

The father reeled. "Murdered? No, this cannot be."

"She was strangled to death."

"Bertha was bitten by a poisonous snake. You were there when we found here. We all saw the marks upon her neck."

"We were meant to, Alwin."

"I do not understand."

Brother Martin relayed the evidence as gently and as concisely as he could. He explained that Helto the Doctor held a contrary opinion but the monk himself had no whisper of doubt. The sheriff had set an investigation in motion.

"They will need to speak to you," cautioned Martin. "I begged them to let me see you first." He heaved a deep sigh. "A lovable creature like Bertha. A girl with no enemies. Who could possibly have wanted to kill her?"

Alwin said nothing. As the horror slowly faded, it was replaced by a lust for vengeance which made his whole body shake. He let out a roar of anger. When Brother Martin tried to calm him, he was pushed roughly away. Alwin snatched up the dagger which lay on the table.

"I want him!" he snarled. "He is mine!"

"Did she not at least give you his name?" asked Ralph.

"No," said Golde. "She would tell me nothing more."

"You pressed her on the matter, surely?"

"I did not feel that I could, Ralph. She is still not well. Eadgyth was distressed enough that she had confided as much as she did. She has been racked with guilt ever since. Bertha made her promise to tell nobody."

"I can understand why," said Ralph. "Everyone thought that Bertha was a fount of innocence and she was careful to preserve that image. It would have cracked in two had people realised the girl had a lover."

" 'A friend.' That is what Eadgyth called him."

"Friends are not kept hidden."

"A *lover*? Bertha?"

"Is that not what every young girl dreams of, Golde?"

"Dreams, perhaps. But rarely more than that."

"Bertha was luckier than most, then."

"We do not know that."

"I think we do," said Ralph to himself.

They were alone in the solar of Osbern the Reeve's house. Ralph had just returned from a long and testing day in the shire hall and Golde was delighted to see him again. She threw her arms around him and kissed him on the lips. He responded warmly.

"That was worth every minute of the boredom I have endured today," he said, holding her by the hands to look at her. "No, that is unfair," he corrected. "There were some lively moments, even some amusing ones."

"Have you been mocking Canon Hubert again?"

"He deserves mockery. So does Brother Simon."

"Spare him, at least," said Golde. "Canon Hubert can strike back but Brother Simon has no defence against you. He is such a gentle, harmless, virtuous creature. I like him."

"Do not tell him that or we will never get him out of the priory. You terrify him, Golde. All women do."

"Why?"

"He feels threatened," explained Ralph. "Brother Simon's body is a temple of purity. He would die rather than let any monstrous females break into that temple."

"Is that what *I* am? A monstrous female?"

"Only in his eyes." He squeezed her hands. "Simon took the cowl in flight from feminine charms. He turned white with horror today when he discovered that the monks in Christ Church Priory had held wild orgies at one time."

"Orgies?"

"Apparently. Wine in quantity and women in abundance. A potent mixture. Archbishop Lanfranc put a stop to all that. He has even enforced celibacy among the secular clergy now. That is why you see so many sad faces in Canterbury." He chuckled, then gave her another kiss before abruptly changing the subject. "I am hungry. When will we eat?"

"They are preparing the meal now."

"Good."

"But we cannot sit down without Gervase."

"Forget him. He may be an hour or more."

"Where has he gone?"

"Harbledown," said Ralph. "I have told him he must not get drawn into this business but my words fall on deaf ears. Under that self-effacing manner, Gervase Bret has an iron will. When he wishes to do something, a whole army could not stop him."

Released from the business of the day, Gervase rode out through Westgate and took a more wide-ranging look at Harbledown. When he came to the archbishop's palace, he slowed his horse to a trot so that he could survey the rambling manor house with its commodious interior and substantial, well-tended garden. It was built of timber and stone on a choice site.

Twenty-seven dwellings had been destroyed to make way for Lanfranc's imposing new home and Gervase paused to wonder what had happened to all those luckless families who had been summarily evicted by religion. A day in the shire hall had given him an insight into the politics of Christ Church Priory and it occurred to him that some of its older monks must have been dismayed when the archbishop first arrived in the city and, instead of living in the enclave himself and sharing in its austerities, sacked their dean, installed Prior Henry in his place, then constructed the palace in Harbledown. The community at St. Augustine's Abbey were probably not alone in harbouring a grudge against Lanfranc.

Gervase rode off at a canter. Having mused on the small human imperfections of the archbishop, he was overwhelmed by a consideration of his good works. Lanfranc had brought a new zest and organisation to the religious life of the city. Centered in the cathedral and the priory, it reached out in all directions and spread slowly throughout the whole kingdom. It was churlish to criticise a man for living in a comfortable house when he had shown such compassion for the poor, the sick and the aged. The hospital of St. Nicholas was only one small monument to Lanfranc's abiding charity.

Alain was sitting outside his hut when Gervase rode up. The leper watched as the newcomer tethered his horse to a yew tree and walked across to him.

"Good day to you, Alain!"

"There is no goodness in any of my days."

"That is not true," said Gervase. "I think that Bertha brought a species of goodness here. Do you miss her?"

"We must learn to live without Bertha."

"Do you not pine?"

Alain fell silent but his sagging shoulders and downcast head were an eloquent answer. Gervase felt a rush of sympathy. The plight of the lepers was piteous. They would not easily find another friend like Bertha.

"We spoke yesterday," Gervase reminded him.

"Not at my behest."

"Do you remember what I said?"

"No."

"You do, Alain. I asked you what you saw when you found Bertha. You wouldn't tell me. I need to know."

"I saw only what you saw."

"Nothing more?"

An insolent pause. "Nothing more."

Gervase nodded. Alain was still unready to trust him. The only person who might get through to him was Brother Martin. It was time to enlist his help to win over Alain. When Gervase looked around, the leper lifted a hand to point.

"Brother Martin is in the church."

"Thank you."

"Do not come back."

Gervase gave up for the second time and strolled up to the litle church, lifting the iron latch on the door. The place seemed empty as he stepped inside and his footsteps echoed in the hollow nave. Brother Martin was not there. Gervase was just about to leave when he caught sight of him at last, seated on a bench up a pillar. With his hood pulled up, his black cowl merged with the dark shadow. The old monk had evidently drifted off to sleep.

It was not surprising. Brother Martin had been like a second father to Bertha and his grief was intense. What made it even more unbearable was the knowledge that the girl had been murdered while returning from the leper hospital. The old monk was bound to reflect that she might still be alive if she had remained in the safety of the city instead of walking alone through the countryside. Loss and guilt were heavy burdens.

Gervase sought to lift some of them from his friend.

"Brother Martin!" he whispered. "It is Gervase."

The monk did not stir. Gervase touched his arm.

"Brother Martin," he said, giving him a firm shake.

Making no sound, the black-clad figure fell softly forward

to land in an undignified heap on the floor. Gervase bent down to turn him over, and shook him again. But he was far too late. Sightless eyes gazed up at him and the mouth hung open.

Brother Martin's selfless life was over.

✑ CHAPTER SEVEN

GERVASE WAS COMPLETELY numbed. He shook his head in disbelief. Brother Martin could not possibly be dead. The monk was old and weary but he had an inner spark which drove him on and which defied the nudging deteriorations of time. He would never leave his charges at the hospital without even the courtesy of a farewell. Brother Martin lived for his work. It animated his whole being. Surrounded by the ugliness of lepers, he showed the true beauty of God's work. The Almighty would never call him so soon from his labours.

That thought made Gervase's mind race. If Brother Martin had gone before his time, it had to be by the hand of another. Unnatural death had taken place in the church. Murder and sacrilege had worked cunningly together. Gervase knelt beside the prostrate form but his own shadow simply deepened the pool of gloom around the monk. Low in the sky, the evening sun was throwing only a meagre handful of light in through the small windows.

A single candle burned on the altar. Gervase swiftly retrieved it and held it close to the face of the fallen man, carefully peeling back the hood until his tonsured head was completely exposed. As Gervase examined him with care, the flame slowly circled the head like a halo but Brother Martin was no slaughtered saint. There was no blood, no bruising, no wound of any kind on the head, face or neck. When Gervase ran the candle over the chest and legs, he found no weapon protruding and no sodden patch of blood to show where one might have been inserted and withdrawn.

Rolling the corpse gently over, he conducted a similar search along the man's back but that, too, showed no signs of violence or foul play. Gervase eased him over once more so that he lay face upward and used tender fingers to close the eyelids. It seemed as if Brother Martin had, after all, exhausted his natural span and slid serenely out of the world. The hospital which had given him his sense of purpose also took it away from him. His ceaseless toil among the lepers had eventually worn him down. Bertha had taken some of the unremitting work onto her young shoulders. Now that it had been shifted back on to Brother Martin, he could no longer cope with it.

Anguish and stress must also have played their part. Shocked by the sudden death of a loved one, he was not able to mourn her passing in privacy. Brother Martin had also taken on the crushing responsibility of setting a murder inquiry in motion, gathering the evidence, submitting it to the sheriff, haggling with Helto the Doctor and then confronting Alwin the Sailor with the truth about his daughter's death. Such strain and tension would have taxed a much younger man.

Gervase replaced the candle, then knelt before the altar

to offer up a prayer for the soul of Brother Martin. When he turned around again, he saw a tall, stooping figure in the doorway. Alain shuffled forward to gaze down through his veil at Brother Martin. When he looked at Gervase with a questioning gesture, the latter gave a solemn nod. The leper lowered his head despondently.

"How long had he been in here?" asked Gervase.

"An hour. Maybe more."

"Alone?"

"I think so."

"Nobody else came or went?"

"Nobody," said Alain firmly.

"How can you be so sure?"

"Brother Martin came to my hut. He makes an ointment with gives some small relief from the pain, and he brought some to apply. When he left, I came out to the place where you found me."

"And Brother Martin?"

"He went into the church and has been here ever since."

"How did he seem?"

"Deeply troubled."

"Was he short of breath?"

"No more than usual."

"Did he mention a pain in his chest?" Alain shook his head. "Was he moving with difficulty? Was there anything you noticed about him that might suggest great strain?"

"Nothing."

Gervase glanced at the body. "The others must be told. It is a sad time. First you lose Bertha; now, Brother Martin himself. It will be hard news to break."

Alain seemed to be wrestling with some inner problem.

"That task will be mine," he said at length.

"Thank you. Help must be fetched at once. Brother Martin's death must be reported so that his body can be conveyed to the priory. Someone will be sent to take charge of the hospital in his stead. Can the door be locked?"

"The key is in his scrip."

"Good," said Gervase. "It is important that the body is not disturbed in any way while I am gone. Brother Martin seems to have died peaceably enough but I am no physician and sharper eyes might note clues that I have missed."

"Clues?"

"Pointing to foul play."

"No," said Alain. "There is no question of that, surely? Brother Martin did not have an enemy in the world."

"Neither did Bertha."

The leper winced at the reminder. Gervase bent down to search for the key in the monk's scrip. When he stood up again, he saw that Alain had gone to start his melancholy peregrination. Gervase locked the church door from outside, then collected his horse. He was soon cantering away from the hospital of St. Nicholas.

As he came over the brow of the hill and began the downward ride, his mind was still bursting with the simple horror of this latest tragedy. The implications for the lepers themselves were highly distressing. Gervase was grateful that it was Alain who had taken it upon himself to spread the grisly tidings.

Eager to reach the city, he paid scant attention to the people he passed on the way and he did not even notice the young man who stepped smartly into the bushes at his approach. When the hooves had thundered past, the man came out of hiding and looked nervously after Gervase.

Reinbald the Priest continued his furtive journey.

Prior Henry responded with speed and compassion. As soon as the news reached him, he dispatched four monks to Harbledown with a horse and cart to bring back the body at a reverential pace. The quartet was accompanied by two more brethren, selected with care and charged with the task of looking after the hospital and comforting the lepers through this second unexpected bereavement.

Brother Martin was known and loved throughout the whole monastic community. Though he spent most of his time at his chosen vocation in the leper hospital, he made regular visits to the priory and took part, whenever he could, in its daily services. Since taking the cowl, Brother Martin had spent the whole of his long life in Canterbury and his conduct had been wholly free from the excesses and liberalities which had tainted some of his weaker brethren in earlier years. Prior Henry had recognised and rewarded his steadfastness.

"He was the epitome of Christian virtue," he said with a wan smile. "Brother Martin was all that a true member of the Benedictine Order should be."

"It was a privilege to meet him, albeit briefly."

"His charitable work will stand as his monument. This has touched me more than I can say. I would lament the death of any of my obedientaries but the loss of Brother Martin occasions a particular regret." He looked up at his guest. "I am most grateful to you for your prompt assistance."

"It was the least I could do, Prior Henry."

"Your visit to Harbledown was opportune. Had you not ridden to the hospital to see Brother Martin, he might have lain for several hours in the church. He would then have been found by one of the poor wretches whom he nursed and that would have thrown the hospital into further turmoil. God save them! They will miss him desperately, Master Bret, but at least they were spared the gruesome shock of discovery."

Gervase was at once surprised and wary at being summoned to the prior's lodging. When he reported the death to the porter at the gate, he expected to be thanked for his help and sent politely on his way. Instead, he was given an immediate audience with Prior Henry himself and questioned at length about the circumstances in which he came upon the dead body and the precise state in which he found it. In view of their tussle in the shire hall, Gervase entered the room with caution, hoping that the prior would not use this chance encounter as a means to exert some subtle influence to advance his cause but the latter did not even refer to the property dispute with the abbey.

"What will happen to him now?" asked Gervase.

"The body will be washed and examined. Then it will lie in the chapel until the time of the funeral. Brother Martin went out to do his good works but we now welcome him back into the enclave. He will be buried in our own little cemetery in the presence of the whole community."

"Will the ceremony be private?"

"Strictly so."

"I would like to attend it."

"That is not feasible, Master Bret. We bury our own here and do so in our own way. I will conduct the service and Archbishop Lanfranc will assuredly preach a sermon."

"That would make Brother Martin feel proud."

"He made us feel proud to have him here." Henry stood up and walked around his desk toward Gervase. "But your kind request is appreciated. The funeral may be closed to you but you may wish to take part in a memorial service for the deceased. It will be held in due course at the hospital of St. Nicholas."

"I will be there," promised Gervase.

"That pleases me."

With a reflective smile, he ushered his visitor out.

Helto the Doctor called briefly at the house that evening to check once more on Eadgyth's condition. He pronounced himself fairly satisfied with her progress. She was much calmer, more easily distracted from her brooding and less prone to sudden outbursts of uncontrollable weeping. Golde's presence was clearly beneficial. She was a patient and resourceful nurse. Helto left another sleeping draught for Eadgyth to ensure a restful night for her and a quiet one for the remainder of the household.

His valedictory words were addressed to her husband.

"She will be markedly better in the morning."

"I am relieved to hear it," said Osbern.

"Keep her in for two or three more days."

"As long as that?"

"Until this arrant nonsense blows over."

"Nonsense?"

"Yes, Osbern," said the doctor testily. "This alleged murder of Bertha. It never occurred. When the sheriff fails to find any trace of a culprit, he will realise the folly of this exercise and abandon it. Why alarm your wife with this wild tale? It will only plunge her into worse melancholy."

"She will not be told. I give you my word."

"Hold to it, Osbern. Or you may rue the consequences."

The reeve paid him his fee, thanked him for calling and showed him out. Mastering his anxiety and remembering his duties as a host, he went into the solar to find Ralph Delchard sitting there on his own with a glass of wine.

"Has he still not returned, my lord?"

"No," said Ralph. "But do not worry about Gervase. He is well able to take care of himself."

"I do not doubt it."

"Your doctor stayed much longer on this visit, I see. Golde tells me that this is his second visit today. Is Helto a

conscientious physician or was he simply in search of double the fee?"

"He came became of his concern for Eadgyth," replied
the other. "She has a delicate constitution and there have
been problems in the past. She buckles under strain and
anxiety. Helto advises that I keep her close for two more
days at least and guard her against hearing the rumours
about Bertha."

"They are more than rumours."

"Not according to Helto."

"Then why has the sheriff initiated an inquiry?"

"I do not know, my lord."

"It is because of Brother Martin's evidence. He and Gervase discussed the case in detail. I agree with them."

"I hope you are wrong. For my wife's sake."

"And for Bertha's, surely?"

"That goes without saying, my lord."

Ralph recalled his earlier conversation with Golde. It
made him probe gently for information about the dead girl.

"Eadgyth must have loved Bertha dearly."

"She did, my lord. Bertha was a girl of rare qualities."

"Did she have other friends?"

"Many of them."

"Admirers, too, I imagine. If she was as comely as report
has it, every young man in the town must have doffed his
cap as she passed. And licked his lips in anticipation. Tell
me," said Ralph artlessly. "Did she have one special admirer?"

"No, my lord."

"A beautiful damsel like that? No swooning youth? No
dashing swain? No secret lover?"

"She had neither time nor inclination for that."

"How do you know?"

"Because I saw a great deal of her. She was often at the house to talk with Eadgyth. When the baby came, Bertha was as delighted as we were. She more or less lived with us for a week or two. It was a difficult time. My wife was exhausted and not able to look after the baby as fully as she would have wished. Bertha was a second mother to it."

"Perhaps because she pined for a child of her own. By the secret man in her life."

"I think it highly unlikely, my lord."

"You only saw what she wanted you to see, Osbern. Maybe she confided in your wife. Maybe she told Eadgyth about her hidden passion."

"She did nothing of the kind," said Osbern firmly.

"You seem very convinced of that."

"I am, my lord. Eadgyth would have told me."

"Not if Bertha had sworn her to silence."

"My wife holds nothing back."

"Even the most intimate confession of a friend?"

"Even that," insisted the reeve. "When man and wife are joined in holy matrimony, they commit themselves to each other without reserve. Is that so with you?"

"Indeed."

"And would your own wife not tell you everything?"

"I hope not!" said Ralph with a hearty chuckle.

"You shock me, my lord."

"I expect her to love, honour and obey me but I do not wish to climb inside her head and watch every thought that passes through her brain." Ralph gave a shrug. "If a close friend unburdened her heart to Golde, it would be a betrayal if my wife then ran to me with the tale."

"It would be a betrayal of you if she did not!"

"We see it differently."

"I think we do, my lord."

"I still believe that Bertha must have aroused great interest among the young men of the city. They are not blind. They probably followed her in droves."

"They would not dare."

"Why not?"

"Because of her father."

"Alwin? Would he object?"

"Most strongly, my lord. He was very strict with her."

"A sailor?" said Ralph with amazement. "Such men are not known for their celibate disposition. They are drawn to their occupation out of a sense of adventure rather than because of any monastic leanings. Is Alwin so devout?"

"No, my lord," said Osbern. "But he made a solemn vow to his wife when she lay on her deathbed. To his credit, he has honoured it ever since." He chose his words with care. "Bertha's parents had a troubled marriage. I do not know why and it was not my business to find out, but Eadgyth spoke of arguments she overheard between husband and wife. This is not to say that Alwin did not love his wife," he added. "He worshipped her. When she became sick, he nursed her devotedly. At the last, she made him promise to keep their daughter on the path of virtue and shield her from the temptations to which the young are often prone."

"How could the sailor do that when he was often away?"

"Bertha was left with a neighbour at first. When she grew older, Alwin took her with him on his voyaging."

Ralph blinked. "She crossed the Channel with him?"

"A number of times."

"Then she had a braver heart than mine. I will fight against any odds on land and meet the strongest foe without a tremor. But do not ask me to sail in rough water. I did that when we took ship on the eve of the Conquest. I still have nightmares about those heaving waves."

"Bertha is a sailor's daughter," reminded Osbern. "Her whole family has been tied to the sea. Two of her uncles have boats of their own, another is a shipwright, a fourth is a wharfinger in Fordwich. Bertha was born to it."

"Then she, too, must have had the spirit of adventure. Might it not have led her into some secret romance?"

"Alwin watched her too closely."

"Not when she went to Harbledown."

"Bertha was unlikely to go astray at a leper hospital."

"No," said Ralph with a grin. "She would be in no danger from Brother Martin. I can see why her father must have encouraged her charitable work."

"But he did not, my lord."

"Oh?"

"It was the one thing on which they disagreed. Alwin tried to stop her going. Mixing with lepers carries all sorts of dangers. He was no doubt fearful that she might contract the disease herself. But she was adamant. Bertha had a strong will."

"Strong enough to defy her father, it seems. Could it not also have prompted her to defy him in other ways?"

"No, my lord."

"I begin to wonder."

"We knew Bertha too well."

"Did you?"

"She would have never have kept something as important as that to herself. She would have confided in Eadgyth."

"Yet you say she did not do that."

"I am positive."

"Could you not raise the matter with your wife?"

Osbern was hurt by the suggestion. "When she is in such distress? It is hardly the time, my lord. Helto has counselled me to try to keep Eadgyth's mind off this tragedy. Why should I take the opposite course and induce further pain?"

"Because she might provide a vital clue."

"Clue?"

"To the identity of Bertha's secret admirer."

"There was no such person."

"There was no murder, according to you," said Ralph. "But Gervase and I have seen the evidence and think otherwise. So does the sheriff or he would not have ordered his officers to look into the case. Let us suppose that there was a killer."

"Impossible!"

"What could have been his motive?"

"There was none. Bertha was liked and respected by all. Nobody had any motive to take her life."

"Nobody you know," persisted Ralph. "That is why we must look for someone whom you do not know. Some shadowy figure in her private life."

"He does not exist!"

"Ask your wife."

"There is no point, my lord."

"It may be the one way to solve this murder. Yes, I know," he said quickly, stilling Osbern's protest with a raised hand. "You do not accept that any murder took place. But we do. A healthy girl like Bertha does not succumb to a snakebite so quickly and in such an unlikely place. Someone strangled her. The trail is cold, Osbern. The only person who may be able to help us here, to give us a name or, at the very least, to confirm that there was a secret lover in Bertha's life, is your own dear Eadgyth. Please talk to her."

"You are asking too much, my lord."

"I am asking on Bertha's behalf."

"There was no man in her life."

"Will you not even consider the possibility?"

"No, my lord," said Osbern resolutely. "We knew Bertha. More to the point, we know Alwin the Sailor. He is the best guarantee here. No man in his right mind would have pressed himself upon the girl."

"Why not?"

"Alwin would have killed him."

Encircled by forest, field and marsh, Fordwich stood at the mouth of the river estuary. The village comprised over seventy houses and a scattered collection of barns, byres and outbuildings. A small church served its spiritual needs and a natural supply of clear spring water contributed to the physical health of the inhabitants. Fordwich gained its status as a borough from its importance as a harbour for seagoing traffic, and the activity around its quays brought in a steady profit from the tolls on goods landed there. Boats and barges, with a relatively shallow draught, came and went every day. Sailors always loitered near its timbered wharves.

When Alwin reached Fordwich, he spoke to everyone he found around the little harbour, interrogating each one in turn with an almost manic urgency.

"Can you be certain of this?" he pressed.

"Quite certain, Alwin."

"Think hard."

"I have done so."

"I must find him!"

"Then you must look elsewhere," said the sailor. "I cannot help you. I have not caught sight of him for months."

"Nor heard mention of the man?"

"Not a word."

"If you do hear news of him, bring it to me at once."

"Why?"

"Just bring it!" insisted Alwin, grabbing him by the shoulders. "I have reasons enough, believe me."

He released the sailor and looked eagerly around but he could see nobody whom he had not already questioned. After passing on his gruff thanks, he walked along the quay to the point where his own boat lay moored and jumped down into it, causing it to tilt and ride in the dark water.

Standing beside the tiller, he gazed around his vessel. Its sail was furled and tied with ropes, its mast sculpted by the wind, its deck pitted and whitened by the endless supplies of Caen stone he had transported. But his mind was on another part of his cargo and the memory of it turned his blood to liquid fire. Snatching at the dagger which hung at his waist, Alwin lifted it high and brought it down with such vicious force that it sank inches into the bulwark.

The return of Gervase Bret brought more sorrow and consternation to the house and disturbed its fragile peace. Coming so soon after one tragedy, Brother Martin's death was a shock to all. Gervase described his audience with Prior Henry and said how impressed he had been with the prompt and loving way in which the old monk had been received back into the enclave.

Osbern was particularly affected by the news but not simply because he had known and admired Brother Martin. The reeve was in a tender frame of mind. His talk with Ralph Delchard had unsettled him at a deep level. He could not believe that his wife had held something back from him, yet he sensed that his guest would not have broached the topic by accident. Ralph obviously knew something and could only have gained such intelligence from Golde. Had Eadgyth concealed a vital piece of information from her husband which she then divulged to a complete stranger?

When he excused himself from the room, Osbern was patently ruffled. Gervase was left alone in the solar with Ralph and Golde.

"What has been happening while I was away?" he inquired.

"Nothing of consequence," said Ralph. "Golde has been running the household with a firm but gentle hand while I have been talking to Osbern."

"What did you say to him?" asked Golde. "When I came in, he seemed a trifle disturbed. I hope that you have not been upsetting our generous host."

"Would I do such a thing, my love?"

"Not by intention."

"I merely fished for some information about Bertha."

"What did you learn?" said Gervase.

"A great deal."

He told them about the girl's relationship with her father and about the way he had resisted her compelling desire to help Brother Martin at the leper hospital of St. Nicholas. Golde was struck by her strength of purpose.

"At her age," she admitted, "I would not have resisted my father's wishes so boldly."

Ralph winked at her. "I hope you will not resist the wishes of your husband, either."

"Bertha was a most unusual daughter."

Before they could speculate further, there was a knock on the door. A few moments later, a servant conducted a visitor into the solar. It was one of the monks who had accompanied Prior Henry during his confrontation with the commissioners. He was panting slightly and perspiration glistened on his brow.

"I have a message for Master Bret," he said.

"An urgent one, by the look of it," noted Ralph.

"Prior Henry ordered me to make all speed."

"What is the message?" asked Gervase.

"You are to return to the priory as soon as you may."

"Why?"

"I do not know, Master Bret. I simply convey the instruction."

"It comes from Prior Henry?"

"From his own mouth. Not five minutes ago."

Gervase was puzzled. He looked inquiringly at Ralph. After a silent discussion, each came to the same conclusion.

"It is the only explanation," decided Gervase.

"I will come with you," said Ralph. "Let us go."

❧ CHAPTER EIGHT

EXPECTING ONLY ONE visitor, Prior Henry was at first disconcerted when two were ushered into his lodging. He found Gervase Bret a more sensitive and congenial person than Ralph Delchard, whose abrasiveness he had already glimpsed at the shire hall and whose lack of respect for the cowl was very disagreeable. Henry quickly adjusted to the surprise. The news he had to impart would in any case have found its way immediately to the leading commissioner. Ralph Delchard might just as well hear it at first hand.

"Thank you for coming so promptly," began the prior.

"Celerity was needed," said Gervase. "You would only have summoned me on a matter of grave importance. We guessed that it must concern Brother Martin."

"It does. Brother Ambrose, too."

"Brother Ambrose?"

"He is our physician here at the priory. He cures our ailments, calms our fevers and sets the occasional bone which gets broken within the enclave." He gritted his teeth. "Brother Ambrose is also responsible for laying out our dead. He is a man of unrivalled experience in this task. It was into his care that we placed Brother Martin."

"What did he find?" said Ralph.

"I must first ask that of Master Bret, my lord." He turned to Gervase with a raised eyebrow. "When you examined him at the hospital of St. Nicholas, you found nothing to arouse suspicion?"

"Nothing at all, Prior Henry."

"How closely did you look?"

"With some care. There were no marks upon him."

"They might not have been immediately visible."

"What should I have seen?"

"It is more a question of what you should have smelt," said Prior Henry. "Did you detect no strange odour?"

"None," replied Gervase. "The church was filled with the scent of herbs. I assumed that Brother Martin had used them deliberately to sweeten the air of a nave where only lepers worshipped. Is that not common practice?"

"It is, Master Bret."

"The aroma was quite pervasive. I think it would have masked any lesser scent."

"Palpably."

"Tell us about Brother Ambrose," said Ralph impatiently.

"He noticed it at once, my lord."

"Noticed what?"

"The smell from Brother Martin's mouth. Faint enough to be smothered by the herbs in the church but strong enough to make its presence felt in the clear air of our morgue." He gave a sigh. "Our dear brother was poisoned."

"Another murder?" said Gervase.

"No question about it. Suicide can be ruled out at once. Brother Martin knew that it was a sin before God to take one's own life. Besides, nobody would subject himself to the pain which he must have endured at the end."

"Pain?"

"Agonies and convulsions. Brother Ambrose has examined the body, searching for the tiny signs which only he would see and cutting open a vein to study the blood. The poison was quick and merciless. Brother Ambrose talks of a herbal compound with belladonna as a main ingredient. It seems that a massive dose was administered."

"How?" wondered Ralph. "Brother Martin would hardly have quaffed the potion obligingly from his chalice."

"Force was used. There is bruising on his chest to indicate that he may have been pinned to the ground while the hideous draught was poured down his throat."

"By whom?" said Gervase. "The church was empty."

"The killer must have left before you arrived."

"He could not have done so without being seen, Prior Henry. One of the lepers watched Brother Martin enter the church alone. Nobody came out."

"He must have done, Gervase," said Ralph.

"The witness was most insistent."

"Is he reliable?"

"I believe so. He sat outside his hut throughout the whole time that Brother Martin was in the church."

"Might he not have dozed off to sleep?"

"I think it unlikely."

"His attention may have been distracted."

"No, Ralph. Not this man. Alain is a solitary person. He does not mix easily with the others. If he had the church in view during that time, his attention would not have wavered."

"Somebody administered that poison," argued Prior Henry. "And with considerable violence. Brother Ambrose showed me the two huge bruises on the chest of Brother

Martin. It seemed as if his attacker knelt hard on him and pressed down with both knees."

"Then how did that attacker escape from the church?"

"I do not know, Master Bret."

"That will emerge in time," said Ralph thoughtfully. "What is more beneficial at this stage is to establish the motive for the murder."

"I am at a loss to imagine what it might be," confessed the prior. "Who could hate Brother Martin enough to kill him in such a savage way?"

"The same man who killed Bertha."

"My lord?"

"These two deaths are linked, Prior Henry. A young girl and an old monk. When Bertha was found on Harbledown, it was accepted by all that she perished by snakebite. That was also the opinion of Helto the Doctor. Only Brother Martin contested that view—with the support of Gervase here."

"It was Brother Martin who activated the sheriff."

"His evidence was crucial," observed Ralph. "They killed him in order to silence him."

"Who did, my lord?"

"That is what we will find out."

"The priory is involved here," reminded Henry, "and we will carry out our own rigorous investigation. Archbishop Lanfranc had been informed and he is rightfully appalled. I have been designated to lead our inquiry. One of our holy brethren has been slain. We will not rest until the fiend responsible has been brought to justice."

"Nor will we," vowed Ralph.

"Then we have a common aim here. It makes it easier for me to ask a special favour of you, my lord."

"Favour?"

"This dispute between cathedral and abbey," said Henry.

"It is a matter of the utmost significance to us and requires my undivided attention. While Brother Martin's murder hangs over us, I will not be able to give it that attention. My plea is that the case be adjourned until this horror has abated and I am more readily available to you at the shire hall."

"A reasonable request," commented Gervase.

"Yes," agreed Ralph without hesitation. "And one with which I concur. We will suspend all work of the commission until this business has been resolved. Along with my dear wife, Gervase and I are the guests of Osbern the Reeve, whose own wife was a close friend of the deceased girl. Bertha's father, Alwin, is a sailor who operates out of Fordwich, the very port at the heart of your quarrel with the abbey. And now we learn Brother Martin, one of your monks, has been poisoned."

"Fate has obviously decreed that we are involved in these misfortunes," said Gervase.

Ralph gave a grim chuckle. "Up to our necks, Gervase. We will do all we can to track down this killer. His methods have been ruthless, his victims defenceless. Such a man does not deserve to breathe the same air as ordinary human beings. We will find this devil somehow."

Bertha's funeral was held next morning at the parish church of St. Mildred's. Alwin and the other chief mourners—the girl's uncles, aunts and cousins—sat on benches at the front of the nave but a sizeable number of friends and neighbours stood behind them. Reinbald the Priest conducted the service and delivered a touching homily, rhapsodising on Bertha's virtues while trying to reconcile the minds of his congregation to the suddenness and awfulness of her demise. The nature of that demise, and the inquiry that now followed it, were nowhere touched upon.

For all his relative inexperience as a parish priest, Reinbald had natural tact.

Mass was sung for the dear departed, and Bertha was lowered into her grave amid copious weeping and painful sighs. Alwin the Sailor threw the first handful of earth on the coffin and closed his eyes tight against the searing agony of separation. There was an added poignancy for him in the fact that his daughter would lie in the church-yard beside his wife, and he berated himself for failing to honour the promise he had given to Bertha's mother on her deathbed.

When he finally looked up again, there was no relief from his torment. It was magnified a hundredfold by the burning eyes which met his across the grave. They belonged to his sister-in-law, a gracious, handsome woman in her forties with braided fair hair entwined around an oval face and a resemblance to his dead wife that was so close as to be breathtaking. Alwin felt that her gaze was like a hot brand on his soul. There was such a fund of remorse and hatred and accusation in her stare that he had to turn away.

Osbern the Reeve suffered discomfort of a lesser order but it still made the sweat break on his brow. Bertha had been strangled. The second murder had forced him to ac-knowledge the first and it left him feeling hurt and guilty. It also obliged him, sooner or later, to tell Eadgyth the ugly truth about the death of her beloved friend and that thought alarmed him the most. As the gravedigger began to shovel earth into the cavity, Osbern could take no more of the anguish and he stole quietly away.

Ralph and Golde stood arm in arm at the back of the en-circling mourners, both deeply moved by the pitiable mis-ery of the occasion. Gervase was close by, caught up in the sadness of it all and yet sufficiently detached to notice a hooded figure who hovered on the very fringe of the burial service. Several monks from cathedral and abbey had come to pay their last respects to someone whose charitable deeds had caused so much favourable comment but the man whom Gervase spotted did not ally himself with either group.

Standing well apart, he kept his hood up and his face concealed. It was when the monk moved away that Gervase became suspicious. Time spent as a novice at Eltham Abbey had accustomed him to the gait of a monastic order. Older monks might shuffle and younger ones stride but all took account of the heavy cowl which swung around their ankles. The measured tread of the cloister was unmistakeable. The man who retreated from the churchyard, however, had such a lithe and hurried step that it was difficult to believe he spent his days within the enclave.

Curiosity made Gervase take a few paces after him but he was immediately distracted by another figure. This one stood a short distance away from the congregation, his head bowed in prayer, his hands clasped together in his lap. It was an affecting sight, all the more so when Gervase realised that Alain the Leper represented the whole community at the hospital of St. Nicholas. On their behalf, he had struggled down to Canterbury to keep his vigil near the graveside.

As the mourners began to disperse, Reinbald the Priest made time for a moment alone with the stricken father.

"My thoughts go with you, Alwin."

"Thank you, Father Reinbald," said the other. "And thank you for your kind words in the sermon. Nothing will ever bring Bertha back but I took some crumbs of comfort from what you said."

"I will visit you very soon to offer more consolation."

"There is no need."

"There is every need," said Reinbald. "You have reached a time of trial in your life. It is my duty as your parish priest and my obligation as your friend to do all I can to sustain your spirit and bring you to an acceptance of God's will."

Alwin's manner hardened. "I do not accept it."

"You must."

"Bertha died because of the will of a cruel murderer."

"Do not look at it that way. It will only lead to endless bitterness and sorrow. Let me visit you, Alwin. You have lost a wife and a daughter now. You need me to ease you through these travails."

"What could *you* do?" said the other sharply.

"Offer solace and guidance."

"How?"

"By understanding your grief."

"How could you possibly understand the sense of loss that I bear? You are a celibate priest. You have no wife and no idea what it is like to bring up a child. Leave me be, Father Reinbald. I want none of your consolation."

"In time, maybe."

"Never!"

"But you need succour."

"Not from the likes of you," snapped the other.

Alwin swung away from the grave and blundered off through the mourners, leaving Reinbald the Priest stung by the rudeness of his departure and wounded to the quick by his harsh words. It was some minutes before he recovered enough to be able to offer condolences to other members of Bertha's family but Alwin's outburst still echoed in his ears.

When Golde had been escorted back to the house in Burgate Ward, Ralph and Gervase collected their horses from the stables and rode off toward Harbledown. Both were still muted by their attendance at the funeral. It was only when they were trotting up the hill that Ralph found his voice.

"Where are we going?" he asked.

"To the hospital of St. Nicholas."

"Why?"

"To put an idea of mine to the test, Ralph."

"What idea?"

"I have been thinking about Brother Martin's death," said Gervase, "and I believe that I may have the answer to the mystery. Brother Martin went into an empty church. An hour or so later, I came along and entered myself, only to find him dead. Yet nobody had come or gone in that time. The explanation is simple."

"Alain the Leper fell asleep on sentry duty."

"No, Ralph. He was vigilance itself."

"Then why did he not see the killer enter the church?"

"Because the man was already inside. He must have gained entry sooner in the evening and lain in wait until Brother Martin came in."

"It is conceivable," said Ralph, weighing the idea in his mind. "And it would certainly explain why Alain did not spot anyone going into the church. But it does not account for the fact that the murderer was not seen leaving either."

"Alain would never have seen him depart."

"Why not?"

"Because the man stayed inside the church."

"He was there when you discovered the body?"

"I believe so."

"Where would he have hidden?"

"That is what we are going to find out now."

Ralph was impressed. "Why did this never occur to me?"

"Because you were not at the hospital. You do not know

the relation between the church and Alain's hut. When I worried away at it long enough, the answer came."

"The possible answer."

"I know I am right, Ralph. What I am not sure about is the exact time of the killer's departure."

"He must have sneaked away as soon as you left."

"I locked the door of the church."

"When was it reopened?"

"By the six monks sent from Christ Church Priory, all of them good friends of Brother Martin. Imagine the scene," said Gervase. "Six shocked and bereaved men, standing around the dead body of a venerable colleague. They would have been far too distressed to notice anyone who slipped out of the church."

"The lepers would have noticed him," suggested Ralph. "Alain must have spread the word by then. They would have come out of their huts to watch Brother Martin being carried away on the cart. The killer must have been *seen*."

An image from the funeral shot into Gervase's mind.

"He was seen, Ralph. Seen but not seen."

"Stop talking gibberish."

"What exactly would the lepers have observed?"

"Six monks going into the church and a stranger sliding out to make a run for it. They could not have missed him."

"They could. Six went in but one came out."

"We are back to riddles, are we?"

"Six monks entered, Ralph. One monk departed."

"One monk?"

"That was the man's disguise," argued Gervase. "Other monks occasionally visit the hospital to help with its work. The killer donned a black cowl so that he would attract no attention if he sidled into the community. He bided his time before stepping into the church unnoticed."

"Yes," agreed Ralph, warming to the theory. "The lepers would have been too heartbroken to count the monks who went in to gather up the body of Brother Martin. When a figure in a cowl emerges, they assume he is one of the party dispatched by Prior Henry. Brilliant, Gervase! How did you work it out?"

"I saw him."

"Who?"

"The man himself. At the funeral."

He told Ralph about the lone monk who had caught his eye with his speedy and irreverent withdrawal from the churchyard of St. Mildred's. His companion became elated.

"By all, this is wonderful!"

"Why?"

"I have learned two things about the man we seek," said Ralph. "First, he has the cunning of a fox and will think through his villainy with care. He made Bertha seem the victim of a snakebite to deflect any suspicion of foul play. And he joins the Benedictine Order so that he can murder Brother Martin and escape through a whole crowd of lepers."

"What is the second thing?" asked Gervase.

"He is still here in Canterbury! We can catch him."

They reached the hospital and tethered their mounts. The two monks who were looking after the place listened to their request and complied at once. Ralph and Gervase were allowed into the church. At first glance, there were no obvious hiding places, especially for a man as tall as the monk Gervase had observed at the funeral. The church consisted of a simple nave and a tiny vestry. Its windows were too high and too small to allow an easy escape.

The vestry was a potential hiding place but its door was

directly opposite the spot where Brother Martin had fallen to the ground. Even six preoccupied monks would have been aware of a seventh member of their Order walking within a couple of feet of them. When Ralph tried the door, it creaked so loudly on its hinges that they ruled out the vestry as the place of concealment.

Gervase began to have second thoughts. An idea which had seemed so convincing on their ride to Harbledown was slowly crumbling. With Ralph's indulgence, he went out of the church, then entered again, retracing the steps he had taken on the previous evening. He came to the pillar against which the old monk had rested, watched him fall to the ground in his mind's eye, knelt to examine him, then recalled that it was too dark to see properly. When his head turned toward the candle, he had the solution.

"The altar!" he shouted.

"Calm down, Gervase."

"Where better to hide?"

Removing the crucifix, the candle and the little vase of flowers from the altar, he lifted the white cloth with a mixture of reverence and excitement. The table was small but a man could conceal himself beneath it without undue discomfort. Even Ralph was shocked by the sacrilege.

"Hiding under an altar to commit murder!"

"The last place from which you would expect danger."

"Brother Martin would have been completely off guard."

"Kneeling in prayer," said Gervase, as his gaze raked the floor underneath the table. "The killer eased himself out, jumped on Brother Martin, overpowered him and . . ."

He broke off as he saw something lying in the crack between two flagstones. Leaning in under the altar, he groped around until his hand closed on the object. When he brought it out, he opened his palm to reveal a small flask.

He held it to his nose and recoiled with disgust. Even the aromatic herbs in the nave could not remove the stink of murder.

"He was here," said Gervase. "We have a trail."

Osbern the Reeve was a decent, hardworking, God-fearing man whose life had hitherto followed a pattern of certainty. When he set himself a target, he always achieved it. When he conceived schemes for the future, they invariably came to fruition. His sense of purpose and his unswerving dedication to the task in hand had earned him an important position in the city, a wife whom he adored and a son on whom he doted. It was almost as if he had planned his happiness like a military campaign, marshalling his divisions to strike at the right point and at precisely the correct moment. Every battle he fought under the flag of domestic bliss had so far been attended by triumph.

The situation had altered dramatically. In the space of a couple of days, some of his certainties had been shattered. His contentment had turned to rising anxiety, his faith in his own good judgement had been undermined and, most disturbing of all, he was being forced to reexamine the assumptions he had made about his wife. Osbern had been too complacent in his happiness.

"May I crave a word or two, my lady?" he said politely.

"As many as you wish."

"Have you spoken to Eadgyth since the funeral?"

"I was just about to do so," said Golde. "She made me promise to describe it to her when I got back here."

Osborn nodded. "Thank heaven we were able to persuade her not to attend in person! It would have been far too harrowing for Eadgyth. She was determined to come. It was Helto who finally talked her out of it."

"He is a sound physician."

"The best."

Golde gave a warm smile. "What did you wish to ask me?"

The reeve hesitated. Golde was an honoured guest and he did not wish to offend her in any way by subjecting her to what she might feel was an interrogation. She had also been immensely supportive to Eadgyth and nursed her through the worst of her ordeal. Osbern liked and respected Golde. She had an essential honesty and would answer his question if only he had the courage to ask it. That was Osbern's other problem. He was torn between wanting to know the truth about Eadgyth and maintaining the illusion that she would never keep anything from her husband.

"Well?" invited Golde.

"How is Eadgyth?"

"You saw her yourself only a few minutes ago."

"Yes, my lady," he said, "but I only see her through the eyes of a fond and worried husband. You have sat beside he bed for hours on end, soothing her troubled mind and giving her relief from her sorrow."

"That sorrow will not easily go away," warned Golde.

"I know."

"It ebbs and flows. Today, as you have seen, Eadgyth is understandably distressed. Your wife desperately wanted to go to Bertha's funeral. She felt it was a betrayal of her closest friend to stay away."

"There was good reason, my lady."

"Yes," said Golde. "It would have upset her beyond measure. Not simply because she loved Bertha so much but because she would have realised that the truth had been kept from her. Reinbald the Priest did not mention the murder in his sermon but it was common talk among the congregation. Eadgyth must surely have caught a whisper of it."

"That was my greatest fear."

"It could easily have been avoided, Osbern."

"How, my lady?"

"By telling her what really happened to Bertha."

"Helto cautioned me against that."

"How long will you keep her ignorant of the truth?"

"I do not know."

"It cannot be held back forever."

"I accept that." He shifted his feet uneasily. "You have spent a great deal of time with Eadgyth," he said. "She is under enormous stress. Given the circumstances, it is only natural that she would talk to you about Bertha."

"Constantly."

"You have shown monumental patience."

"I have been interested in all that she told me."

"My lady," he said, running his tongue over his lips before blurting out his question. "Did my wife ever mention that Bertha had a secret romance?"

"Romance?"

"An admirer whom nobody knew about. A lover. Did she?"

"Not in those terms."

"There was someone, then?"

"Eadgyth only referred to him as 'a friend'."

"What was his name?"

"Your wife did not say," explained Golde. "Indeed, she did not really mean to confide anything of the relationship to me. It slipped out unwittingly. Once she had told me that Bertha had this special friend, she refused to say another word on the subject. It is a secret she is determined to keep."

"Yes," said Osbern ruefully. "Even from me."

"What harm has it caused you?"

"It was wrong, my lady. I should have been told."

"This secret belonged only to Eadgyth and Bertha."

"I am Eadgyth's husband. There should be no deception between us."

"Do you not keep secrets from her, Osbern?"

"Never!"

"You take her into your confidence about everything."

"It is an article of faith."

"An admirable one in many ways," said Golde. "Marriage should blend two people completely together. But you must not blame Eadgyth for harbouring this secret. Although you profess to be honest with her, you have clearly not been so."

"I have, my lady! I swear it."

"Then why have you not told her the truth about Bertha's death? That is a dreadful secret to keep from your wife. Eadgyth may never forgive you."

The visit to Harbledown was highly productive. Ralph Delchard and Gervase Bret were pleased with their progress and rode back toward the city in good humour. As they approached Westgate, they saw a hooded figure sitting outside the town wall with a begging bowl at his feet. Gervase found a coin in his purse and tossed it down as they passed.

Alain caught it expertly in his bowl and looked up to nod his gratitude. Recognising Gervase, he rose from the ground and dipped a hand deep into his sleeve. He brought out something wrapped in a piece of cloth and handed it over before moving away. Gervase was puzzled. He flicked back the folds of cloth and held the object in his palm. Wrinkling his nose in distaste, Ralph urged him to hurl it after the leper, but Gervase felt that it had a significance. He turned it around to examine it more closely.

It was an apple out of which one large bite had been taken.

ᴄ᷾ᴥ Chapter Nine

CANON HUBERT WAS profoundly disappointed by his visit to Canterbury, and he was left with the uncomfortable feeling that his hopes had been ridiculously high. Having regaled Brother Simon with more or less continuous anecdotes about Archbishop Lanfranc all the way from Winchester, the boastful canon fully expected to be summoned into the presence of his erstwhile friend within a short time of his arrival at Christ Church Priory. Instead, he was kept at arm's length by the archbishop and treated to a highly unsatisfactory interview with Prior Henry, whose barbs were wounding and whose cold Italian charm was a poor substitute for Lanfranc's glowing benignity.

There was a second blow to Hubert's self-esteem. When his ecclesiastical status was not given the recognition that he felt it deserved, he at least had a role as a royal commissioner by way of compensation. In the judicial arena of the shire hall, he and his colleagues were able to weigh the competing claims of cathedral and abbey in the balance. It was an important role and Canon Hubert played it with a dignified enthusiasm, savouring in particular the chance to gain some mild revenge on Prior Henry when the latter was called before the tribunal. Now that the activities of the commissioners had been suspended, Hubert's position of power had temporarily vanished and he was thoroughly jaded.

Brother Simon, by comparison, was suffused with joy.

"We are blessed, Canon Hubert. Truly blessed."

"In what way, Brother Simon?"

"Being sent here to Canterbury. I had doubts at first, I must confess, but your prophecy was so accurate. This is indeed the Heavenly City made manifest."

"I would never use such florid language."

"Is it not all that you envisaged it would be?"

"In some respects," said Hubert grudgingly. "In others, I have to register a sense of slight disillusion."

"With Canterbury?"

"With our reception here."

"When we have had such a cordial welcome?"

"It was not untinged with reservation."

"I have no complaint whatsoever," said Simon with a pious smile. "Events have so fallen out to our advantage. Now that the work of the commission has been postponed, we may stay here in the enclave to share in the life of this wondrous community. Is this not a gift from God?"

"Most certainly not!" scolded Hubert. "Those events which you portray as beneficial to us include the murder of an innocent young girl and the poisoning of one of the obedientiaries here. Are we to profit from the misfortune of others, Brother Simon? Is that a Christian attitude? Two people lie dead and we are to rejoice at the advantage it brings to us? Shame on you!"

It was shortly after Sext and they were ambling side by side around the cloister garth. While one was beginning to see the priory as a form of prison, the other was wholly liberated by it. The cruel irony was not lost on Canon Hubert. While he had talked about seeking the new Jerusalem in Canterbury, his companion had actually found it.

Brother Simon squirmed under the stinging criticism.

"Do not misunderstand me," he begged. "I am as appalled as anyone by these terrible murders. I have prayed for both victims and will continue to do so as fervently as I may. Especially for Brother Martin."

"Why? The girl equally merits your petition to God."

"I agree, Canon Hubert, but the other tragedy has more resonance for me. A holy brother, cut down in the very church where he ministered to the unfortunate souls of Harbledown. A place of sanctuary turned into a slaughterhouse. It does not bear thinking about."

"But it does," argued the other. "It is a most fit subject for meditation. It reminds us that Canterbury is not quite the hallowed retreat you seem to think it. The spirit of evil hovers over this city and its corruption has been seen at the heart of this enclave."

"You are right as ever," apologized Brother Simon.

"Put your own selfish desires aside."

"I will do so henceforth."

"Think of the girl who was buried this morning and the holy brother who lies in the morgue. God rest their souls!"

"Amen!"

They walked on in silence. Brother Simon was completely subdued by the reprimand and looked down at the flagstones but Canon Hubert remained watchful, still hoping that his stay at the priory might be redeemed by a summons from the archbishop. When a figure suddenly came out of a doorway and hurried toward them, Hubert's spirits rose. Had Lanfranc finally found a moment in a crowded calendar to embrace his old friend?

Hope turned instantly to irritation. The man approaching them was no dutiful messenger but a disgruntled Prior Gregory. He accosted them with a truculent stare.

"Good day to you both!" he said.

"And to you, Prior Gregory," replied Hubert. "What has brought you away from St. Augustine's Abbey?"

"Archbishop Lanfranc sent for me."

"Oh," gulped the other, trying to control his envy.

"He sent for me," said the prior angrily, "he kept me waiting, then he decided that he did not have time to see me, after all. I was summarily dismissed."

"I am sure that was not the case."

"I have just come from him, Canon Hubert."

"No disrespect was intended to you. Archbishop Lanfranc is much preoccupied with the murder of Brother Martin. You must have heard of this disaster."

"Heard of it and suffered the consequences."

"Consequences?"

"The abbey wanted an early settlement of our dispute with the cathedral," explained Prior Gregory. "Our case is stronger and we have the charters to support it. Because of these shocking crimes, your work at the shire has been suspended until further notice."

"That was not my decision."

"Whoever made it, we are the losers."

"Why?"

"Delay favours the cathedral. Abbot Guy is due to arrive in the city any day now. We will resist him hard but the archbishop has the power to override our wishes. What hope do we have that Abbot Guy will take up this fight for us against the very man who consecrated him?" He thrust out a combative chin. "We need a judgement *now!*"

"I cannot give it to you here," said Hubert tartly, "and it is most improper even to discuss such matters outside the shire hall. You will have to wait, Prior Gregory."

"At least take note of his latest strategy."

"Strategy?"

"Dragging me all the way here from the abbey and making me wait outside the archbishop's door like a naughty schoolboy. Insult and intimidation are combined here, Canon Hubert. We were winning the battle in the shire hall."

"The issue is unresolved."

"We were," asserted the prior. "That is why Archbishop Lanfranc summoned me today. To remind us of his superiority. To put the abbey firmly in its place."

"This is lunacy!" warned Ralph Delchard. "Throw it away!"

"No," said Gervase. "It could be important."

"A rotten apple from a festering leper?"

"I see something rather different, Ralph."

"And what is that?"

"A clue."

They were sitting astride their horses outside the parish church of St. Mildred's, waiting to see its priest. Gervase studied the apple which had been given to him by Alain, certain that it must have some significance. Ralph was equally certain that the gift was dangerous.

"It is probably riddled with disease, Gervase."

"Then why is it so carefully wrapped up?"

"He gave it to you as a gesture of contempt."

"Had that been the case, he'd have hurled it at me."

"Get rid of it!"

"Before I have divined its meaning?"

Gervase turned it over then held it close to sniff it.

"Stop!" howled Ralph. "Have you taken leave of your senses? The man was a leper. Unclean, unclean!"

"Yet this apple is red and shiny."

"Except where he has taken a bite out of it."

"No, Ralph. Alain did not touch it. Bertha did."

"Oh, I see," mocked Ralph. "Bertha took one bite out of the apple, flung it up into the air at the leper hospital and Alain was the first to catch it. Is that how it came into his possession?"

"He found it by that clump of holly."

"Where the girl herself was discovered?"

"Yes," said Gervase with growing certainty. "I knew that Alain had seen a clue of some kind. He was the one who first spotted Bertha." He held up the apple. "And this is what he saw on the ground beside her."

"How do you know?"

"Why else would he give it to me?"

"It was pure chance. If some other kind soul had tossed him a coin as you did, he might have given them his apple instead."

"No. Alain was waiting for me. He knew that I would ride in or out of the gate sooner or later. When I asked for his help before, he refused to give it to me. Something has changed his mind."

"What?"

"The death of Brother Martin."

"Perhaps the old monk took the bite out of the apple."

"This is serious, Ralph," said Gervase, still turning it slowly in his hand. "I would wager anything that this was found beside Bertha's corpse."

"Then why did the leper pick it up?"

"As a keepsake."

"A half-eaten apple? It would soon decay."

"Even then he would have cherished it. Bertha was one of the only two friends he had in the world. This keepsake was all that he had to remember her by. It must have been a huge sacrifice to give it to me."

"But where does it get us?" said Ralph. "Even if your guess is right—and I am very sceptical—what are you actually holding in your hand?"

"I told you, Ralph. A clue."

"To *what*? Bertha's eating habits? That is all that it tells us. The girl liked apples. Shortly before she was killed, she took a bite out of this one. It fell to the ground beside her. Where is the revelation in that?"

Gervase pondered anew until the answer slowly emerged.

"That snake!" he exclaimed.

"Snake?"

"Found near the clump of holly."

"Ah!" teased Ralph. "So it was the snake which took a bite out of the apple, was it? That explains everything."

"You have forgotten your Bible."

"I have certainly done my best."

"Yet even you must remember Genesis."

"Adam and Eve?"

"Yes, Ralph. The Garden of Eden. Who persuaded Eve to eat the apple from the Tree of Knowledge?"

"The serpent."

"Exactly. And what did they discover by that clump of holly? A young woman, an apple and a serpent. It was a deliberate warning, Ralph. A sign that Bertha had gained some forbidden knowledge and forfeited her life as a result."

"You are reading too much into this."

"Am I?"

"What murderer would make such use of Scripture?"

"One who disguised himself as a monk."

Ralph was jolted. He was compelled to accept that there might have been something emblematic about Bertha's death. There was a strange logic to Gervase's argument. In giving him the apple, Alain the Leper might indeed have provided an invaluable clue.

"A final proof," said Gervase. "Bertha did not touch this apple. Look at the size of the bite. A much larger and stronger mouth left that damage on the fruit. It was placed beside her, along with the snake, after she was strangled. A careful tableau was arranged."

"A biblical villain!" noted Ralph. "It makes me even more determined to catch the rogue. We will have some local Noah murdered in a makeshift ark next!"

"This information must be given to the sheriff."

"Not if we wish to make best use of it."

"We must not withhold evidence, Ralph."

"Who found that evidence? We did. Why should we do the sheriff's work for him, then let him have the credit? No, Gervase. It would take his officers a month to learn what we have rooted out in a single day."

"We have certain advantages over them."

"Intelligence, for a start."

"I was thinking of poor Brother Martin," said Gervase. "I was with him when we examined the place where Bertha was hidden. And, unhappily, I was the one who found him dead. I also have a witness at the hospital."

"Witness?"

"Alain the Leper. He trusted me. He gave me a keepsake that he was sorry to lose because he thought it would somehow help in the pursuit of the killer."

"It will," said Ralph, slapping his thigh. "Two corpses, but only one murderer. We must divide our strength to stalk him. You follow his spoor from Brother Martin and I will begin my hunt here at Bertha's grave. With luck, we should close in on him from two sides."

Gervase took one last look at the apple before wrapping it in its cloth and slipping it into his saddlebag. When they had arranged to meet later, he set off in the direction of the cathedral.

Ralph looked sadly across at the churchyard. The mound of fresh earth that marked Bertha's last resting place was encircled by wreaths and posies. An irreverent raven landed inquisitively at the grave and pecked at the earth. Ralph was about to dismount to find a stone to hurl at it, when it suddenly flew away.

Reinbald the Priest came out of the church and closed the door behind him. He spread his arms in apology.

"I am sorry to have kept you waiting, my lord," he said. "But I had to give instruction to my churchwarden. We have another funeral this afternoon."

"Bertha's is the one that concerns me."

"How may I help?"

"By telling me something of her family," said Ralph, as he got down from the saddle. "Osbern has spoken about the father but there were other relatives here this morning."

"Mostly from Alwin's side of the family. They live in Fordwich and, like him, are tied in some way to the sea. Visit the port and mention his name. You will have no difficulty finding one of his brothers."

"What about his wife's side of the family?"

"They are few in number, my lord."

"No parents still alive?"

"I fear not."

"Brothers or sisters?"

"One sister. Bertha's aunt. She was at the funeral."

"I would like to speak with them all," decided Ralph. "And with Alwin himself, of course, when he is through the ordeal of today. I will start in Fordwich, then talk to this aunt of Bertha's."

A faint smile threatened. "Take care, my lord."

"Why?"

"Juliana is a prickly conversationalist."

"Is that a polite way of saying that she does not like Normans? If that is so, I will take my wife with me. Golde is a Saxon and will act as interpreter. What is the problem with this aunt Juliana?"

"She is something of a shrew."

"Not married, then?"

"No man would take on such a belligerent partner."

"How well did she know Bertha?"

"Very well," said Reinbald. "Juliana had a soft spot in her heart for her niece. The biting tongue was reserved for her father and his side of the family."

"Why?"

"I do not know, my lord. But this I can vouchsafe. When her sister died, Juliana stopped visiting Canterbury. She and Alwin have not spoken for years."

"What of Bertha?"

"When she wanted to see her aunt, she went to Faversham. On foot, my lord. A walk of eight miles."

"That shows an eagerness to visit this aunt Juliana. I would like to meet the lady, shrew or not." He glanced over his shoulder. "We passed a sign for Faversham on our way here. How would I find this termagant?"

"If I had a horse, I would teach you the way myself," offered the priest with sudden enthusiasm. "But you might think me an encumbrance to your work."

"Not at all, Father Reinbald. You know Faversham?"

"I was born there."

"Then I will find you a horse and employ you as my guide." Ralph hauled himself back up into the saddle. "A celibate priest is less likely to inflame an unmarried shrew than a Norman lord. You will take me to Faversham."

An involuntary grin flashed up on Reinbald's face only to vanish just as quickly. Ralph was surprised. It was an odd thing to see on a priest who was between two funerals.

Anticipating the effect of the funeral upon her, Helto the Doctor called at the house to see Eadgyth once more. Grief had sent her back to her bed and her condition seemed to have deteriorated. His calming presence was a comfort and he stayed with her until she driftly quietly off to sleep. When he came down to the solar, Helto used crisp reason to settle the argument that was still in progress.

"Eadgyth must not be told," he decreed. "It would be both unkind and dangerous."

"Is there not unkindness also in deceit?" said Golde.

"No, my lady. Not in this instance. Eadgyth is rather unstable at the moment. I talk of her mind, not her body. Confront her with news of this alleged murder and you may cause her untold harm. That will rebound on the whole household and everyone will suffer, especially the child." He gave a peremptory shake of the head. "It is too dangerous. Time is the true healer here. We must wait."

"You still call it an alleged murder?" noted Osbern.

"I stand by the results of my own examination."

"Yours is a lonely voice here."

"That is nothing new, Osbern," said the other with a resigned smile. "But my opinion is immaterial here. The cry of murder has been taken up and that is what we must keep from Eadgyth's ears."

"Until when?" asked Golde.

"Until the time is ripe, my lady. I am her physician. I will judge when that moment has come. Until then," he stressed, "I would ask you to abide by my instructions."

"We shall," promised Osbern.

"Thank you."

"What more may I do to help?" offered Golde.

"You have already done so much of value, my lady. I wish that all my patients had such a caring nurse. Do as you have been doing. Sit with her, encourage her to eat, let her have the baby in her arms whenever she asks. And if there is any change for the worse, send for me at once."

"You are very kind, Helto," said Osbern.

"I am at your disposal." He inclined his head politely then looked across at the reeve. "But why are you at home today? Should you not be at the shire hall to marshal witnesses for the royal commissioners?"

"They have suspended their work for a while."

"Why?"

"The murder of Brother Martin brought everything to a halt. My understanding is that Prior Henry is looking into the circumstances of the death and is therefore unable to represent the cathedral in a property dispute."

"The tribunal has other cases to consider, surely? Why do they not simply postpone this particular one and deal with another in its stead?"

"I cannot say, Helto."

"I may be able to throw some light here," volunteered Golde. "My husband feels that they are entangled in these two inquiries and wants these murders solved before they can proceed without hindrance."

Helto was curious. "And in the meantime, my lady?"

"They will lend their help to the investigations."

"I trust they will not discuss them under this roof?"

"My husband is tactful."

"And Master Bret even more so," added Osbern.

"I am relieved to hear it," said Helto with emphasis. "Whatever happens, Eadgyth must not suspect for one moment that her dearest friend may have been murdered."

There was a loud gasp from outside the door. Osbern pulled it open in time to see his wife standing there. She had clearly overheard them. Eadgyth was on the verge of hysteria. Her face was white, her eyes rolling, her mouth twitching violently and her body shuddering. She emitted a weird, wild, high-pitched scream which swept through the entire house. Before anyone could catch her, she slumped to the floor in a dead faint.

When Ralph Delchard rode to Fordwich, he took four of his men-at-arms with him. Norman soldiers were a familiar sight at the port but they were still far from welcome. The usual glances of muted antagonism met the posse. Coming in search of Bertha's relatives, Ralph was astounded to see her own father sitting alone on the quay. The chance of a word with him was too enticing to miss. He approached slowly.

"Good day to you, friend," said Ralph, ignoring the hostile glare which he had provoked. "My name is Ralph Delchard and I am in Canterbury on royal business. You, I know, are Alwin the Sailor and you have my deepest sympathy. We lodge at the home of Osbern the Reeve and have heard nothing but good words about your late daughter."

Alwin's manner changed from open resentment to a defensive silence. He studied Ralph with distant interest.

"The sheriff is searching for her killer," continued the other softly. "I have loaned him eight of my men to speed up that search. The others I have kept to assist me with my own inquiries into this sad business."

"Why?" muttered Alwin.

"The villain must be caught."

"But why should you help?"

"For personal reasons."

"We do not need you, my lord."

"The wider the search, the more chance we have of catching the murderer. Bertha, alas, was not his only victim."

"Who else?"

"Brother Martin. Have you not heard?"

"I heard that he died and that the monks brought him back to the priory in a cart but that was all. My mind has been on someone else's death."

"I understand."

"Do you?"

"Yes," sighed Ralph. "I know the grief that fills the mind until it is ready to burst apart at the seams. I lost my own wife and child, Alwin. By natural means, it is true, but the pain is still intense. In some sort, I do understand."

The sailor was taken aback. He had never heard a Norman lord speak to him so considerately and he had certainly never heard one confide in him so easily. Ralph had the bearing of a soldier but his battle scars were not only on the outside. Alwin still distrusted him but he was now more ready to talk to his visitor. He spoke in the halting French he had picked up in the course of his seafaring.

"How was Brother Martin killed?" he asked.

"Poisoned."

"Why?"

"Because he raised the alarm about Bertha."

"Alarm?"

"Yes, Alwin. Everybody else believed that she had died from snakebite. Helto the Doctor gave that as his medical opinion and Reinbald the Priest accepted it without a qualm. Brother Martin was the man who ferreted out the truth. We are convinced that he was murdered for his pains."

Apprehension flooded into Alwin's eyes. He stood up.

"Who will look after the leper hospital?" he said.

"It is in good hands."

"Brother Martin was their father."

"They mourn him with deep sorrow."

"But what of those he left behind, my lord?"

"Two monks were sent from Christ Church Priory."

"The lepers are properly cared for?"

"They are," assured Ralph. "Do not distress yourself."

Alwin relaxed. "I am bound to worry," he explained. "My daughter devoted her life to that hospital. So did Brother Martin. I would hate to see their work come to nothing."

"They lit the torch. Others will carry it on."

"Good."

There was a lengthy pause. "I did not expect to find you here in Fordwich," said Ralph.

"Where else?"

"Locked up in the privacy of your home."

"This is my home."

"When my wife died, I did not leave the house for months. I lacked the will to do so."

"I have will and need, my lord."

"Need?"

"To find the man who killed Bertha."

"We are ready helpers in that quest," promised Ralph. "Do you have any idea who that man might be?" Alwin shook his head. "Are you sure?"

"Quite sure."

"How will you know where to look for him?"

"He will turn up."

"And you will recognise him?"

"Yes."

Ralph could see that he was lying but there was no point in trying to dig out information that the sailor would never yield. Alwin was a powerful man who was determined to mete out his own justice. The only way to find out what he was hiding from Ralph was to try to extract it from his friends and relatives. Most of them lived there in Fordwich but the one who interested Ralph came from farther afield.

"This has been a shock to the whole family," he said.

"It has ruined our lives."

"I saw you all at the funeral."

"You were *there,* my lord?" said Alwin.

"We were anxious to pay our respects to Bertha."

"I thank you for that."

"No thanks are needed. She seems to have been a remarkable young woman. I only wish that we could have met her. It was a large congregation," recalled Ralph. "A real tribute to her popularity."

"Bertha had many friends."

"Her aunt was there, too, I believe."

"Which one? She had a number."

"Aunt Juliana from Faversham."

"Yes," groaned Alwin. "Juliana was there."

"I hope to talk to her sometime."

"Why?"

"She may be able to tell us something of value."

"All that Juliana will give you is a flea in your ear! She has a tongue like a rusty sword and a temper to match."

"It does not matter," said Ralph. "Bertha used to visit her in Faversham. She will know things about your daughter that even you might not know. I will endure a torrent of abuse from Juliana in order to get at them."

"Stay away from her!"

"I am entitled to speak to the woman."

"No, my lord. This is family business. Keep out."

"But if Bertha and her aunt were close—"

"This is nothing to do with you!" roared Alwin, losing all control. "You must not speak to Juliana. She will tell you nothing. I hate the woman. I never wish to see her again. Keep away from Juliana and her vile tongue! Leave us alone!"

ꙮ Chapter Ten

EADGYTH WAS CARRIED gently back to her bedchamber and left to the ministrations of Helto the Doctor. Golde waited outside the door with the frantic husband, reassuring him as best she could and trying to relieve his sense of guilt. Osbern the Reeve was beyond the help of mere words. Deeply shaken by his wife's collapse, he feared that she might have suffered some irreparable damage. When Helto finally came out of the chamber, Osbern clutched at his arm.

"Well?" he implored.

"She is conscious again now, Osbern. I have given her a potion to still the demons inside her head."

"Will she recover fully?"

"It is too soon to say."

"What must we do?"

"Be very tender to her," advised Helto. "She is in a highly delicate state. Eadgyth has sustained a terrible shock." He flicked a glance at Golde. "As I warned you she would. Now you will realise why I urged you to protect her from such a discovery. You saw the result for yourselves."

"May I go to her?" asked Osbern.

"Please do. Sit with her and soothe her. Make her feel loved and wanted. Do not upset her in any way. Whatever she asks, humour her wishes. I will call again this evening."

"Thank you."

When Osbern went into the bedchamber, Golde showed the doctor out of the house. She felt unjustly rebuked by his comments and wanted to defend herself but she bit back the words. Eadgyth was Helto's patient. It was not her place to question his treatment of her or to start an argument with him.

Helto left the house and Golde repaired to the kitchen to give the servants their orders. She was surprised when Osbern came searching for her. He was pale and harassed.

"Eadgyth is asking for you."

"Now?"

"She will speak with nobody else, my lady."

"Let us go at once."

"No," said Osbern uneasily. "She asks for you alone."

"But you are her husband."

"Eadgyth insisted. The doctor told me to obey her whims."

Golde could see the agony of rejection in his face. After touching his arm in sympathy, she went upstairs to let herself into the chamber. Eadgyth was lying in the bed and staring up at the ceiling. Golde took the stool beside her.

"How are you?" she asked.

Eadgyth turned to look at her with large questioning eyes. She held out a hand and Golde took it between her own to squeeze and stroke it. Eadgyth's fingers were icy cold.

"Why did they lie to me, my lady?" she whispered.

"They did it for the best."

"I could not believe that Osbern would be so false."

"He was only trying to save you from pain, Eadgyth."

"He deceived me. My own dear husband."

"It was on the doctor's advice."

"Helto lied to me as well," said the other in distress. "He told me that Bertha had died from the venom of a snake."

"That is still the opinion to which he holds."

"But it is untrue! I am not stupid, my lady. I *knew* that there was something wrong. Bertha and I grew up together. We played on Harbledown a hundred times. Our parents warned us about snakes and other poisonous creatures. We were careful." Her eyes grew moist as they widened earnestly. "Bertha would never have been caught un-awares."

"Not by a snake, perhaps."

"Then, by what? By whom?"

"We do not know, Eadgyth."

"Tell me the truth."

"I will."

"I know that I can trust you," said Eadgyth. "Osbern loves me but he still fobbed me off with lies. Tell me exactly what happened, my lady. How did Bertha die?"

"She was strangled." Eadgyth winced, and Golde gave her a moment to recover before she continued. "A snake did bite her neck but it seems that may have been after she was dead. It was a means to conceal the fact that she was murdered."

"Bertha! Of all people!"

"Nobody deserves to die in that way."

"But why her? She never harmed anyone in her life."

"Someone had a reason to kill her."

"Who?"

"They will find him."

Eadgyth began to weep silently and Golde reached out to hug her. An ugly truth had been kept from the young wife and she had learned it in the most heartrending way. To realise that Bertha had been murdered was an overwhelming horror and it was linked to a second hideous shock. Osbern had lied to her. In losing a dear friend, she also lost something of her love for her husband. Golde sensed her recrimination.

"Do not blame Osbern," she said. "He is a good man and he worships you. He only acted on the doctor's counsel. Your husband has been through his own tribulation these past few days. Be kind to him. Understand his pain."

She sat back on the stool as Eadgyth dabbed at her tears. Golde looked sadly down at her. It was a paradox. Everyone had kept back knowledge of the murder from her and yet Eadgyth might be the one person who knew the identity of the murderer. It was time to fish in the rivers of her memory.

"You told me that Bertha had a friend," whispered Golde.

"Oh, no, my lady!"

"You did, Eadgyth. I heard you clear."

"Then I was speaking out of turn. Bertha swore me to secrecy. It was a solemn vow."

"Her death absolves you. Who was he?"

"I could never tell you that."

"Even if it meant that you were shielding a killer?"

"He would never lay a finger on her!"

"How do you know?"

"He loved her!"

"Is that what Bertha said?"

"They were soon to be betrothed."

"Then maybe jealousy in the motive here," opined Golde. "Another of her admirers heard of her plans and murdered her out of envy. Could that be the case?"

"No, my lady. I was the only person who knew about him."

"Then we must start there. What is his name?"

"She never told me."

"What *did* she confide?"

"It was a secret, my lady."

"And will you let her take it to her grave?" Golde held her hand once more. "Listen, Eadgyth. We must track down this man. He may not even know that she has been killed. If he loved Bertha, he will be desolated by the news. But he has a right to know it. Will you keep the truth from him as it was kept from you?"

"No, my lady. That would be a cruelty."

"Then tell me how to find him."

"I do not know."

"Does he live in the city?"

"No, my lady. He hails from France."

"Is that where he dwells?"

"Much of the time," said Eadgyth. "Bertha only saw him when he came to Kent and he would not stay in Canterbury for long. He travelled around the whole county."

"Why? What was his occupation?"

"Bertha did not say."

"How did she describe him?"

"As the most wonderful person she had ever met. Kind, loving and very handsome. Somewhat older than she. She was entranced by him. It is the first time I have seen Bertha truly happy."

"Why such secrecy about her lover?"

"Because of her father."

"Alwin the Sailor?"

"He would have stopped her at once." She gave a little shrug. "That is all I know, my lady, I swear. Do not press me further. It distresses me to recall the joy in her voice when she talked about him. All that hope, strangled out of her."

"One more question, then. That is all. May I?" Eadgyth gave a reluctant nod of assent. "When did Bertha last speak of her friend to you?"

"Four or five days ago. She was very excited. Bertha had not seen him for months but word had finally come. It gave her such delight." Her face was shining at the memory but it soon lost its glow. Eadgyth's voice was dulled by sorrow again. "He was due to arrive here this week."

Gervase Bret spent a long time at Christ Church Priory. Having been given permission to speak with Brother Ambrose, he sought out the monk and introduced himself. They adjourned to the privacy of the garden so that they could talk. Ambrose was a round, red-faced, affable man in his fifties, with a zest for life which was quite unmarked by his regular contact with death.

When Gervase showed him the flask which had been found at the hospital of St. Nicholas, the monk needed only one sniff to confirm that it had contained the poison which had ended Brother Martin's life. Gervase was not allowed to view the cadaver in the morgue but he was given a most detailed inventory of its contours and its condition by the beaming Brother Ambrose. The bell for Vespers brought the conversation to a close and Gervase watched the monks converge on the chapel for Evensong. Special prayers would be said for the soul of the dear departed, and Canon Hubert and Brother Simon joined the obedientiaries to add their personal supplication.

Instinct sent Gervase back to Harbledown. In the hope that the scene of the crime might yield more clues about the murder, he rode steadily up the hill in the cool evening air. When he caught sight of a tall, stooping figure far ahead of him, he recognised Alain at once. The leper was dragging himself toward the crest of the hill and Gervase was chastened by the thought that a journey which would take no more than fifteen minutes on a horse had been an excruciating crawl throughout most of the afternoon for Alain.

Gervase overhauled him and dropped down to walk beside the leper. Alain did not even look up or check his stride.

"You are back, Master Bret," he grunted.

"How did you know that it was me?"

"Who else would walk so close to a leper?"

"I came to thank you for your gift."

"Gift?"

"The apple."

"Was it of any help?"

"We think so."

"I do not see how."

"Where exactly did you find it?" asked Gervase. "Beside the body? Under the holly close by?"

"It was in her hand."

"Of course!" It confirmed his theory. He reached up to take the apple and its wrapping from his saddlebag. "I have brought it back to you, Alain."

The leper stopped and turned to him, clearly touched but unable to find the words to express his gratitude. When the apple was handed over, he held it as if it were a bag of gold, then secreted it once more inside his voluminous sleeve. Gervase did not have the heart to tell him that the apple had not belonged to Bertha but had probably been put into her fingers after she was dead. It held a special meaning for Alain and should be allowed to go on doing so until the apple rotted slowly away like the man who coveted it.

"You must have cared deeply for Bertha," said Gervase.

"She was a friend."

Alain trudged off again and Gervase kept pace with him.

"Did you ever speak to her alone?"

"Now and then."

"What did you like about her?"

"She was not afraid of me."

"How long have you had leprosy?"

"Most of my life," said Alain without any trace of self-pity. "I have got used to the effect I have on others. Bertha was different. She did not turn away."

They walked on without speaking until they came to the hospital and turned off the track. One of the monks was distributing food to some of the other lepers. Seen from behind, the man looked so like Brother Martin that the two of them came to a sudden halt and blinked. When the monk turned to smile a welcome, they realised their mistake. The incident served as a reminder to Gervase.

"Were you here when they took Brother Martin away?"

"I was."

"You saw them arrive with the cart?"

"We stood around the door of the church throughout."

"How many monks were there, Alain?"

"Five or six."

"What happened when they went into the church?"

"Why do you ask?"

"It is important. Did one come out again on his own?"

"Yes."

"And where did he go?"

"I do not know," said Alain. "We were only interested in Brother Martin. They put his body on the cart and covered it with a shroud. Then they took him away."

Gervase was quietly exhilarated to have his guesswork transformed into fact. He thanked Alain and let him join the others for the meal, watching him shuffle away and knowing that he carried an item of food inside his sleeve which would never be consumed and yet which would provide constant nourishment.

The door of the church was open. When Gervase went into the empty nave, he stood at the rear and looked at the spot where Brother Martin had been propped against the pillar. He then gazed across at the altar with its crucifix, its flowers and its single candle in an iron holder. By putting an apple in her hand and a serpent beside her, the murderer had used Bertha's death as a means of sending a hidden message. Gervase wondered if a similar sign was contained in the manner and the venue of Brother Martin's demise. He was still standing there when one of the monks joined him.

"Are you looking for something, my son?" he asked.

"Yes," said Gervase. "A scene from the Bible."

Cradled in his arms, Golde lay naked in bed beside her husband. It seemed to her almost sinful to share so much love in a house filled with so much pain and remorse, but Ralph was plainly untroubled by any feelings of guilt. He caressed her hair before running his hand down the smooth skin of her back. There was no responsive purr.

"What is the matter, my love?" he asked.

"Nothing."

"You are unhappy."

"After that? Of course not."

"I know you too well, Golde."

"I am tired, that is all."

"Your mind is elsewhere. So is your heart. Is it my fault? Something that I did or said? What ails you?"

"Nothing that cannot wait until morning," she said,

snuggling into him and placing an apologetic kiss on his chest. "I am sorry if I was not as welcoming as you have every right to expect."

"You were miles away, Golde."

"Was I?"

"Or maybe only five yards or so."

"Five yards?"

"In the next bedchamber. With Eadgyth."

Golde sighed. "She is much in my thoughts, Ralph."

"Can she not move over and leave some room for me?"

"There is always room for you," she said, rolling on top of him to kiss him on the lips. "Have I not proved that to you time and again?" He rubbed his nose against hers by way of reply. "But I fret about Eadgyth."

"She has a husband and doctor to look after her."

"After today, she will not trust them so implicitly. That is one of the sad consequences of Bertha's death. It has come between husband and wife. Osbern is a devoted husband yet she now views him with suspicion."

"That will change in time."

"I hope so. For both their sakes. When we stepped into this house, it was brimming with happiness. Where has it all gone, Ralph?"

"Right here," he said, hugging her close. "Have you so soon forgotten? Besides," he continued, "Osbern's loss has been our gain. When his wife felt betrayed by him, she turned to you and confided things we would never otherwise have known. Bertha *did* have a lover, after all. We have no name and no occupation for him as yet but we know he exists. My own information supports that."

"What did you find out at Fordwich?"

"That I could never be a sailor."

"Why?"

"The very sight of water makes me feel seasick."

"Even this far inland?"

"Yes," he said. "I went to Fordwich and was astonished to chance upon Alwin himself, sitting on the quay. He told me little enough and his brothers were even less forthcoming. They had obviously been warned to say nothing."

"What did you do?"

"I hung around the harbour and spoke to people who were not his kith and kin. My helm and hauberk made them reticent but I coaxed it out of them eventually."

" 'It'?"

"There *was* a man in Bertha's life and Alwin has been hunting him. He was down at the harbour only yesterday, accosting all and sundry and demanding to know if anyone had seen him."

"Was a name given?"

"No, Golde. Only a description. But it tallies with the one that Eadgyth gave you. A handsome Frenchman in his thirties, who might recently have arrived at Fordwich by boat. Alwin was most anxious to trace him."

"I can understand why."

"Nobody had seen him."

"But he was due to land here this week."

"He may well have done so," said Ralph, "and one of those captains may well have ferried him across the Channel on his boat."

"Why did he not admit as much to Alwin?"

"His passenger probably bribed him into silence. Bertha's lover—or killer, or whatever he is—likes to cover his tracks. I will take up the search again tomorrow."

"Where?"

"In Faversham. With the girl's aunt."

"How will you find the way?" she asked.

"Reinbald the Priest is my navigator," said Ralph with a chuckle. "You see how desperate I have become, my love? I have to turn for help to the Church!"

He picked his way through the undergrowth with the sure-footed confidence of someone who was very familiar with the terrain. Moonlight gave him some assistance but he did not really need it. When he passed the leper hospital, he did so in a wide arc so that there was no possibility of his being seen by anyone spending a sleepless night outside one of the huts. Leprosy kept different hours from the rest of world.

His route brought him back to a narrow track that meandered down the hill through thickening woodland. The sound of an approaching horse made him step quickly into the bushes nearby. Crouched in his hiding place, he waited until the rider had cantered past, wondering why anybody should be out so late and why he was going toward Harbledown. The question soon faded from his mind as more immediate and inspiring thoughts rushed to take its place. He allowed himself a smile.

There was not far to go now. After half a mile at a steady jog, he came around the edge of a copse to catch his first glimpse of the light in the distance. He quickened his pace at once. An owl hooted, a wildcat screeched and some other animal darted across his path but he was neither distracted nor dismayed.

Reinbald the Priest ran on toward Faversham.

Osbern the Reeve lay on the straw pallet in extreme discomfort and wondered why the master of the house was occupying one of its meanest rooms. He had done so at the suggestion of Helto the Doctor, who felt that Eadgyth's condition would become less volatile if she were allowed to spend the night alone. Her husband offered to keep a vigil in a chair at her bedside but he was overruled. Eadgyth refused to take the sleeping draught prescribed for her, and Osbern's presence, it was felt, might incite rather than soothe. Helto believed that a combination of isolation and fatigue would ensure a restful night for his patient. That same combination had the opposite effect on her evicted husband.

What had he done wrong? That was what he kept asking himself. Why did Eadgyth look at him in such accusatory silence? Would they ever recapture the joy which had brought them together and made their home such a haven of peace and love? He was still reflecting on his misfortunes when sleep stole up on him and, taking pity on him at last, claimed him for a couple of short hours.

He came awake with a start. His body was still aching and his pride was still wounded by the fact that he had been relegated to a chamber normally used by the most menial of the servants. During the trials of childbirth, it was natural for him to vacate the marriage bed for a short duration but this was a very different situation. Eadgyth was unwell and in need of succour. His place was beside her.

A distant *bang* made him sit up. As he tried to work out if the noise had come from inside or outside the house, a second *bang* was heard, louder and closer. It sounded like the front door. He swung his legs off the pallet and pulled himself upright, striking his head against the rafter as he did so and almost losing his balance. Groping his way out into the passage, he strained his eyes against the darkness. A board creaked beneath his foot but the rest of the house was in silence.

He crept across to the bedchamber he shared with his wife and put his ear to the door. There was no sound from within. Helto's advice had been wise. Left alone, Eadgyth was enjoying a deep and untroubled sleep. Osbern could not resist the opportunity to look in upon her and he eased her door open as gently as he could. When the aperture was wide enough, he peered through it to take some comfort from the sight of his slumbering wife.

His blood congealed. Eadgyth was not there. A finger of moonlight came in through the gap between the shutters to point down at an empty bed. Flinging the door open, he lunged into the room to see if she had fallen to the floor but there was no sign of her. Panic deprived him of all consideration for the guests in the household.

"Eadgyth!" he yelled. "Where are you, Eadgyth!"

He went stumbling out into the passage and felt his way down the oaken staircase, creating even more disturbance.

"Eadgyth! Are you downstairs? Answer me, Eadgyth!"

A servant was the first to react, trotting down from the attic room with a lighted candle and confirming Osbern's worst fear. The little flame illumined the front door and showed that its bolts had been drawn back. The reeve pulled it open and stepped out into the street.

"Eadgyth! Come back! Please, Eadgyth!"

It was Ralph Delchard who brought him back into the house and rescued him from the protests of his neighbours. Another servant brought a second candle, then Golde came downstairs with a third. Gervase Bret was behind her.

"What has happened?" he said.

"My wife has disappeared," gasped Osbern.

"We do not know that for sure," argued Ralph. "Let the house be searched from top to bottom before we raise any alarm." He pointed to a servant. "Take the candle and scour every room with care. Bring a report at once."

"Yes, my lord."

"I'll help," said Golde, following him upstairs.

"She is gone," moaned the Reeve. "I know it."

"At this time of night?" said Gervase.

"Eadgyth has run away."

"That is foolish talk," said Ralph, trying to calm him. "She has no cause to run away. This is her home."

"My wife is sick. She does not know what she is doing."

"We must find her at once," said Gervase, lighting another candle from the one held by the servant. "I'll try the kitchen and the solar."

"Do not forget the stables," said Ralph.

"Where *is* she?" demanded Osbern.

Snatching the candle from his servant, he went off on his own wild inspection of the ground floor, running from room to room and even climbing down the cellar to search for his wife. The frenetic activity was in vain. Eadgyth was definitely not in the house. As her husband was trying to cope with the horror of one loss, another was forced upon him.

Golde came hurrying down the stairs in consternation.

"Dear God!" she said. "The baby has gone as well!"

Still in her night attire, Eadgyth clutched her son to her breast and walked unsteadily along a rutted thoroughfare. Her hair hung loose and her feet were bare. Darkness took away the Canterbury she knew and replaced it with a bewildering maze of streets and lanes that led her in every direction but the one which she wanted. When she paused at a corner to take her bearings, the baby awoke and cried its disapproval of the cool breeze around its head. Hugging him tight, she hummed a lullaby and rocked the child to and fro until it dozed off.

Night had its own collection of unexplained noises but

she heard none of them. Even the occasional yelp of a dog did not penetrate her ears. Eadgyth blundered on, stopping from time to time to study the silhouette of a building which she thought she recognised, then choosing another wrong direction. Frustration only made her walk faster, impervious to the pain in her feet as they trampled indiscriminately over hard stones, discarded animal bones and the accumulated refuse of the city.

The impulse which drove her on eventually became a more reliable compass and guided her toward her destination. Familiar houses loomed up, shops acknowledged her acquaintance and a horse trough was a reassuring landmark. She was back home.

"We are coming!" she called. "We are here!"

Her cry woke the baby again and its complaints were more boisterous this time. It took her several minutes to lull it back to sleep with gentle rocking and warm kisses. As she moved on, the boy still in her arms, her words came out in an urgent whisper.

"Wait for us! We have not forgotten you!"

She was back in the Canterbury of her youth now, lifted by its memories and reassured by its certainties. The baby was her future but she carried him back into the safety of the past. When she turned a corner, Eadgyth saw the solid mass of the parish church of St. Mildred's against the night sky. She paused to stare up at it with simple awe.

Most of her life had been circumscribed by its stone walls. Baptised in its font and married before its altar, she had been an ardent member of its congregation for all the years in between and, although she now worshipped beside her husband in the daunting glory of the cathedral, it was the little church which still held her in thrall.

"We are here," she murmured. "Do you see? We have come."

It was almost dawn when they found her. Eadgyth was fast asleep in the middle of the churchyard, her back against a tombstone, her feet almost touching the fresh mound of earth beside it. The baby was fretful in her arms. Golde took it gently from her to wrap in a warm blanket. Osbern the Reeve knelt down to enfold his wife in the tenderest embrace.

Her eyes opened and she gave a smile of explanation.

"Bertha wanted me," she said.

❧ CHAPTER ELEVEN

NOTHING DISTURBED THE even tenor of Canterbury Cathedral. A murdered monk lay within its priory, a bitter dispute awaited it in the shire hall and an even more violent controversy threatened it from the abbey of St. Augustine but the cathedral went about its business at the same pace and with the same unassailable sense of purpose. It was the still centre at the heart of the city, a spiritual fortress that was proof against any upheaval from within and any siege from without. Archbishop Lanfranc was invincible.

Nobody had managed to convince Prior Gregory of this fact.

"The abbey will not be browbeaten. We will fight the archbishop with all our strength and resources. And we will win!"

"Lower your voice. This is hallowed ground."

"He has done it again, Canon Hubert!"

"Done what?"

"Hauled me to the cathedral to keep me waiting."

"Have you been sent away unseen?"

"Not this time," said Prior Gregory. "When I had cooled my heels for an hour or two, Archbishop Lanfranc deigned to give me an audience. It lasted five minutes. I was hardly permitted to speak. Five minutes, Canon Hubert!"

Hubert was about to remark that it was five minutes more than he had contrived to spend with the archbishop but his pride held him back from that damaging admission. In his present mood, the disenchanted canon would have settled for five seconds in the presence of the head of the English Church in order to feel that his journey to Canterbury had been worth the effort and that the most significant and influential friendship in his long career had, albeit briefly, flickered back into life.

The aggressive religiosity of Prior Gregory was not to his taste. It was the second time they had met in the cloister garth and this encounter was no more pleasant than the first. Canon Hubert struck what he considered to be an apostolic pose but his response sounded more like that of a Pontius Pilate.

"This is nothing to do with me, Prior Gregory."

"It is," insisted the other. "Do not try to wash your hands of the matter. You and your fellow commissioners are involved to the hilt."

"The cloister is for meditation, not for acrimony."

"Tell that to Archbishop Lanfranc."

"Would that I had the opportunity!"

"Do you know what he told me this morning?"

"It is no concern of mine."

"During our meagre five minutes together, that is."

"You are violating my impartiality."

"Abbot Guy is on his way to Canterbury."

"Let me hear no more, Prior Gregory."

"Our express wishes are being ignored."

"Desist!"

"Abbot Guy will be no father of St. Augustine's Abbey. He is a one-man army of occupation sent in by a tyrannical archbishop. He must be stopped at all cost."

"And so must you, Prior Gregory!"

Canon Hubert's intemperate yell lifted the heads of every monk within earshot and raised their eyebrows in censure. The prior was undeterred but his portly companion was seething with embarrassment.

"Let me impress upon you once more," he said through gritted teeth. "We will not take sides and we will certainly not be swayed by arguments thrust at us in this bellicose fashion. The property dispute between cathedral and abbey will be settled in the shire hall when we reconvene. Any other disagreement between you is an irrelevance to us."

"Disagreement?" echoed the other. "An unworthy and wholly unacceptable abbot is to be forced upon us and you characterise this as a mere disagreement? Our spiritual lives are at stake here, Canon Hubert."

"Raise the matter with Archbishop Lanfranc."

"We have been doing so for weeks on end!"

"His word has the force of law."

"Not at the abbey."

"You defy him at your peril," said Hubert, lapsing into pedagogic mode to terminate the exchange. "Obedience is a precept of the Benedictine Order. That may sometimes mean an acceptance of unpalatable commands. Monastic institutions are ruled from above and not from below. Where would we be if every decision of an archbishop was flouted and every appointment of an abbot was contested? That is the high road to anarchy, Prior Gregory. Even you must realise that."

162

There was a hissing power in his rebuff which made his companion step back a pace and glower at him resentfully. Prior Gregory claimed the right to the last word.

"So be it," he said. "I see that we have to fight King as well as cathedral. An impartial judge? You are no more than a hired lackey of the archbishop."

Canon Hubert's cheeks turned to ripe plums and he throbbed with righteous indignation but he had no opportunity to defend himself against the insulting charge. The angry prior was already striding toward the main gate to carry yet more bad tidings to the abbey of St. Augustine.

It had been a bruising confrontation and Hubert was left feeling both hurt and misunderstood. His discomfort was sharply increased when he saw the slim, erect figure of Prior Henry bearing down on him with a dignified tread. Christian fellowship and social niceties were swept aside by the impassive Italian. His question was a knife at Hubert's throat.

"What exactly did Prior Gregory say to you?"

"How did Eadgyth know where to find the grave in the dark?"

"It was beside that of Bertha's mother, my lord."

"When did the mother die?"

"Several years ago," said Reinbald. "Before my time as priest at St. Mildred's. Bertha has been an assiduous visitor to our churchyard. She treats her mother's grave like a shrine."

"What about Alwin the Sailor?"

"Whenever he is in Canterbury, he comes daily to pay his respects. I have watched him stand before his wife's grave for an hour or more in the most inclement weather. It is almost like a penance."

With four men-at-arms at his back, Ralph Delchard rode

toward Faversham with his cloak trailing in the stiff morning breeze. Reinbald was beside him on a borrowed mount which was too mettlesome for such an inexperienced horseman. The priest hung on grimly to the reins as he was bounced along in the hard leather saddle and the following escort were greatly amused by his predicament. Ralph used the journey to gather more information even if it came out of Reinbald's mouth in frightened gasps.

"Tell me about this Juliana," said Ralph.

"I told you all when I said that she was a shrew."

"Not so, Reinbald. A woman is not that forward without some cause. Few are born shrewish. How did she become so?"

"I do not know, my lord."

"Is the woman deformed or ill-favoured?"

"Far from it," said Reinbald, trying to ignore the pounding saddle beneath him. "She and her sister both had their share of grace and beauty but their characters were as different as chalk and cheese. One was wild and obstinate while the other was soft and gentle."

"Yet not so gentle, I hear."

"My lord?"

"Bertha's mother often argued with her husband. Perhaps she kept her softness only for show and turned into a second Juliana when indoors."

"Oh, no," said the priest. "There is only one Juliana!"

"You speak with feeling."

"I grew up in Faversham. It is not a big town."

"The lady bulks large, then?"

"She is certainly no shrinking violet."

Reinbald the Priest let out a howl of pain as his horse leapt over a fallen log and treated his buttocks to the worst pummelling yet. Ralph led his men in a chorus of mirth.

"Thank God you are not married," he said, giving the

priest a slap on the back. "By the time we get there, your chances of procreation will have been cracked open like a pair of hot chestnuts at Christmastide."

Raucous laughter took them on a mile or more. Reinbald the Priest suffered his martyrdom in agonised silence.

Eadgyth's plight threw the whole house into disarray. Osbern the Reeve was tortured by anxiety, the servants were in a frenzy and the guests were caught up in the general alarm. Helto the Doctor came running and his immediate concern was for the baby, a lusty-enough infant but one whose nights should be spent in a warm crib rather than in a cold churchyard. Miraculously, the child seemed to be largely unharmed by its nocturnal excursion and went happily to sleep once it had been fed and wrapped in a blanket. Helto was able to turn his full attention to the mother.

Never more needed, Golde's help was all-embracing. She committed herself wholeheartedly to the tasks in hand and was, by turns, mother, nurse, cook, housekeeper and doctor's assistant. Having run her own household and business in Hereford, she had an easy authority. When the crisis was at its height, it was Golde who brought the calming influence.

At her suggestion, Gervase Bret took the husband aside and tried to bolster his morale.

"You may relax now," he said. "The ordeal is over."

"I fear that it has only just begun, Master Bret."

"The doctor is with her. He will know what to do."

"Yes," agreed Osbern. "But what happens when Helto has gone? Eadgyth is an unruly patient. She left her bed in the middle of the night to roam the city. Think of the danger."

"It seems to have been averted."

"This time, perhaps. What of the next?"

"There will be no next time," Gervase assured him. "Your wife did not roam the city. She went with a clear purpose and that was to visit the grave of her friend."

"Thank heaven she did not join Bertha *in* that grave!"

"Her need is satisfied now, Osbern."

"I pray that it is."

"She will not desert the house again."

"I hope not, Master Bret. We cannot mount a guard on her twenty-four hours a day. This is a home and not a dungeon."

Gervase let him pour out his heart. Osbern the Reeve was now more tormented than ever by guilt. Having concealed the truth about the murder from her, he had estranged his wife. Having kept her from the funeral, he had implanted an irresistible urge in her to visit the grave. Nothing had ever vitiated the harmony between husband and wife before. Osbern had moved from concord to chaos in one giant leap.

"Are you married?" he asked.

"Betrothed."

"Learn from my example, Master Bret."

"Yours is a sound and joyful union."

"It was, it was."

"And will be so again in no time at all."

"Eadgyth will never forgive me."

"She must," said Gervase confidently. "There is so little to pardon. No husband could have been more caring toward his wife. What you did was purely out of concern for her. Eadgyth will come to appreciate that."

"I beg leave to doubt it."

"Her crisis is past. Healing can now begin."

"How can I help that process?" he asked quietly. "Helto the Doctor will tell me how to restore her bodily health but it is Eadgyth's mind which disturbs me. To snatch our child and rush out of the house like that! It is not the act of a rational person, Master Bret. I fear for her sanity."

"Try to understand what prompted her," said Gervase. "Only the most powerful impulse could have made her behave the way that she did. What was it?"

"A rebellion against her husband."

"No, Osbern."

"A wild urge to escape from me."

"That was not the reason."

"A hatred of the way that I deceived her."

"There is no grain of hatred here."

"Then what?"

"Love."

"Of whom?"

"Bertha. They were friends, their lives intertwined from birth, their hopes shared, their joys celebrated together and their disappointments taken upon each other's shoulders. Could any two young women have been closer?"

"No, Master Bret."

"Then there is the real explanation of her conduct in the night. Eadgyth could not rest until she had made one last contact with the person most dear to her after you."

"But why do so in such a frightening way?"

"Your wife was not frightened," argued Gervase. "Love is its own best protection. When she stepped out into the night, she did not even think what hazards might lurk in the darkness of the city. Her desire to be with Bertha was strong enough to sweep all such thoughts aside."

"That may indeed be so," conceded Osbern as he thought it through. "But did she have to take our son with her?"

"I think she did."

"Why?"

"Did you not tell me that Bertha more or less moved into the house when the child was born? She was second mother to baby Osbern. She helped your wife when that help was vitally needed."

"That is very true."

"And she nurtured the child like her own."

"You are right," said Osbern. "He had to go. Eadgyth and our son took their leave of Bertha together."

The reeve was now more reconciled to the shock of his wife's unheralded departure in the night but his conscience was still sorely troubled. Gervase whispered some advice.

"Helto is not the only doctor in the city."

"Should I call in another physician?"

"One who can medicine her soul."

"Whom do you mean?"

"Reinbald the Priest. Though she dwells here in the shadow of the cathedral, your wife will always look towards St. Mildred's. That is where Bertha lies. Call in Reinbald. He is young but earnest in his ministry. He will be a visible link between Eadgyth and Bertha."

"You counsel well. It will be arranged."

"A priest may cure where a doctor fails."

"I will bear that in mind." Despair brought a sudden groan out of him. "What a change there has been! A week ago, there was not a cloud on our horizon. Then lightning strikes. Bertha is killed, then Brother Martin, and—but for the grace of God—my wife and child might have ended up in their coffins as well. Four possible victims!"

"Five."

"Who was the fifth?"

"Alwin the Sailor."

"Expiring from grief, you mean?"

"No," said Gervase. "He was set to take a bloodier exit

from the world than that. According Brother Martin, he tried to kill himself by smashing his head on the flagstones at the church of St. Nicholas. It was all they could to to save him from his own rage. Alwin was demented. Brother Martin did not realise he had so much violence inside him."

"Tell me!" shouted Alwin, kicking him again. "Tell me!"
"There is nothing to tell," gasped the man.
"You're lying!"
"No, Alwin."
"Tell me the truth!"
Alwin kicked him once more and the sailor doubled up in pain. They were alone in one of the warehouses at Fordwich. It was a private place. Blocks of stone were stacked all around them to await transport to the cathedral. The door was closed. No cries for help could be heard outside.

The man was bigger and stronger than Alwin but he was no match for his assailant. Lying in wait, Alwin had felled him from behind with a stout length of timber, then kept him on the ground with a succession of blows and kicks. Blood was oozing from the man's chin and from his temple. One of his eyes was already puffed up and encircled with a darkening ring. Alwin was in no mood to temporise.

"Tell me!" he ordered, jabbing the timber into his victim's stomach. "Or you'll never get up alive."
"Have pity, Alwin!" whimpered the other.
"This is your last chance!"
"I have a wife and child."
"I had a daughter of my own until a few days ago!" said Alwin with a surge of fury. "That is what it is all about."
"Believe me, I only wish that I could help you."

"You will!"

Alwin belaboured him with the timber until the man was writhing in anguish, then he sat heavily astride his chest. Hands well apart, he pressed the timber against the other's throat until the man was spluttering. He exerted relentless pressure. The victim's eyes bulged, his veins stood out like whipcord and his face slowly changed colour. He used his last ounce of energy to signal agreement with a raised hand.

Lifting the timber, Alwin kept it an inch from the throat by way of a warning. The man coughed and panted.

"When did you bring him?" demanded Alwin.

"At the start of the week," confessed the other.

"From Caen?"

"Yes, Alwin."

"I knew he was here. Why did you lie?"

"He paid me."

"Yes," said Alwin darkly, "that was always his way. Money and soft words. Bring him over and take him back. No questions asked, no answers given."

"I needed the money. What else was I to do?"

"Nothing. Did he talk to you on the voyage?"

"Hardly a word."

"Did you agree to take him back?" A defensive look came into the man's eye. Alwin brought the timber back into play. "Did you?" he said, pressing down hard. The man nodded at once and he was liberated again. "When?"

"Next week, Alwin."

"What day?"

"Wednesday."

"Where must you take him?"

"Boulogne."

A spasm of pain shot through Alwin and he dropped the timber on the ground. He clambered to his feet and brooded in silence.

Released from his ordeal, the man sat up and took stock of his wounds. No bones were broken but his whole body was a mass of aches and bruises. Blood was now dripping down on to his chest. Alwin offered a hand and pulled him up.

"Thank you," said the man.

"Wednesday?"

"We arranged a time to meet."

"I will be here."

Faversham was a colourful mixture of thatched cottages, civic buildings, shops, stables and hovels, running down to a creek. In earlier centuries, it had been the administrative centre of the whole Lathe and a vanished dignity still hung from it like a tattered robe of office. The town had a wooden church, a mill, two salt pits and a busy harbour, but most of the inhabitants worked the surrounding land. Ploughmen, cowherds and shepherds lived on the outer fringes of Faversham but sent their wives into its bustling market. Over a hundred pigs foraged for acorns in the woodland.

Ralph led the canter across the meadow. His men-at-arms fanned out to ride beside him but Reinbald the Priest was left well behind. Still struggling to stay on the horse, he did not want to goad any more life out of it than the animal was already showing, and tugged on the reins with all his might. His hands were raw from the effort but it was another part of his anatomy which bore the most vivid memories of the journey. For all that, he arrived at his birthplace with a brave smile and looked eagerly across at the tiny church.

They came to a halt near the mill and watched the swift waters of the River Swale turn its noisy wheel as they waited for the laggard rider to catch them up. Ralph noted the marshland to the north of the village and saw that flooding was an annual problem. Faversham was in a pleasant spot. After the teeming streets of Canterbury, it was a relief to be in a more rural community.

Reinbald arrived but needed a further two minutes to bring his horse under control. When it finally stopped, he slipped his feet from the stirrups and dropped to the ground. His legs almost buckled beneath him.

"Where does Juliana live?" said Ralph.

"In the main street, my lord, but she will not be there."

"Where will we find her?"

"Follow me," he said, walking gingerly and leading his horse along the riverbank. "Juliana inherited one of the salt-houses from her father. That is where she will be."

A shriek of outrage soon confirmed the prediction.

"No, no, no, you dolt!"

They were fifty yards from the place but Juliana's voice cut through the air like a scythe through dry grass.

"Put it there, man! Put it there, you imbecile!"

An unseen servant was mishandling blocks of salt and being reprimanded by his mistress. The loud, ringing tones were like the discordant chimes of a cracked bell. When they reached the salt-house, Reinbald went in to talk to her. An eerie silence fell. Expecting some kind of monster to come snarling out of the building, Ralph was taken aback to see a trim woman of middle years sail out with poise and take up her position in front of him. He looked at the full lips in the harsh beauty of her face and decided that one of the Faversham bachelors had lost a prime catch in his courting days. Juliana was a woman of some style.

She dropped the merest replica of a curtsey and smiled.

"My lord?" The voice was low, almost melodious. "Reinbald says that you wish to speak to me. If you have ridden all the way from Canterbury, it must be important. As you see, I am busy. I would not wish to be kept too long away from my work here."

The priest had been brought as a guide and interpreter but he could now be relieved of the latter role. Ralph could understand the woman perfectly, not simply because she spoke with slow emphasis but because she accompanied her words with the most expressive gestures. Even had he been stone deaf, he would have had no trouble picking up the gist of what she said.

Dismounting from his horse, he escorted Juliana across to the comparative privacy of a beech tree. Though he had learned much of her language from his wife, he could still not speak it with fluency and wanted to be out of earshot of his men before he plunged into its tangled verbiage. The priest followed them but stood some yards away, detached from the conversation but ready to intervene if required.

"I want to ask you about Bertha," said Ralph.

"My niece?" she asked guardedly.

"I believe you were at the funeral yesterday."

"Yes, my lord." She lowered her head. "The sorrow will always be with me. Bertha was a lovely girl. She was the only member of that family I cared about. They are worthless. Alwin is the most miserable of them all."

"Why, then, did your sister marry him?"

"I warned her against it."

"But she went ahead?"

"He talked her into it somehow," she said bitterly. "No man would ever do that to me. Least of all, a sailor. They are the worst. I told her what she was taking on but she ignored me. My sister was a fool. She paid for her folly."

"How did she die?"

"He killed her."

"Alwin?"

"Yes," she asserted, getting into her stride. "The doctor said that she was carried off by a fever but I talked with her and I know the truth. My sister died of a cracked heart. Her husband treated her abominably."

"He beat her?"

"Not with his fists, my lord. But there are other ways to wound. She was too soft and submissive with him. By the time she learned to strike back, it was too late." She let out a screech of anger. "Ha! He would not have found me soft and submissive. I'd never have let him touch me after that. If Alwin had come anywhere near my bed, I would have sliced his manhood off with a carving knife!"

Once started, there was no holding her. Juliana railed against her brother-in-law for several minutes, waving her hands as she did so and working herself up into such a temper that she was almost frothing at the mouth. Ralph recoiled before the torrent of abuse without really under-standing what had provoked it.

"Clearly you have no love for Alwin," he observed, drily.

"He is the most loathsome man alive."

"Your sister did not think so."

"She came round to that view at the end."

"What about Bertha?"

"Poor child! She was left alone with him."

"Was Alwin unkind to her? Violent?"

"He would not have dared to be either!" she growled. "Or he would have answered to me. I would have taken Bertha away from him. I told her that."

"Yet she stayed with him."

"He was her father."

"Did she not respect him in any way?"

"Bertha was an innocent. She did not understand the ways of the world. I have lived longer and know the depths to which men can sink."

"Some men, Juliana."

"That is a matter of opinion."

"I think I know yours."

"It is honestly held, my lord."

"And very forcefully expressed," he said with a wry smile. "But there is something missing here. You tell me that you despise Alwin for what he did to your sister but I still do not know what it was."

"Nor will you."

"Is it, then, so shameful?"

"It is past. Let us forget it."

"But it runs through everything you say. Alwin is your brother-in-law yet you bear him such ill will that you would wish him dead. Is that not so!"

"Yes, my lord. Drowned in the deepest ocean!"

"Why? What was his crime?"

"He is a man!"

"So am I. So is Reinbald. So are at least half of the population. Would you condemn us all on that account?"

"Alwin was cruel."

"In what way?"

Juliana shook her head to indicate that she would say no more on the subject. He turned to Reinbald to see if the priest could offer any enlightenment but the man had vanished. Ralph was mystified by the disappearance. He looked back at the formidable lady in front of him.

"Help me," he said. "Your niece was strangled to death. I want to find the villain who killed her. Anything you can tell me about Bertha or about her parents may be of value. You loved your niece, Juliana. I sense that. And she loved you or she would not have walked all the way here simply to be with her aunt."

"Yes," she admitted. "There were some happy times."

"When you and Bertha were alone together?"

"When she was away from the contamination of her father!"

"Is Alwin really so wicked? I have met him and he did not seem so to me. What is it that he *did*, Juliana?"

"He drove my sister into her grave."

"But how?" pressed Ralph. "Tell me how!"

Lips tightly pursed, Juliana put her hands on her hips in an attitude of defiance. Her mind was a whirl of scalding memories that would be shared with nobody. Ralph withstood her fierce scrutiny with patience. She could never like him but there was a nobility in his bearing which she had to recognise, even if she could not bring herself to admire it. He seemed brave, honest and just, but those qualities were not enough to make her trust him completely.

"It is a long ride, Juliana," he said, trying to coax her with a smile. "Do not send us back empty-handed. Think of your niece. Surely, you want her death avenged?" He took a step closer. "Tell me about her father. What did Alwin do?"

Juliana folded her arms as she pondered. She had turned her back on her brother-in-law forever, but his shadow had followed her to Faversham. To make it go away again, she might have to confide at least some of what she knew.

"Return to Canterbury, my lord," she said.

"And?"

"Speak with Helto the Doctor."

ᕤ CHAPTER TWELVE

IT WAS INCREDIBLE. Canon Hubert would never have believed that a time would come when he was glad to be rescued from Christ Church Priory. He had come to Canterbury with such high hopes and they had been systematically dashed. It was galling to be so close to Archbishop Lanfranc and yet so impossibly far away. Brother Simon immersed himself in the cloister with the deep joy of a true obedientiary but Hubert was finding it a distinct strain. Robbed of ecclesiastical status and deprived of function as a royal commissioner, he was at the mercy of Prior Henry's beady watchfulness. When Gervase Bret offered him a chance of escape, he grasped it willingly.

He was less excited about the prospect when he realised that it involved a ride to Harbledown on his donkey. Gervase led him first to the spot where Bertha had been found and they dismounted to examine it. When the situation had been explained to him, Canon Hubert simmered with disgust.

"A woman, an apple and a serpent?"

"Is it too fanciful to imagine a reference to Genesis?"

"No, Gervase," he said sternly. "But this was no mere reference to the First Book of the Old Testament. It is a shameful travesty of it. The Bible is being mocked."

"That was my feeling, Canon Hubert."

"Genesis tells of the Creation and yet one of its central images is here used to mark a scene of destruction. That is an act of the most foul blasphemy."

"Who might have put it there?"

"Some mindless heathen."

"He is not mindless," said Gervase. "There is calculation here. And why did he go to such trouble to present Bertha's death as the result of snakebite? It is confusing."

"What I perceive is the utmost profanity."

"But did the killer *expect* it to be perceived? He wanted the girl to be found, the cause of her death to be ratified as snakebite and no further inquiry made. This strike at the Bible was for his own benefit."

"It was certainly not for mine!"

"Nor for anyone else's but the man himself," said Gervase. "It tells us much about his mind. This tableau was a personal seal. A signature on a death warrant."

"There may be a double meaning here, Gervase."

"What is that?"

"Genesis. Chapter three. Consider the opening verse," he said, translating from the Latin in his memory. "Mark it well. 'The serpent was more crafty than any wild creature that the Lord God had made.' There is vile craftiness at work here. The killer is a serpent in himself."

"Brother Martin certainly tasted his poison."

After further discussion, they mounted up and rode on to the leper hospital of St. Nicholas. They arrived as one of its charges was about to take his leave.

"Good morrow to you, Alain!" greeted Gervase.

The leper paused to look up at them and gave a faint nod. When Canon Hubert was introduced, he passed a kind remark to Alain but took great care not to get too close to him. Gervase made a point of showing that he was not frightened by proximity to the unfortunate young man. Dropping down from his horse, he strode over to him.

"Where are you going?" he asked.

"To be on my own."

"You can do that here."

"Not anymore."

"You have your own hut."

"Bertha does not come to it now," said Alain wistfully. "Nor does Brother Martin. Both are gone."

"Others have taken their place."

"They can never do that."

"They will try."

Alain shrugged. "I must go."

"Where?"

"Away from here," he said, pointing to a path through the bushes. "Somewhere quiet where I can sit in the shade and where nobody will bother me. Somewhere that is mine."

"What will you do there?"

"Pass the time."

"Nothing else?"

Alain fingered the apple that was deep in his sleeve.

"I will remember."

Gervase watched him until he disappeared from sight.

"Strange fellow!" said Hubert. "Lepers lead a twilight existence. Poor creatures! Yet God put them on the earth for a purpose. How do you know him?"

"Alain found the body at the place we have just been."

"Was it he who gave you that apple?"

"Yes, Canon Hubert."

"Does he guess at its meaning?"

"I think not."

Hubert dismounted again. "What is it you wish to show me here?" he said. "I must not delay too long. Brother Martin's funeral will be held this afternoon. I have to be back in time for that."

"Let me show you where and how he died."

Gervase led the way into the empty church and took up the position that had been occupied by Brother Martin at the moment of discovery. Hubert paid no heed to him. He was hypnotised by the tiny altar, gazing at its white cloth with a blend of reverence and revulsion, thinking of its Christian significance and recalling the black heart it had hidden beneath it on the day of the murder. The sacred and the profane had been conjoined just as they had been at the scene of Bertha's death.

Canon Hubert stared on, his heart pounding and his breath coming in short, irregular pants. Here was something worse than a simple mockery of Holy Writ. A blameless monk had been murdered in the House of God but it had been no random act. There was malignant preparation.

The killer had emerged from the altar itself to commit the deed. The very sacraments themselves were being abused. Canon Hubert was overcome with a sensation of complete horror when he realised the perfidy of what had taken place. The service of Holy Communion had been murdered just as ruthlessly as was Brother Martin. Instead of preserving body and soul unto everlasting life, the Body of Christ had been an instrument of death. The chalice which contained the Blood of Christ was a flask of poison.

Perspiration broke out on his face and body as he contemplated the magnitude of the desecration. Shielding his eyes from the hideous sight, Canon Hubert recited the Credo aloud to erect a further screen between himself and this blinding act of violation.

" 'Credo in unun Deo. Patrem omnipotentem, factorum caeli at terrae, visibilium omnium et invisibilium. Et in unum Dominum Iesum Christum, Filium Dei unigenitum. Et ex Patre natum ante omnia saecula. Deum et Deo . . .' " His mouth went dry but he forced himself on. " 'Deum et Deo . . . Deum et Deo . . .' " It was no use. The comforting phrases would not come. In the presence of such evil, Canon Hubert could not even affirm his faith. " 'Deum et Deo . . . lumen de lumine . . .' "

His voice trailed meekly away. Lowering his hands, he looked at the altar again and was overwhelmed once more by the enormity of the sacrilege. When the Credo could not come to his aid, he put all his strength and sense of outrage into a word that came hissing out of his mouth like hot steam.

"HERESY!"

"Where did you find him?" asked Golde.

"In the church. He slipped away while I was speaking with Juliana. *Listening* to her, rather," he corrected, "for she did most of the talking. She is a fearsome creature in full flow. I can see why the men of Faversham shrink away."

"Did you learn anything from her?"

"Yes," said Ralph. "I discovered things about Alwin that nobody else would have told me. The journey was worthwhile. Reinbald felt that, even though his buttocks are raw from the ride and he walks sideways like a crab. He thanked me for taking him."

"He was glad to see Faversham again."

"A pretty place," he said. "For all her thunder, I enjoyed

meeting Juliana. I admire a woman with spirit and she has enough for ten. Like you." He gave her a fond kiss. "But what has been happening here?"

They were in the solar. Golde told him how the problems of the household had been addressed throughout the morning. The baby was now asleep, Eadgyth more quiescent and Osbern less fraught. A brittle peace had been restored to the house. Golde was determined that it would not be shattered again.

"I cannot apologise enough to you, my love."

"Apologise?"

"For thrusting all this upon you," he said. "Had we stayed at the castle, it might not have been as comfortable as here, but at least you would not have been expected to take over the running of the establishment."

"That is no hardship to me, Ralph."

"Are you sure?"

"I like it here. Osbern and Eadgyth are good people who are caught in a bad situation. I am only too pleased to help them out of it. And there is a huge compensation."

"Yes," he said with a grin, "I am here with you."

"I was thinking about the baby."

"Baby! I take second place to a child?"

"You can look after yourself, Ralph. He cannot."

"Is that your excuse?" he teased.

"Do I need one?"

"Of course not."

Golde sighed. "He is a pure delight!"

"You used to say the same about me."

"Whenever I hold him, I do not want to put him down."

"We will have to take him with us when we leave."

"No," she said. "He belongs here. They adore him. Baby Osbern will help to bring his parents close together again."

"Then we will have to seek another way."

"Another way?"

"To find you a child."

Golde caught her breath and looked up into the smiling face. She flung her arms around him to hug him close. The embrace was short-lived. Footsteps could be heard clattering down the stairs and voices filtered through the door. Ralph's ears pricked up immediately.

"Is that Helto?"

"Yes. He has been here for the best part of an hour."

"I need two minutes of his time myself."

"Then I will leave you alone."

When Ralph came out, Helto was standing at the front door with Osbern, giving the reeve careful instructions. The doctor agreed to speak with Ralph and was led back into the empty solar.

"How is she?" asked Ralph solicitously.

"There is still cause for mild alarm."

"You have been an attentive physician, Helto."

"Not attentive enough, alas," said the other. "I did not foresee that crisis in the night. Mother and baby might both have suffered some injury, blundering about in the darkness like that. I am partly to blame for the fright."

"You?"

"If I had forced her to take that sleeping draught, none of this would have happened. Eadgyth would have passed a restful night in her bed and Osbern would not have been put through that ordeal." He clicked his tongue. "What drove her to do such a thing?"

"The death of her friend has upset her profoundly," said Ralph. "Eadgyth will never rest while the murder remains unsolved. It is one of the reasons why we have taken an interest in this business."

Helto was curt. "I wonder that you do not leave it in the hands of the sheriff and his officers, my lord. That is their function. What can you possibly find out that they cannot?"

"A great deal. You can help me to find out more."

"Me?"

"Tell me about Alwin."

"What is there to tell?" asked the other. "The man is overcome by grief. He has turned in upon himself."

"That is not my observation," said Ralph. "But I am not talking about Bertha's death. I am more interested in that of her mother. Was she a patient of yours?"

"Yes, my lord."

"What was the cause of death?"

"Fever. It carried her speedily off."

"Yet she was not old or frail."

"She had no will to live."

"Why was that?"

"I do not know, my lord."

"I think you do," pressed Ralph. "A doctor sees the inside of a marriage. Alwin and his wife were both your patients. You saw the effect that each had on the other."

"What I saw is no business of yours, my lord."

"It is if it touches on this murder."

"I do not fully accept that the murder took place."

"Something was seriously amiss with that family. What was it, Helto? Enlighten me."

"I will not discuss my patients like this. It is unethical. Improper."

"It all comes back to Alwin the Sailor."

"You will have to excuse me, my lord."

"What happened between husband and wife?"

He moved away. "I have tarried long enough."

"Tell me!" ordered Ralph, grabbing him. "Tell me the truth!"

Helto the Doctor looked at him with withering scorn.

"No, my lord. It is where it belongs. In the past."

Hood back and veil removed, Alain forced his blistered feet on through the undergrowth. His muscles were aching and his skin was on fire but his eyes remained alert, scanning every tree, shrub and outcrop of bushes that bordered the twisting path. When brambles leaned over to block his way, he did not duck beneath them. His bare hand brushed them aside and flakes of skin were left impaled on the tiny spikes that had no power to hurt him. Alain was cloaked in a deeper pain that nothing could reach or soothe.

As he stepped into a clearing, a pig looked up from its meal and grunted in annoyance. It trotted toward him with a token pugnacity before scampering off into the undergrowth. Alain moved on with a resigned smile. A leper was spurned even by animals. His search took him on through more woodland, then brought him out near an orchard. Through its trees, he caught a glimpse of a manor house, a long, low building with its thatch bleached by the bright sun.

Alain crept slowly through the orchard. Ripening apples hung all around him in wholesome abundance but he would not have exchanged the one in his sleeve for any of them. As he fondled it with his hand, cherished memories came flooding back. Long conversations with Bertha echoed in his brain. The joys of friendship and understanding were briefly rekindled. His reverie was disturbed by the approach of a horse. Alain immediately took cover, lurching forward to lower himself down behind some bushes, his face pressed close to the ground. The rider passed close by but the leper remained unseen.

Voices were heard outside the house. Alain took fright. It was time to steal away to the safety of the wood and the reluctant company of the pigs. As he hauled himself upright, however, he saw something out of the corner of his eye. It was caught on a twig and danced in the breeze. He reached out to detach it with the utmost care then inspected it more closely. Alain was content. It was hers.

Canon Hubert was anxious to return to the city as quickly as possible, not simply because of the funeral of Brother Martin and the chance, at last, of a distant glimpse of Archbishop Lanfranc, but because the experience in Harbledown had shaken him badly. He was deeply offended by what he had seen, and felt almost tainted. Christ Church Priory offered him the sanctuary he needed and the solace he craved. It would cleanse him.

Gervase rode back to the cathedral precinct before parting company with him. He reached the house as Ralph Delchard was leaving and their discussion took place in the narrow passage than ran to the stables. When Gervase recounted all that had taken place on his latest visit to Harbledown, his friend was cynical.

"I would not trust Canon Hubert's instincts."

"He felt the presence of evil, Ralph."

"Who would not? Brother Martin was poisoned to death in that church. Murder is bound to leave its effect."

"It was more than that," said Gervase. "A malevolence hangs in the air. I sensed it, too. It is almost tangible. Canon Hubert was so shocked that he is going to seek a meeting with Prior Henry to report his findings. There was definitely something in the atmosphere, Ralph."

"Is it surprising?"

"What do you mean?"

"The church is used only by lepers, Gervase. They are not the most fragrant of human beings. Even sweet herbs and strong prayers will not wholly disguise the corruption of their flesh. Canon Hubert is used to the clean air of the cloister in Winchester. That is why he took offence."

"It struck him at a profoundest level. He believes that the church should be exorcised."

"That will happen when we have caught this killer," said Ralph. "We will drive the devil out of Harbledown."

"We have to find him first."

"We are getting closer."

"All we know for certain is that he mocks the Christian Church. Wearing the cowl was not just a convenient disguise. It was a deliberate act of contempt."

"That narrows it down, Gervase. I still believe that our villain may be this mysterious lover of Bertha's. Her father thinks the same or he would not be so eager to track down the man. Put together what we already know of him with what you and Canon Hubert have added today, and what do we have?"

"A handsome Frenchman in his thirties with a scorn for the basic tenets of Christianity."

"Who likes to hide behind a cowl," said Ralph with a grin. "Pull back the hood of every monk in Canterbury and we will find the one without a tonsure. You take the priory and I will search the abbey."

"Be serious, Ralph. We must catch him another way."

"Alwin is still our surest guide."

"But he refused to help you."

"I'll be more forceful this time, Gervase. My visit to Faversham has given me a powerful threat to use against him."

"Threat?"

"Juliana. If Alwin will not tell us all he knows, I'll set his sister-in-law onto him." He chuckled merrily. "Juliana would beat the truth out of him with her bare fists."

The first punch broke his nose and sent him staggering back with blood streaming down his lips. A second caught him on the ear and made his head ring. Third, fourth and fifth punches were delivered to the midriff and knocked all the breath out of him. It was the sixth blow which felled him, a vicious uppercut to his chin which made his teeth rattle. After that, he lost count.

Alwin the Sailor slumped to the floor in a flurry of punches and kicks. He was a strong man but all resistance was beaten out of him by the flailing fists and the swinging feet. It was no covert attack. Alwin was sitting in his boat when the two men accosted him. There were several witnesses near the quayside in Fordwich but none dared to intervene. Most turned their backs out of fear or indifference. Some felt that Alwin was getting no more than he deserved.

The punishment continued long after the victim was senseless. It only stopped when the two assailants began to tire. Sweating profusely from their exertions, the brawny young men swayed over the body on the deck, their shoes stained by the blood now gushing from a dozen wounds. As a final act of violence, they suddenly grabbed hold of him and lifted him in the air before hurling him into the river with a loud splash. Their work was done. Heedless of his fate, they walked away from the quay.

It was only then that others leaped into action, rushing to save the drowning sailor. One man dived into the water to reclaim the body while another threw a rope after him. Two more lent their aid and the victim was hauled slowly back into his boat. Alwin lay face-up on the deck, soaked to the skin, streaming with fresh blood, expelling water from his mouth and threshing wildly about like a beached whale.

Canon Hubert could not contain his sense of outrage. As soon as Brother Martin had been laid to rest in the cemetery at Christ Church Priory, the monks dispersed with dignified sorrow to mourn their loss in their own way. Hubert sought an immediate audience with Prior Henry and the two of them adjourned to the private parlour in his lodgings.

Behind the mask of impassivity, Henry was fuming.

"Could this not wait at least a decent interval?"

"I fear not, Prior Henry."

"Brother Martin has only just been lowered into his grave."

"This concerns his murder."

"I find your conduct most unseemly, Canon Hubert."

"You may not do so when you hear my explanation."

"Pardon will not come easily from me."

"Hear me out, Prior Henry. That is all I ask."

The prior lowered himself into his chair and put the tips of his fingers together, regarding his visitor with an icy disapproval which would have quelled most people. Canon Hubert was made of more durable material. Standing before the table, he inhaled deeply and began his denunciation. He described exactly what he had experienced in Harbledown.

Henry's reservations quickly melted and, once roused, his curiosity moved through keen interest and utter fascination to a controlled horror. By the time that Hubert had finished his account, the prior was back on his feet to put him under close questioning.

"Whom else have you told about this, Canon Hubert?"

"Gervase Bret was with me at the time."

"Was he likewise scandalised?"

"Yes," said Hubert. "But not to the same degree. He is a layman and does not have the same spiritual insight as someone who has spent his whole life in the Church."

"He had the sense to take your opinion and for that we must be grateful. I have had vague warnings of all this from Brother Bartholomew and Brother Vitalis. They were sent to Harbledown to take over the running of the hospital when Brother Martin was killed. The urgency of the situation meant that have spent most of the time placating the lepers but they have obviously taken services in the church."

"Did they not feel its malign influence?"

"They spoke only of a sense of unease."

"Heresy is writ large across the altar cloth."

"It has taken your sharper eye to decipher it. I will view the place myself in time but this is too sinister a development for independent action on my part. Archbishop Lanfranc must be informed at once."

"I am gratified by your response, Prior Henry."

"Your report is alarming," confided the other. "All the more so because it is matched by intelligence we have gathered from other sources. Suffice to say that a threat has been identified more clearly. For such evil to appear anywhere would be a cause for dismay. But when it arrives on the very doorstep of Canterbury Cathedral, when it defies the anointed head of the English Church, when it hurls such vile abuse at Christianity itself, it must provoke an instant and merciless reaction."

"I heartily endorse those sentiments," said Hubert.

"Archbishop Lanfranc will say no less himself."

"Please convey my warmest greetings to him."

"You may do so yourself, Canon Hubert."

"Myself?"

"The archbishop will want to hear your testimony in full. You will imagine his distress when he first heard that Brother Martin had been killed within the hallowed walls of a church which Archbishop Lanfranc himself founded. When he comprehends the full extent of the desecration, he will strike back like an avenging angel."

Prior Henry snatched up a bell on his desk and rang it decisively. A monk entered at once, received a whispered message and hastened away. Canon Hubert savoured the sudden improvement in his fortunes. He would not only meet Lanfranc in person, he would now do so with the status of a loyal intelligencer for the Church. It was impossible to bear any real affection for Prior Henry but Hubert disliked him considerably less. Uniting in the face of a common enemy, they clearly had distinct affinities.

Hubert stalked the room and washed his hands in the air, nervously awaiting the summons from Lanfranc. He soon worked himself back up into a lather of indignation.

"Jesus warned against false prophets who would take His Name in vain," he said querulously. "We have one in our midst."

"He will be exposed."

"Where can such foul heresy have originated?"

"We may have the answer to that."

"Was this devil sent from Hell itself?"

"No, Canon Hubert. We believe he comes from Orléans."

They sat in a large circle around him with heads bowed and minds awaiting the illumination of his word. There was one empty chair. Someone was missing. The man who stood at the centre of the circle showed no sign of impatience. He was tall, slim, well-favoured and unobtrusively commanding. His white robe accentuated the black beard, which in turn threw the sallow skin and the piercing green eyes into relief. There was a quiet charisma about him which everyone around him felt even when they were not looking at him. His presence seemed to fill the room.

They were in the parlour of the manor house. Shutters were closed to guarantee privacy and servants were posted outside to prevent any intrusion. The figures in the circle were drawn closer together by a common faith and a shared purpose but everything radiated out from their leader like the spokes of a wheel. He was the hub of all activity. They could feel him as surely as if he were reaching out to touch them.

Distant hoofbeats approached the house. Nobody moved until the horse came to a halt outside the front door. The leader then broke the circle by stepping out of it. A long, graceful stride took him out of the room and into a passageway where he saw the rider being admitted into the house. He gave him a welcoming nod. The latecomer was deferential.

"I am sorry to that I was delayed."

"We knew you would come."

"There are problems, I fear."

"Still?"

"They have picked up a trail and sniff it like hounds."

"Throw them off the scent."

"That is not easy. They are very persistent. They are getting closer all the time."

"We will deal with them," said the other easily.

"They worry me."

"Leave them to me, my friend. All will be well."

"Good."

"And the other problem? Alwin the Sailor?"

The newcomer smiled. "He will not trouble us again."

⟡ Chapter Thirteen

RALPH DELCHARD WAS shocked at the state in which he found the man. Alwin the Sailor was a hideous mass of bruises and swellings. One arm was in a splint, one leg heavily bound up. Bandages covered part of his face and head but the swollen eyes and the shattered nose were dramatic reminders of the ruthless beating he had taken. They had brought him home from Fordwich in a cart, wrapped in old sacks which were now crimson with blood. At one point they thought he had died.

Helto the Doctor cleaned him off and tended his wounds. The patient revived slightly but was far too weak to protest when his arm was reset. The pain rendered him unconscious again. By the time that Ralph arrived, the doctor had gone and Alwin was being cared for by the old woman who lived in the adjacent house. She sat beside the bed, watching her neighbour in frightened silence, wondering why a new calamity had befallen a household which had already suffered the death of a wife and the murder of a beloved daughter.

After letting Ralph in, she withdrew to the kitchen to leave him alone in the bedroom with Alwin. There was nowhere to sit and the low ceiling obliged the visitor to duck his head but he ignored the discomfort. In the presence of such extensive injuries, it was churlish to complain about a crick in his neck. As Ralph's shadow fell across him, Alwin half opened his eyes and made a gurgling sound in his throat. Ralph knelt down beside him and gave him time to come fully awake.

"Who did this to you?" he said at length.

"I . . . don't . . . know."

Each word was a separate effort, forced out between lips that had been split open by teeth which were now knocked out of his mouth. Alwin experimented with the same answer until he found a way to speak without moving his lips at all.

"I don't know."

"How many were there?"

"Two."

"Here?"

"Fordwich. On my boat."

"In broad daylight?" said Ralph. "Were there not witnesses at the quayside? Did nobody come to your aid?"

"No."

"What about your friends?"

"Nobody."

The pain of recollection sent him into a long bruised silence but Ralph waited. Alwin could not be rushed. Judging the moment, the visitor tried again.

"This is something to do with him, is it not?" he said.

"Him?"

"The man you are after." Alwin closed his eyes. "Do not pretend to fall asleep," warned Ralph with soft jocularity. "I know that you can hear me perfectly well. When I saw you in Fordwich, you were lurking in the harbour, hoping to catch news of a certain person. You were saving him for yourself. That was your plan, was it not?" He gestured at the injuries. "You are in no state to crawl out of this bed, let alone to conduct a search. You *need* me, Alwin. We must work together."

The eyes opened to regard him with a suspicion that was tempered with a reluctant admiration. Alwin could never bring himself wholly to trust a Norman but Ralph had earned his respect. The murder investigation was nominally headed by the sheriff. His officers had been diligent in their inquiries but they had so far achieved little success. With no reason to be personally involved, Ralph Delchard had taken it upon himself to pursue the killer and to brave the dangers that that would obviously entail.

Harsh truths had to be faced. Alwin could never wreak revenge on his own. He would not be fit to intercept a passenger on a boat the following Wednesday. Helto had talked about keeping the splint on his arm for a month at least and warned him that the damage might leave him with a permanent limp. The way he felt at that moment, Alwin began to wonder if he would ever recover.

"He killed Bertha," Ralph reminded him. "Are you going to let him get away with it?"

"No, my lord."

"Then let me help. Who is he?"

"I'm not sure."

"I think you are."

"It could be him. There is nobody else. She liked him."

"Bertha?"

"Yes."

"How did she meet him?"

"On my boat. In Normandy."

"You were collecting more stone from Caen?" Alwin gave a perceptible nod. "Who was this man?"

"A stranger. He wanted to cross the Channel."

"In that old boat of yours?" said Ralph in surprise. "Why did he wish to sail with a cargo of stone when he could have taken a bigger and faster vessel that would have offered more comfort?"

"I did not ask. He paid well."

"You brought him to Fordwich?"

"He had business in the area."

"What kind of business?"

"He did not say."

"Can you describe him?"

A rueful sigh. "Tall, fine-looking, dark beard."

"A Frenchman, I hear."

"And well-dressed. In the French fashion."

"What did you learn from him?"

"Very little. He hardly spoke."

"He talked to Bertha. You said she liked him."

"Yes."

"What did you do?"

"Pulled her from him. Spoke sharply."

"Why?" said Ralph. "Did you not trust her?"

"Him. The passenger."

"Was he too attentive?"

"Bertha was young, innocent."

"What happened when you landed at Fordwich? Did he pay you his money and come ashore?"

"Yes, my lord."

"Where did he go?"

"I don't know."

"And you never saw him again?"

"No."

"What about Bertha?" The swollen eyes closed in agony. "You assumed that she had never seen him again, either, but now you think differently. Is that it?" Alwin's pain was answer enough. "He must have been a remarkable man if he had such an effect on her. A brief meeting. Few words. Only smiles and glances passing between them. Yet he somehow persuaded her to defy her own father."

"No!"

Anger made the sailor roar and squirm for a few moments but he soon subsided once more, wracked by physical anguish and tortured by remorse. Ralph had pushed him to the limit of his strength and endurance. It would be a cruelty to continue. When he asked a final question, Ralph felt as if he were jabbing the man with a sword but it had to be done.

"What was his name, Alwin?"

The sailor was sobbing quietly. He turned his head away to escape. Ralph leaned over to him to whisper in his ear.

"Give me his name, man. His *name.*"

It came out through the shredded lips as a distorted grunt.

"Philippe."

"Philippe Berbizier," said Lanfranc. "Have you heard the name?"

"No, Your Grace."

"It is one they have cause to loathe in Orléans."

"Who is he?"

"A renegade priest. A notorious felon. A heretic."

"And this man is here in England?"

"We believe so, Hubert."

For the first ten minutes of the audience, Canon Hubert was too overwhelmed to do anything more than stand, listen and nod in agreement. The situation in which he found himself surpassed his most ambitious imaginings. In company with Prior Henry, he was in the exalted presence of no less a personage than Archbishop Lanfranc, primate of the Holy Church of Canterbury and the appointed voice of Christianity in the kingdom. Hubert was in a state of high exhilaration.

There had been nothing formal about Lanfranc's welcome. He had risen from his seat to embrace Canon Hubert with warm affection, apologising for not being able to see him before and assuring him that their happy days together at Bec were often in his mind. Hubert was overjoyed. Lanfranc had aged considerably since their last meeting but he was still recognisable as the inspirational prior of Bec under whom Hubert had served with such love and alacrity.

Now in his late seventies, he was worn down by the cares of state and by the immense ecclesiastical responsibilities which he carried. Rounded shoulders, a curving spine and silver hair told one tale but it was contradicted by the vitality in the wrinkled face and by the astonishing power of his mind.

They were in his parlour. While his visitors stood before him, Lanfranc was sitting in his high-backed carved chair, a large gold crucifix on the wall behind his head. He made the self-effacing gesture which Hubert remembered so well.

"I was content as prior of Bec," he said. "I was even more content as abbot of Caen. What more could a man want on this earth? Nothing! Why should I choose to leave all that and come to Canterbury? When the King invited me, I tried to decline. When Pope Alexander, of blessed memory, sent his legates to enforce that invitation, I pleaded in vain my incapacity and unworthiness, my ignorance of the language and of the barbarous people here. King William would have me."

"The English Church has been the beneficiary," said Henry.

"I have done my best, ill-suited as I am."

"No man could have done more, Your Grace."

"They could, they could, Prior Henry." He held his palms up to heaven. "The miseries I endured when I came here! The suffering, the harshness, the avarice, the lust and the baseness I saw all around me! Why was I dragged from the monastic life I love into this wilderness? Without Henry as my prior and Ernulf of Beauvais to teach scholarship, I never could have survived. Yet by the grace of God, and by His divine mercy, I did."

"With honour, Your Grace," said Hubert.

"We tried. And there have been successes. We have built and we have educated. We have brought the fruits of civilisation and culture to a land devoid of both when we first arrived. When I depart this world—and God cannot put off the call much longer—I wish to leave the English Church in a far healthier state than when I found it." A note of rancour was injected. "And I cannot do that when it is threatened by the worm of heresy."

"Tell Canon Hubert about Orléans," suggested Henry.

"Oh, dear! Yes, Orléans. Philippe Berbizier."

"They drove him out in time."

"He should have been caught and burned to death like the rest of them. Fire consumes evil. It is the only way to rid ourselves of it." The furrows deepened in his brow. "Philipe Berbizier is a monster. Orléans is a centre of learning and a city of great spiritual worth. It was into this place of beauty that Philippe Berbizier crawled like a serpent, tempting the weak-minded and corrupting the young. He even drew one of the canons of the church of Holy Cross into his circle of damnation."

"What was the nature of their heresy?" asked Hubert.

"They spurned orthodoxy," said Lanfranc. "They claimed that Christ was not born of the Virgin Mary."

"God preserve us!"

"They said that Christ did not suffer on the Cross for mankind. He was not buried in the sepulchre or raised from the dead. And," he continued, grasping the arms of his chair, "that the sacraments themselves had no validity."

"This is intolerable."

"There is worse, Canon Hubert. It involves carnal acts with young women as part of their ritual. One of the accused even talked about the ashes of a murdered baby, born to a woman who had been unwittingly drawn into the circle."

"Horrors!" gasped Hubert, swaying at the contemplation of such wickedness. "These are abominations!"

"But exposed," said Lanfranc. "The heretics were caught and interrogated in chains in Holy Cross before an assembly of king, queen and bishops. Confessions were wrung out of them. They were condemned and properly burned to death."

"All but Philippe Berbizier," noted Prior Henry.

"All but him."

"He looked elsewhere for converts."

"Here in Canterbury, it seems," said Lanfranc with foreboding. "That is what has brought him to the city. The search for those he can convert to heresy."

"Converts," added Henry. "And unsuspecting young women."

Canon Hubert thought of Bertha and shuddered.

The girl dressed without once raising her eyes to him. When she knelt before him, he offered his hand and she kissed it with reverence before leaving the room. Philippe Berbizier got up from the bed and yawned with satisfaction. He kept them waiting for a long time before he finished his glass of wine, put on the white robe and went back into the parlour.

The girl had taken her place in the circle and sat, like the others, with her head bowed. Berbizier brushed a hand against her shoulder as he stepped back into the centre of his followers. Restored to his place, his power was stronger than ever, flowing out like waves to lap over each one of them. When he chanted a prayer, they sang the responses in unison. The service ended with his benediction.

As the members of the circle left the house, Berbizier stood at the door to bid them farewell and to have a private moment with each. The last man to arrive at the service was also the last to depart. Berbizier waited until everyone was completely out of earshot.

"I have been meditating on our problem," he said.

"It will not easily go away."

"What are their names?"

"Ralph Delchard and Gervase Bret."

"Who is the greater threat to us?"

"The lord Ralph. He is the soldier of the two."

"How many men does he have?"

"Twelve," said the other. "Eight of them are helping the sheriff while four stay with their master."

"He is well-protected, then?"

"Yes, Philippe. That is not the way. The lord Ralph is impregnable. You would tangle with him at your peril."

"Every man has a weak spot."

"That is true."

"Every woman, too," said Berbizier with a smile. "That is their attraction. However well-defended they may seem, any woman can be conquered if you know how to lay a siege."

"You have taught me much in that respect, Philippe."

"You will learn much more before I have finished."

"My eyes have been opened to the flames of passion."

"Good. This turbulent soldier . . ."

"Ralph Delchard?"

"We must divert his attention."

"How?"

"Where is *his* weakness?"

Golde was deeply grateful to Reinbald the Priest. His arrival was a surprise and his time spent alone with Eadgyth was immensely beneficial. He was not only able to offer her a sustenance and understanding outside the capacity of any doctor, his presence in the house reassured Osbern the Reeve and released Golde to get on with the domestic management. She liked Reinbald. His relative inexperience was offset by a dedication to his ministry which bordered on obsession. Before he left, Golde made sure that she spoke to him.

"Thank you for coming, Father Reinbald."

"It was a duty which brought me pleasure, my lady. I have known Eadgyth since the time when I became a deacon at St. Mildred's. She is a decent, honest, God-fearing person. I only wish that all members of my congregation were so."

"How is she now?"

"Becalmed by my visit and that is very heartening."

"Your words were a much-needed balm."

"I said little," explained Reinbald. "It was Eadgyth herself who did most of the talking. She wanted to tell me about her youth in Worthgate Ward and I encouraged her reminiscences. Anything which touches on St. Mildred's is of great interest to me and I was moved to see how steadying an influence my church has had on Eadgyth's life."

"And on Bertha's, presumably."

"Yes, my lady. Until this last few months."

"Oh?"

"Her attendance was not as regular as it had been."

"Did you not tax her about that?"

"Eventually, my lady."

"Eventually?"

"I do not stand at the porch to count my parishioners in. That office I leave to my churchwarden. It was one of them who first called Bertha to account."

"Did she explain her absences?"

"Yes," said Reinbald. "She told him that she was spending more time at the leper hospital and taking part in services there. I had no complaint about that. Evensong led by Brother Martin at St. Nicholas is every bit as valid as my own service at St. Mildred's. I thought no more of the matter until I chanced to meet Brother Martin himself."

"Had Bertha lied?"

"I fear so, my lady. When I teased Brother Martin about stealing one of my parishioners, he took it in good part. But he also denied that she was spending quite as much time at Harbledown as she claimed."

"It was then you taxed her?"

"Sternly."

"What did she say?"

"She promised to mend her ways."

"No explanation of where she had been when she was neither at St. Mildred's nor at the hospital?"

"None, my lady. Just an urgent plea."

"Not to tell her father," she guessed.

"Yes," he said. "I acceded to her request on condition that we saw her in St. Mildred's more often. And I held a warning over her head. If she strayed from us again, I would tell her father all. Fear is a powerful weapon. It worked on Bertha. Alwin never knew the truth about her absences." A haunted look came into his face. "In the light of what has occurred since, I think I was wrong to deceive him."

"You spared her certain punishment at his hands."

"But helped to forfeit her young life."

"No, Father Reinbald!"

"Had her father known the truth, his vigilance would have been increased, Bertha would never have been allowed the licence to climb up Harbledown Hill to the hospital whenever she chose. She would still be *alive,* my lady."

"You cannot be sure of that," said Golde.

"It gnaws at my conscience."

"You did what you felt was best at the time."

"Yes," he said dolefully. "I knew how Alwin would react and I did not want to introduce any more discord into a house that has had more than enough." He opened the front door, then turned back. "Family is the most blessed thing. But it can sometimes be a curse. Look how this little family here has been blighted. Eadgyth sick, Osbern anxious and their dear child without their mutual love to enfold it."

"The baby has not been neglected."

"I know. You have been mother and father to him these past couple of days. But it is not the same, my lady."

"I accept that," said Golde. "My role is temporary. Eadgyth improves. With your help and that of Helto the Doctor, she will recover completely and this family will soon knit back together again."

"I earnestly hope so, my lady. We will do all we can. But there is one thing that a priest and a doctor can never do."

"What is that?"

"Find Bertha's killer," he said. "Until that is done, Eadgyth will never fully recover and this family will suffer more woe."

Gervase Bret responded to the summons immediately. When the message came from Canon Hubert, he hurried to the priory and was admitted by the porter. The still trembling Hubert and the ghostly Brother Simon were waiting for him inside the gate. They conducted him to the garden and sought out a quiet corner where they might pass on their frightful tidings. Hubert had already confided in his companion and it had made Brother Simon wish that he never had to stir outside the safety of the enclave again.

"What is the problem, Canon Hubert?" asked Gervase.

"Greater even than we feared."

"In what way?"

Hubert took a deep breath. "I had an audience with Archbishop Lanfranc himself," he said, managing to combine a fulsome boast, a reverential whisper and a statement of fact into one short sentence. "Prior Henry was also present. Our discussion was long and intense."

"Did it concern our visit to Harbledown?"

"It did, Gervase. My instinct was sound."

"As ever, Canon Hubert," praised Brother Simon.

"We are dealing with heresy!"

"Is that what the archbishop confirmed?"

"He did more than that," said Hubert. "He gave me details of this man's immoral, criminal and profane history."

"This man?"

"Philippe Berbizier."

"Who is he?"

"An ogre who corrupts minds and hearts."

"A devil incarnate," added Simon.

"He formed a sect in Orléans and led them in rites which were almost satanic. And now, Archbishop Lanfranc fears, this creature is searching for converts here."

"At the heart of the Christian Church?"

"Where better to strike?" replied Hubert, rolling his eyes. "Do you see the boldness of the villain?"

Simon shivered. "Nothing is sacred to him!"

"At the hospital of St. Nicholas, you will only see leprosy of the body. A disease which attacks from outside. Philippe Berbizier is far more insidious. He works from within. He infects his converts with a leprosy of the soul."

"How?" asked Gervase. "Be more specific, please. You call him a heretic without first defining his heresy. What sect did he form in Orléans? Who were they?"

"Gnostics!" boomed Hubert.

"Pagans!" bleated Simon.

"That is not so," said Gervase. "Correct me if I am wrong, but is not Gnosticism a crude mix of Paganism and Christianity? They do not deny the existence of Jesus Christ. They teach that he was a mere mortal and not the Son of God."

"Blasphemy!" said Simon with his hands over his ears.

"Gnostics are the caterpillars of Christianity," ~~Gervase~~ HUBERT said, borrowing a phrase from Lanfranc. "They eat their way through it and leave only the remnants behind. If we do not stamp them out, they will crawl over all of us."

Gervase let him find his way through the extended metaphor and rid himself of more vituperation against the sect. He then pressed for details.

"What exactly did Philippe Berbizier preach in Orléans?"

"That divine truth is only revealed to the select few," said the scowling Hubert. "Berbizier claimed to be one of that elite. He argued that neophytes could only attain illumination through him, leaving the darkness and opening their eyes to the light of the true faith."

"That is Christianity!" affirmed Simon.

"Gnosticism is a perversion of it, shot through with Paganism and mixed with other heathen elements. Philippe Berbizier, it seems, adopted the view of the Docetics, a Gnostic sect, that Christ did not die upon the Cross at all. According to Berbizier, he was a mere phantom upon which Jews and Romans alike wreaked an ineffectual vengeance."

"What happened to the sect in Orléans?" said Gervase.

Canon Hubert was delighted to have another chance to haul in the name of Archbishop Lanfranc and to remind them that it was his evidence which provided conclusive proof to the primate that Philippe Berbizier was in England. He told Gervase about the arrest and burning of the heretics in Orléans, and of the escape of their leader. Rumors about Berbizier had surfaced in other parts of France and many sightings were reported but he could never be caught.

"He will stop at nothing to further his aims," said Hubert. "Intimidation, theft, seduction, even murder. Prior Henry told me that one of the accused confessed, under torture, that it was Berbizier who killed the infant whose body was used in one of their macabre rituals."

Brother Simon yelped and resolved to hear no more. Closing his ears, he began to recite the Credo to himself. Gervase's mind was on Bertha, an innocent and impressionable girl who might well have been drawn to the amalgam of charm and spiritual intensity which Philippe Berbizier patently had. A heretic who could convert nobles, commoners and even a member of the clergy in Orléans, would find a defenceless creature like Bertha an easy target.

The more he heard, the more convinced he became that Berbizier was indeed the man they sought. To the essentials of Gnosticism, he seemed to have added refinements of his own, which bound his neophytes ineluctably to him and allowed him to reap a harvest of sexual favours from the female members. Gervase feared that Bertha had yielded up her virginity to him before she surrendered her life.

"What action is Archbishop Lanfranc taking?" he asked.

"The strongest," said Hubert. "He has alerted the sheriff and he has summoned his own knights. They will scour the city and the surrounding towns and villages. Berbizier has gone to ground somewhere in or near to Canterbury and must be smoked out at once."

"Will he not try to flee?"

"Sentries have been posted on the roads and a watch has been put on the port. He will not sneak away as easily as he did at Orléans."

"Did you warn the archbishop about his disguise?"

"Yes, Gervase."

"He may use that black cowl of his again."

"It will not advantage him. The villain will not escape under the pretext of Christianity. The archbishop's men have orders to stop and question everybody, including monks of the Benedictine Order."

"These are swift precautions."

"A net has been thrown around the whole area. Philippe Berbizier must be caught and arraigned as soon as possible. He tears at the whole fabric of the Church."

"And he has two murders to answer for," said Gervase. "It is a strange kind of faith that condones the killing of blameless people. How does he justify that?"

"He is above the need to justify anything."

"A man with no moral precepts. Above the law."

"That is how he sees himself and convinces others to perceive him. A true heretic. But we will get him. Well over a hundred man have been committed to the pursuit. With so many chasing at his heels, he is bound to be taken. God will not be mocked. His vengeance will be terrible."

He had to wait until night to make his escape. Soldiers patrolled the streets. The city gates were closed and guarded. He had never seen such activity in Canterbury and it made him extremely wary. When he finally ventured out from his hiding place, his black garb blended with the darkness to make him no more than a fleeting shadow. He picked his way along streets and down lanes until he came to the town wall.

Having reached it, he cowered quickly against it as a patrol passed nearby, six mounted men-at-arms with bright torches to pierce the darkest void and the promise of a bounty if they took their quarry. Their eyes were paid to be keen. They did not see him this time but his luck could not hold. He had to get out of the city at once. The wall was high but earth was banked against it farther along. Clambering up the mound, he got within reach of the top. Long arms reached up and he got a strong enough purchase on the top to haul himself slowly up.

He took a furtive inventory. More soldiers were circling the perimeter of the city with torches. Crouched on the wall like a cat, he waited until the coast was clear then hung by his fingers before dropping into oblivion. The ground came sooner than he expected and he was jolted badly by the impact. But he was quite uninjured. After stretching his back a few times, he was able to move on. Making his way to the northwest, he kept to the shadows and walked with great stealth. When he got within sight of

Westgate, he saw the brazier lighting up the faces of a dozen men. Avoiding action was needed. If they caught him, they would strike first with the swords and spears. He swung left in a wide and cautious semicircle, falling to his knees at one point to grope his way along the ground like an animal.

It was a harrowing experience and it brought cold perspiration out all over him. He was accustomed to a life of secret movement and had developed his skills but he had never encountered such a vast search party. Escape was vital. Once clear of the patrols, he broke into a gentle trot, using trees and bushes as continuous cover. It was only when he was halfway up Harbledown Hill that he paused to catch his breath and dared to look back. The city lay below him, ringed with fires, lit by torches and bristling with armed men. Only someone with real audacity could have eluded the watching soldiers. He could afford to take satisfaction from that. Lanfranc's knights and the sheriff's officers had failed to imprison him in the city. It gave him a sense of quiet triumph. He moved off again.

Confidence gradually returned. Freed from what lay behind, he could reflect on what waited for him ahead. His mind raced and his concentration wavered. Ears and eyes were no longer as keen as they had been. He was off guard. Stars speckled the sky to give him a measure of guidance. A drizzle began to fall. It did not dampen his expectation in any way.

He did not even see him. As he descended the hill, he started to trot once more and hit an easy rhythm. He noticed the tree but not the figure hunched up against it. Passing within a yard of the man, he was still totally unaware of his presence. But his own approach had not gone unremarked. The man looked up, caught a glimpse of his face, then retreated back inside his hood.

Alain had something to think about during a long, wet night.

❧ CHAPTER FOURTEEN

DAWN LIFTED THE black shroud of night and the oppression of the curfew from Canterbury. Soldiers still guarded the various gates, questioning all who came and went, but the citizens no longer felt incarcerated in their own homes and the stallholders who brought in their produce from the surrounding farms were allowed to set up the market. An air of normality returned, though it was still a city on edge.

Searches had been thorough and security tight yet the wanted man was still at liberty. The common opinion was that he was still somewhere in Canterbury itself, hidden by friends or lurking in some secret refuge of his own. It would not be easy to find him among a population of a few thousand or more. Several hundred houses and countless other buildings offered a bewildering array of places where he might shelter. Canterbury would need to be systematically combed.

Ralph Delchard was determined that he would not miss

out on the action. He was up at first light, putting his hauberk on over his tunic and strapping on his sword-belt. Gervase had given him full details of the manpower which had been assembled for the hunt but Ralph was not surprised when a new day rose with Philippe Berbizier still at large. The Frenchman was too cunning to be caught easily and the hullabaloo of his pursuers was so loud that it gave him ample forewarning of their approach.

"A troop of soldiers will never catch him," he said.

"Then who will?"

"One or two, moving in subtler ways."

"You and Gervase?"

"For preference, it would be me alone. I would love to meet this villain face to face." Ralph reached for his helm. "But I am not greedy, my love. I will let Gervase have his share of the honours."

"Where will you go now?"

"To check the sentries, confer with my men, see if anything untoward occurred in the night. I hope that they do not ask that question of me or I would blush."

Golde laughed. "Be off with you!"

"Pine for me."

"Just take care, Ralph," she said, giving him a kiss. "This man is dangerous. He will not scruple to kill."

"Nor will I."

He let himself out of the house and she waved him off through the open shutters. Golde was about to go into the kitchen when she heard the baby crying upstairs again. It was a noise which had punctuated much of the night. Osbern came down the stairs in a state of consternation.

"What is the matter?" she asked.

"The baby. Something ails him."

"Do you wish me to go to him?"

"Eadgyth is nursing him in her arms. That seems to soothe him from time to time. But the pain returns."

"Pain?"

"In his ear," said Osbern. "He keeps putting his little hand up to it. I slept in a chair beside Eadgyth. The crib was in the bedchamber with us. We must have woken a dozen times in the night to see to the baby."

"Poor little child!"

"I'll send a servant for Helto the Doctor."

"There are none here, Osbern," she said. "Two have gone to market to buy food and the third is saddling my husband's horse in the stables. Let me go for Helto."

"You do not know the way, my lady."

"Teach me."

"This is too menial a task for you. I'll go myself."

"You are needed here," argued Golde as a fresh burst of noise came from above. "Stay with your wife and child. Now, where does Helto live?"

"At the end of King Street. It is not far."

"Give me directions."

When the reeve had explained the route to her, Golde put on her gown, adjusted her wimple and slipped out of the house. She was soon caught up in the morning throng. Anxious to do what she could to relieve the recurring anxieties in the household, she thought only of Eadgyth and the baby. After such a disturbed night, both would need the services of a doctor. Golde was so preoccupied with helping them that she forgot to consider herself. As she pushed her way through the gathering crowds, it never occurred to her that she was being followed.

Fortune favoured them. They had not expected to get their opportunity so soon. Instead of having to contrive a way to lure Golde out of the house, they found her a willing accomplice in their scheme. They moved in closer. She had almost reached King Street when they struck. Stopping to check her bearings, Golde was suddenly grabbed from behind by strong hands and shoved down a muddy alleyway. Her struggles were pointless against two burly men and her scream went unheard as a large hand was clamped over her mouth.

They were proficient at their trade. She was bound and gagged in less than a minute and an evil-smelling sack was dropped over her head. One of them lifted her bodily and carried her over his shoulder while the other led the way down the alleyway and into a narrow lane to avoid being seen. Hundreds of people were within earshot but Golde could call to none of them. When a bell rang nearby in the parish church of St. Alphege, it sounded to her like a death knell.

Golde had been kidnapped. She did not know why or by whom but she was in serious danger. Yet even in the blind panic of her abduction, the thought that was uppermost in her mind concerned others. What would they think at the house when the doctor did not come to attend to the baby?

Alain heard the commotion from a mile away. It was not just the daily tumult of the city. It had a military ring to it. As he got closer, he could pick out the jingle of harness and the march of feet. Westgate seemed to have been turned into a small garrison. A troop of soldiers came trotting toward him and he scurried off the road at once, hiding his face from them as they passed, and being spattered by the lumps of mud thrown up by uncaring hooves. He struggled on his way.

He was forty yards from Westgate when the soldier ambled toward him with his hands on his hips. The man spat on the ground with contempt.

"Be off with you!" he snarled. "We want none of your filth here! Go to the wood and graze with the other swine."

Alain was not unused to such abuse. It went hand in hand with the fear of leprosy that everyone felt. Some gave alms to assuage their conscience, some passed by on the other side of the street and some took pleasure in treating him like a stray dog who had to be chased away. Alain felt no anger. Resignation was an easier way to cope.

The soldier took a few menacing steps toward him.

"Take your rotting arse away from here!" he yelled.

"I have come to see someone," said Alain.

The man was taken aback at first to hear the sound of French coming from a creature he assumed must be Saxon. It did not increase his sympathy or lessen his scorn.

"Find somewhere else to beg!"

"But I have to see a friend in Canterbury."

"You have no friends."

"His name is Master Gervase Bret."

"Crawl away, you cur!"

"He is a royal commissioner."

"Ha!" The man let out a peal of mocking laughter. "You'll be asking for the Archbishop of Canterbury next!"

"I must see Master Bret."

"Meet him at court in Winchester."

"I have an important message for him."

"I have one for you—fart off!"

"Let me wait at the gate until he comes out."

"And infect the rest of us?" sneered the man, taking his sword from his scabbard. "Disappear before I help you on your way. Go! Go!"

He rushed at Alain with his sword flailing and the leper

turned tail at once, rushing away so fast that he tripped and fell headlong into the mud. The soldier bellowed his coarse amusement. When Alain got up painfully to skulk away, the man hurled a final taunt at him.

"I'll give your regards to the royal commissioner!"

Alain had never missed Bertha more than at that moment.

Concern set in after thirty minutes. When there was no sign of Golde or the doctor after an hour, that concern turned to great agitation. Osbern the Reeve stood outside his front door to look up and down the street. Gervase Bret was with him.

"They should have been here long ago," he said.

"Perhaps Golde lost her way," suggested Gervase.

"It would be difficult."

"What if Helto was not at home? She might be waiting for him at his house."

"She is much more likely to have left a message for him and come back here to explain the delay. I am worried, Master Bret. I'll hasten to King Street this minute."

"Then I'll keep you company."

On the hurried journey to the doctor's house, Gervase tried to reassure Osbern but he knew that he was really hoping to reassure himself. Golde's disappearance was ominous. When Eadgyth vanished, it was on impulse. This was very different. Golde was running an errand which should have taken her no more than ten or fifteen minutes.

When they got to Helto's house, neither she nor the doctor was there. The servant told them that his master was making his first call of the day on Alwin the Sailor in Worthgate Ward because of the seriousness of the patient's condition. Nobody had come in search of the doctor while he was away.

Gervase and Osbern were baffled. They left instructions that Helto was to be sent to the reeve's house immediately on his return, then they made their way slowly back, scouring every street, lane and alleyway they passed in case Golde had strayed into one of them by mistake. The search was fruitless. When they reached the house in Burgate Ward, they were more dismayed than ever.

"This is dreadful!" said Osbern, wringing his hands. "I cannot believe that any harm would befall her on the short journey to Helto. Unless she herself was taken ill."

"No," said Gervase. "Golde was in the best of health."

"Could she have met with some accident?"

"I think it unlikely."

"Then what is the explanation?"

"I do not know."

"Assault? Foul play?"

Gervase turned over the possibilities in his mind. None of them brought comfort and most induced deep apprehension. The conclusion seemed inescapable. On her way to the doctor's house, Golde had been intercepted.

"I'll find Ralph," he said.

When Prior Gregory arrived, his usual combative demeanour had been replaced by a deep distress. His head was down, his brow troubled and his hands clasped inside his sleeves. He all but collided with Canon Hubert. Greetings were exchanged, then Hubert tried to detach himself in order to evade yet another outburst on the subject of the abbey's property dispute with the cathedral. But a new imperative had brought the prior on this occasion and it pushed his differences with the archbishop into the background.

"Heresy in our midst, Canon Hubert!"

"It is profoundly alarming."

"We must all be thankful to you for helping to bring it out into the open. The archbishop sent word of what has transpired and I have been summoned to discuss how the whole monastic community of Canterbury can best meet this crisis."

Hubert relaxed, enjoying the unexpected flattery. "We have taken decisive steps already, Prior Gregory," he said easily. "Archbishop Lanfranc and I were equally appalled by this shocking development."

"Who is this Philippe Berbizier?"

"A proselytising Gnostic."

"Has that been established without question?"

"Why do you ask?"

"The archbishop's letter gave little detail of the man's heretical opinions, stating only that his sect taught that the body of Christ was an illusion and rejecting the notion of a resurrection."

"That is at the heart of Gnosticism."

"And part of the Bogomil tradition, too," reminded the prior. "Their dissidence has spread to many parts of the Byzantine Empire and—who knows?—may have insinuated itself into France. Bogomils could easily be confused by the untutored eye with Gnostics."

"Not in this case," explained Hubert. "Berbizier formed a sect in Orléans which was exposed and destroyed. He alone escaped the sentence of death."

"How was the sect denounced?"

"From the inside, Prior Gregory. When rumours of its existence began to grow, a spy was introduced into their circle as a neophyte. He gathered sufficient information, then revealed it to the secular and ecclesiastical authorities. Arrest and trial were immediate."

"That is heartening."

"It will happen here when Philippe Berbizier is taken.

Every member of his sect will be hunted down but he is the prime target. This priory has a special reason to see the man brought to justice. Brother Martin was buried here only yesterday."

"His death was a warning to us all, Canon Hubert."

"The manner of it was so calculated."

"That is what I mean," said Gregory. "It serves as an image of the heresy which threatens us."

"I do not follow."

"Brother Martin was poisoned inside a church."

"The ultimate desecration!"

"That is their way, Canon Hubert. What else is heresy but a poison which spreads through the body of Christianity? That message is inherent in the nature of the murder. Why was he not stabbed, bludgeoned or strangled to death? Why was the crime perpetrated in that particular place?" The prior's voice darkened. "Heresy is a poison that works from within."

Canon Hubert was so impressed with the vivid phrasing that he made a mental note to use it himself in conversation with others. It dawned on him that he had misjudged both Prior Henry and Prior Gregory. The former had been almost supercilious toward him and the latter overtly truculent. Under the pressure of a crisis, however, both men had emerged as committed Christians with a horror of any threat to their beliefs. It superseded all other considerations. Like Hubert himself, they were true defenders of the word of God and that gave all three men a solidarity which was quite invigorating.

"I will not detain you," said Hubert, ushering him on his way and falling in beside him. "This will be a critical discussion with Archbishop Lanfranc."

"That is why I came so promptly."

"What steps have been taken at St. Augustine's Abbey?"

"Prayer and vigilance. The whole community has been praying for the early capture of this fiend. And those holy brothers who leave the enclave will use their eyes and ears in support of the swords and spears. Philippe Berbizier must have made more than one visit to Canterbury."

"A number, Prior Gregory. That is evident."

"Then *somebody* must have seen him come and go."

"Tell me all that you know about him," said Ralph Delchard.

"I know nothing at all, my lord."

"Is that the truth?"

"I swear it."

"Your memory must be at fault."

"No, my lord."

"It will come back in the castle dungeon."

The man blenched. "Dungeon?"

"That is where I'll have you thrown."

"But I must sail for Sandwich this afternoon."

"You will be lying in chains instead."

"My boat is expected."

"I'll have it impounded," warned Ralph. "If the stench of the castle dungeon does not revive your memory, I'll burn the boat and send the ashes to you. Speak, you vermin!"

The sailor's name was Leofstand. His face still bore the evidence of Alwin's fist but he had sustained nothing like the injuries of the man who had attacked him. He was fit enough to work at his trade and was loading baskets into his boat when Ralph arrived with his men-at-arms. The assault on Leofstand was only verbal this time but it was just as effective.

"I hate liars," said Ralph, fixing him with a glare. "Every-body in Fordwich knows what Alwin was trying to beat out of you. And you must have told him something or you would not be standing before me. Now, Leofstand. Let us try once more, shall we? If you want to spend a month in the dungeon, inhaling the stink of your own excrement, I will make sure that the castellan can accommodate you. But he, too, has a wayward memory." Ralph put his face inches from the sailor. "He may forget completely that you are there."

Leofstand's resistance turned to dust. Ralph had the power to do all that he warned and he was obviously not a man who made empty threats. The sailor capitulated.

"I brought the man from Normandy," he admitted.

"When?"

"We sailed into harbour on Monday morning."

"Did he say why he was coming here?"

"He said nothing, my lord. He never did. I was not paid to hold a conversation with him. Safe passage was all he craved. I gave him that."

"How many times?"

"Three or four."

"When was the last occasion?"

"A month ago, my lord."

"You carried him here and back?"

"Each time."

"So you were his chosen captain."

Ralph could see why. Leofstand was a big, solid, taciturn man who scraped a living from the sea. Money would easily buy his loyalty and seal his lips. Philippe Berbizier had used Alwin the Sailor on his first voyage but the friendship with Bertha made it impossible for her father's boat to be brought into service again. It was crucial that Alwin had no idea of the Frenchman's whereabouts or of his deepening involvement with the girl.

"This last voyage," resumed Ralph. "Was it from Caen?"

"Nearby, my lord. My boat sprung a leak. I had it repaired in the shipyard at Dives-sur-Mer. My passenger joined me there."

Ralph knew the area well. The invasion fleet had sailed from the mouth of the River Dives. He had been part of a large and impatient army which waited for a favourable wind.

"Did he always embark there?"

"No," said Leofstand. "I twice picked him up at St. Valery at the mouth of the Somme. And once returned him there. He pays me well enough to nominate the port."

St. Valery was another name Ralph heard with displeasure. Duke William's army had anchored off there on its way to England, held up once more by unhelpful winds and contrary tides. One difficult voyage had been enough to convince Ralph he was no sailor. If Philippe Berbizier could cross the Channel so readily, he must either enjoy sailing or be impelled by a purpose which made light of any discomfort at sea.

"Did you agree to take him back?" said Ralph.

"No, my lord."

"Then how will he return?"

"I do not know."

"I think you do, Leofstand. That is what Alwin came to knock out of your skull. The date of Berbizier's departure. Alwin wanted to be here to bid him farewell."

"He will not do that now," said the other with a grin.

"Tell me about your passenger."

Leofstand hesitated again. "My lord . . ."

"Take him away to the castle!" ordered Ralph.

"No!" yelled the sailor as he was seized.

"You are lying to me."

"I'll tell you all you wish to know."

On a signal from Ralph, his men-at-arms released Leofstand but stayed in menacing proximity. There was no hope of escape. Ralph understood the man's quandary.

"It is not just a question of money, is it?" he said.

"No, my lord."

"What did Berbizier say to you?"

"If I betrayed him, he would have me killed. And he will, my lord. Look what happened to Alwin. When he asked too many questions, they tried to silence him forever."

"We are on the alert now. You have more protection."

"I do not feel that."

"When is he leaving Canterbury?" barked Ralph.

"On Wednesday next."

"To sail back to Normandy?"

"No, my lord. Boulogne."

"What time will he arrive in Fordwich?"

"At first light."

Ralph was satisfied. Philippe Berbizier was still somewhere in the vicinity. If all else failed, an ambush could be set for him when he tried to set sail. Deciding that Leofstand had told him all that he knew, Ralph turned on his heel to walk away. The sailor grabbed at his arm. The bruises from his beating still hurt. His attacker had been severely punished but Leofstand wanted more vengeance.

"Talk to Alwin again," he suggested.

"About this villain, Philippe Berbizier?"

"No, my lord. About another passenger of his."

"From France?"

"Yes."

"A disciple? Another heretic?"

Leofstand shook his head. "Alwin will tell you."

"What should I say to him?"

"Ask him about Boulogne."

Gervase Bret had some difficulty in tracking him down. It was only when he thought to call at the castle that he established where Ralph had gone. His turned his horse toward Fordwich. The ride gave him time to reflect more deeply on Golde's predicament. It had to be linked to the investigations that he and Ralph were conducting. No other explanation served. To halt their inquiry, someone had lain in wait outside the house to abduct Ralph's wife.

It was proof that they had got close enough to Philippe Berbizier to force him to strike back but that was little consolation in the present circumstances. Golde's safety was paramount. A man who would strangle a young woman and poison an old monk would not draw back from a third murder. If Golde were still alive—and he prayed that she was—she had to be rescued with the utmost urgency. Dozens of armed soldiers were patrolling the streets of the city and yet she had been kidnapped under their noses. That argued skill and preparation on the part of her captors.

The five of them were just leaving the quayside when Gervase arrived at Fordwich. He reined in his horse without acknowledging Ralph's cheerful wave.

"More progress at last, Gervase!" he announced.

"At some cost, I fear."

"Cost?"

"Golde has disappeared."

"What!" growled Ralph, his smile congealing.

"The baby was sick," explained Gervase. "Golde went to fetch the doctor. It is only a short walk but she had not returned after an hour. Osbern and I rushed to the house ourselves to discover that she never arrived there."

"Could she not have got lost?"

"In the event, she would surely have asked the way."

"What was she doing in the streets alone?" demanded Ralph. "Why did Osbern not send one of the servants?"

"I will tell you on the way."

"Do, Gervase. There is nothing to keep us here."

The destrier felt his spurs and galloped away. All six of them kept up a fast pace in the road to the city. It made conversation difficult but Gervase managed to give his friend all the relevant details. Their madcap route took them past St. Augustine's Abbey and in through Burgate, where they slowed to a canter but still scattered the people who thronged Burh Street. Ralph led them toward Osbern's house and dismounted to hammer on the front door. The reeve opened it himself and his expression told them that Golde had still not returned.

"Where is my wife?" howled Ralph.

"We do not know, my lord."

"Why did you send her on a servant's errand?"

"I did not. It was her own decision. She insisted."

"Is this the way to treat your guests, Osbern? By giving them chores that lead them into danger?"

"My lord . . ."

Gervase interrupted to point out that their host was not to blame. The reeve was mortified by the turn of events. On top of the other blows he had suffered, this one was crippling. Ralph was calmed enough to shift his ire to the abductors themselves and he warned what would happen to them if his wife came to the slightest harm. Blind rage was then replaced by speedy action. His men were ordered to search every turning on the way to King Street and to question people along the route to see if anyone remembered seeing Golde earlier on. He turned back to Osbern.

"What was she wearing when she went out?" he asked.

The reeve looked more uncomfortable than ever. Stepping back into the house for a second, he reappeared with Golde's gown in his hands and held it up.

"She was wearing this, my lord."

"Where did you get it?" said Ralph, snatching it away.
"They sent it back. To let you know."

Golde tried to control her fear in order to work out where
she might be. On the journey to her prison, she had kicked
and fought in protest, taking no note of the twisting route
her captors followed. She was bundled through a door and
taken down some steps. Dropped into a chair, she was tied
securely to its arms. When the sack was lifted from her
head, a blindfold was quickly put in place. It was pulled
very tight and dug into her but the gag on her mouth
smothered her complaint.

The dank smell and the sense of oppression told her that
she was in a cellar. When the two men left, she heard a trap
door close. A heavy bolt slid into position. She was still inside the city and close enough to the cathedral for its bell
to reach her, albeit with muffled effect. What it gave her
was a purchase on time. If the bell was ringing for Tierce,
she had been held captive for over two hours.

They had taken her gown but made no attempt to harm
her. Once she had been restrained, their job was done and
that was a faint reassurance. Had they meant to kill her,
they would already have done so. The chair was another
tiny source of consolation. Instead of flinging her down on
the bare earth, they had thought about her comfort. Not
many houses in Canterbury would have such a stout chair
with carved arms. The property above her head belonged
to a man with a degree of wealth.

Something ran across her foot to bring her speculation
to a sudden halt. She could not work out if it was a mouse
or a rat but the contact unnerved her. Golde braced herself
for more evidence that she was sharing the cellar with vermin. To take her mind off her own plight, she tried to think
about others who would now be suffering. Ralph and Ger-

vase would be distraught. Osbern and Eadgyth would be skewered by guilt, blaming themselves for having been indirectly responsible for her disappearance. The baby caused her less worry. Helto the Doctor must have been summoned by now and he would have treated the child.

A snuffling noise at her feet showed her that the animal had returned and she kicked out. Above her head, the bolt slid back and the door to the cellar was lifted. Footsteps descended the stone steps. Someone came to stand over her and she flinched when she felt the touch of cold steel on her cheek. But no wound was inflicted. The dagger was used to cut her wimple free from the encircling gag and blindfold. Her braided hair was exposed. The warmth of a flame kissed her face as it was held up for someone to inspect her.

An admiring sigh came. Her visitor stroked her hair.

"My lord Ralph is fortunate," said a voice. "Let us hope that he has the sense to protect his good fortune."

↪ CHAPTER FIFTEEN

RALPH DELCHARD HAD been shaped in the warrior mould of his ancestors. When faced with an enemy, his first instinct was always for attack. Diplomacy was something he left to others, believing that a sword and a lance were the best weapons with which to negotiate a peace. Seated astride his destrier, he would ride into battle against any foe and had yet to be on the losing side. But his opponents had always been visible before, flesh-and-blood soldiers with blades as keen as his own and a simple urge to vanquish by means of superior strength and skill.

This time it was different. He was pitted against a shadow. He knew its name, its reputation and something of its appearance but nothing more substantial. The shadow had already moved across the face of Harbledown and killed twice without mercy. Golde might well become the third victim if she were not soon released. How could Ralph lead an assault on an enemy he could not see, who was holding his wife hostage in a place he could not find? It was an unfair fight. Keyed-up to lead a charge, he felt as if his warhorse had been hobbled and his sword arm tied behind his back. Thick fog was obscuring the whole battlefield.

"God's tits!" he yelled in frustration.

"Try to stay calm, Ralph."

"How can I when Golde is in their hands?"

"That is one of the reasons they abducted her," said Gervase. "To provoke your ire. To make you act in wild and unconsidered ways. Taking a decision in anger is like firing an arrow without first taking aim. It will never hit its target."

"We *have* no target, Gervase. That is the trouble."

"We do and we are closer to it than we think."

"Is that why he is trying to frighten us off?"

"Why else?"

"I'll tear him to shreds when I catch him!"

The council of war was held in the solar at the house. While Ralph's men-at-arms searched in the streets, Gervase tried to urge stealth. Ralph sat with Golde's gown across his lap, stroking it absentmindedly and shifting between rage and nostalgia. It was a gown he had bought as part of the wardrobe for her wedding. Having been offered as a token of his love, it had now come back as a token of hate and dire warning.

"Where can she be?" he whispered.

"Still in the city. Of that we can be certain."

"Can we?"

"Yes," said Gervase. "Golde was seized somewhere between here and King Street. They would not have taken her far in case they were seen. And how could they smuggle her out of Canterbury when every gate is guarded and every person arriving or leaving is challenged to identify themselves? No, she is here. And not too great a distance from where we are now."

"I'll pull down every house in the city to find her!" vowed Ralph, bunching a fist for emphasis. He put the gown aside and got up. "I cannot sit here. I must get out there and direct the search."

"No, Ralph. Stay where you are."

"It irks me so."

"Leave the house and you will be watched. Do you want them to know exactly what your movements are? Besides," said Gervase, "you must be here to receive the message."

"What message?"

"From Philippe Berbizier. His terms."

"Ransom?"

"All I know is that he will be in touch. The gown merely told you that he held the advantage. He will want to use that advantage to dictate the situation. To make you call off the hunt."

"It is not within my power, Gervase. The sheriff's officers and the archbishop's knights are outside my command. I cannot stay their swords."

"They are no threat to Berbizier. We are."

"So what must we do?"

"You remain here. I continue the search alone."

"That puts you at too great a risk."

"No," said Gervase. "He does not fear me. I have ridden to Harbledown more than once. He has spurned the chance to ambush me. You are the one who troubles him. Since he cannot attack you directly, he strikes at your Achilles' heel."

"My dear wife!"

"I will find her."

There was a tap on the front door and they both turned expectantly as they heard the servant open it. But it was no missive from Philippe Berbizier. Helto the Doctor had called back. Gervase slipped out into the passage to speak to him.

"How is baby Osbern?" he asked.

"Grievously sick," sighed Helto. "He has an infection in his ear, which causes him pain and upsets his balance. I fear that his night in a cold churchyard may be to blame."

"Can he be cured?"

"I hope so, Master Bret. When I came earlier, I gave him a draught to make him sleep through the discomfort. I went back to my house to mix a potion that must be administered with care into the ear itself."

"I will not keep you from your patient."

Helto thanked him and trotted up the stairs. Gervase went back into the solar to find Ralph holding the gown against the side of his face. Even the finest doctor could not mix a potion to remedy his ills. Only the safe return of Golde would effect a cure for him.

"Tell me about Fordwich," said Gervase.

"Fordwich?"

"You said that you had learned much there this morning. If I am to follow the trail alone, I will need every signpost that you can give me. Whom did you see at the port?"

"His name was Leofstand."

Ralph described everything which had passed between him and the sailor. Gervase absorbed the information readily. He was especially glad of an excuse to visit Alwin the Sailor because he felt there was still much to be gleaned from him that had a bearing on the murder of his daughter.

The second knock at the front door was louder and more authoritative. Certain that news had come for him, Ralph reached for his sword but Gervase held up his arms to prevent him from leaving the room. The front door was opened, voices spoke, then Brother Simon was admitted to the solar. He was trembling beneath the weight of the message he bore. It was directed at Gervase.

"He wishes to see you at the cathedral."

"Canon Hubert?"

"No," said Simon, barely able to get the summons out. "His Grace the Archbishop of Canterbury."

Oblivious to the presence of his companions, Lanfranc sat in his chair and pondered, his eyelids drawn down, his lips pursed and his brow striped with concentration. He toyed with a large ring on his left hand as if fumbling with a device to open some secret compartment in his mind. But the compartment remained shut and its contents inaccessible. His lids suddenly lifted and a distant despair showed in his eyes.

"We have so far failed," he announced gloomily. "Hundreds of men were committed to a manhunt yesterday but they have had no sight of their quarry. The sheriff's officers have searched in vain, my own knights have made equally fruitless forays into the city's environs, and the concerted prayers of our priory and St. Augustine's Abbey have not produced one glimmer of assistance from above. I make no criticism of divine disposition," he added solemnly. "God wishes us to make amends on His behalf. To do that, we must be more sedulous in our pursuit of this heretic and more subtle in gathering the clues that will lead us to him and his foul sect."

"We are doing our best, Your Grace," said Prior Henry.

"It is inadequate."

"If you say so, Your Grace."

"If heresy thrives, we are all inadequate. This man has

been prosyletising at the very gates of the cathedral and we did not detect him until it was too late. How many has he led from the paths of righteousness? How many has he shown into the valley of sin?" His voice croaked. "How many has he debauched?"

"Too many, Your Grace," said Canon Hubert.

"One is too many. One reproves our vigilance."

"Philippe Berbizier is very cunning."

"Heretics always are."

Prior Henry nodded in agreement and Hubert quickly followed suit but Prior Gregroy stood motionless between them, his features grey with a swirling anguish and his pugnacity drained completely away. Lanfranc toyed with the ring once more as his reminiscences flowed.

"When I was at Caen," he began, "that dear, beautiful abbey which I loved so much, there were faint rumblings of heresy in Rouen. Members of a sect were caught, practising some fearful rituals in a wood. Fire was involved. And bestiality of a kind I dare not mention within this hallowed place." His jaw tightened. "When I was asked to determine whether it was unorthodoxy or witchcraft, I argued that it might be some hideous mixture of the two, for heresy and necromancy have always gone hand in hand like illicit lovers, proud of their lasciviousness. I examined him."

There was a long pause. Canon Hubert and Prior Henry were eager to hear more. Prior Gregory remained subdued and detached. The recollections started up again.

"I do not remember his name," said Lanfranc. "But he was their leader and their unholy priest, just as Philippe Berbizier is—the two, I imagine, hewn from the same tree of falsehood. I examined him closely but his answers were guileful. He hid behind such a shield of words that I could scarce get at him. The man was like a veritable serpent which more easily eludes the grasp the more tightly it is held in the hands."

"What happened, Your Grace?"

"God came to my aid. He gave me the strength to wrestle with the serpent until I squeezed a confession out him." He mimed the action then became peremptory. "We must treat this serpent of our own with the same show of might!"

Henry and Hubert agreed in unison. A monk interrupted the audience to bring a whispered message to Lanfranc. The archbishop snapped his fingers and the monk scuttled away to fetch in Gervase Bret. Canon Hubert seized on the opportunity to ingratiate himself with Lanfranc by introducing his fellow commissioner. Gervase was poised but humble in the presence of the archbishop. Lanfranc's reputation towered over ecclesiastical affairs, as solid and massive as the cathedral he had rebuilt in Canterbury. Even at his advanced age, he exuded an awesome intellectuality.

"Canon Hubert has spoken well of you, Master Bret."

"I am flattered, Your Grace."

"You are a lawyer like me, I hear."

"A poor replica of one beside Your Grace."

"There is a beauty and a logic in the law which has always appealed to me. Order. Purpose. Symmetry. Just like the heavens themselves as created by the Almighty." He saw the defensive look in Gervase's eye. "No, Master Bret. I have not brought you here for a legal confrontation. Though Canon Hubert stands beside you as your companion on the tribunal and though Prior Henry and Prior Gregory contest the respective rights of cathedral and abbey, this audience will not concern itself with a minor property dispute. Especially when it no longer exists."

Prior Henry was startled. "No longer exists?"

"I cede the land in question to the abbey."

"But it is ours, Your Grace."

"Say no more, Henry. My decision is made."

The prior bowed and backed slightly away, dismayed by a decision in which he had no part and which he strongly opposed. Gervase was pleased to hear that days of wrangling in the shire hall had now been obviated and he expected Prior Gregory to be showing the satisfaction of a victor. All that Gregory could raise, however, was a mild interest. Instead of wishing to race back to the abbey with the glad tidings, he looked as if he might forget to mention them.

"It is a gesture of goodwill toward the abbey," explained Lanfranc. "I look for a reciprocal gesture."

They all knew what he meant. In return for the right to retain the controversial land, the abbey had to reconcile itself to their new abbot. Prior Gregory was dismissed with a gracious smile and bowed to the archbishop before leaving the chamber. Hubert sensed an archiepiscopal reprimand.

"Prior Gregory was unusually quiescent, Your Grace."

"We discussed his future, Canon Hubert."

"His future?"

"He has been such an effective prior at the abbey that I felt his abilities could be put to excellent use here. Needless to say, it will be in a less-exalted office, as we already have a prior." He indicated Henry. "I am sure that Gregory will soon learn the ways of Christ Church Priory and give us the loyalty he has shown to St. Augustine's Abbey."

The soft plausibility of Lanfranc's voice disguised the ruthlessness of his action. Because the abbey opposed his wishes, he removed its recalcitrant prior. Invited to discuss heretics with the archbishop, Gregory found himself treated like one. He had been examined, reproved, stripped of his monastic rank and removed summarily from the abbey. Gervase was chastened by the sight of such chilling brutality.

Archbishop Lanfranc appraised his young visitor.

"I wish to talk to you about Harbledown," he said.

"Harbledown, Your Grace?"

"A place so green and tranquil that I chose to build my own palace there. But its grass has been stained with blood and its tranquillity has been violated. You, I believe, know the exact spot where the poor young girl was found."

"I do, Your Grace."

"And it was you who first saw the fallen body of Brother Martin at the hospital of St. Nicholas. Is that not so?"

"It grieves me to recall it, Your Grace."

"Accompany Prior Henry to the scenes of both these crimes. Show him, if you will, what you revealed earlier to Canon Hubert. There is a sound reason for this request."

"No reason is needed, Your Grace," said Gervase with a polite nod. "Your request justifies itself. I had thought to visit Harbledown again on my own account. My journey now has a double purpose and value."

"I am ready to leave instantly," said Prior Henry.

"Then I am at your service."

"Thank you, Master Bret," said Lanfranc. "We are indebted to you. The scourge of heresy must be burned to cinders. Help us to light the torch that will do it." He rose from his chair and held his arms wide. "My blessing goes with you."

Gervase and Prior Gregory bowed, then moved toward the door. The archbishop's voice made them come to a brief halt.

"Abbot Guy is due to arrive here tomorrow," he said. "I want him to come into a city that is cleansed and purified.

What will he think if he discovers that Canterbury is a den of heresy? When he rides over Harbledown Hill, he must not hear the hiss of this vile serpent. Two innocent people have been killed already. I do not wish to welcome Abbot Guy with a third dead body lying near my palace."

Gervase thought at once of Golde and his resolve stiffened.

"That will not happen, Your Grace," he promised.

"*Deo volente!*" added Prior Henry.

Patience did not come easily to Ralph Delchard. When it was forced upon him by a turn of events, he was even less likely to embrace it. Strutting up and down the solar at the house in Burgate Street, he cursed royally and banged one fist into the palm of his other hand.

"There must be something I can *do*!" he insisted.

"Watch and pray," suggested Osbern, tentatively.

"I have watched too long and prayer has never gained me anything more than a crick in my neck and a pain in my knees. Hell's teeth, man. My wife is in danger! How would you feel in that situation?"

"I know only too well, my lord."

Ralph's anger was checked. While bemoaning his personal quandary, he had completely forgotten the reeve's own suffering. Osbern, too, was a husband whose wife had mysteriously disappeared and left him on tenterhooks. Eadgyth was still unwell and their son was also seriously ill. Osbern's anxiety was divided between his wife and child. The fact that Helto had already made two visits to the house that morning showed how concerned he was at the condition of the baby. The child was in jeopardy.

"My apologies, Osbern," said Ralph. "I am too full of self-affairs. You will understand why."

"I share your worries, my lord."

"If only I knew that Golde was safe!"

He paused at the window to peer out yet again. Ralph had been surveying the street at regular intervals, waiting for word to come from Philippe Berbizier and hoping to pounce on the messenger to beat information out of him. All he saw was the normal human traffic of the day, moving past on its way to and from the main thoroughfare of Burh Street. Ralph stamped his foot to relieve his tension, then stalked away from the window. He was beginning to believe that no further message would arrive. His wife's gown had been an explicit-enough missive in itself.

There was a soft tap on the door and Osbern opened it to admit his manservant. When Ralph saw what he was carrying in his hand, he snatched the item at once to examine it. Golde's wimple was slit to ribbons.

"Where did you find this?" he demanded.

"In the stables, my lord."

"When?"

"Even now," said the man nervously. "I saddled Master Bret's horse for him, then saw him off. As I was cleaning out the stables, I discovered the wimple." He held up a scroll. "This was wrapped inside it, my lord."

Ralph grabbed the letter from his hand and unfolded it. The message it contained was short and unequivocal.

Call your men off and your wife will stay alive.

While Ralph assimilated the warning with glowering rage, Osbern dismissed the servant. The reeve waited in silence until Ralph had scrunched the letter up, hurled it at the wall, then paced restlessly up and down.

"Why did nobody see this delivered?" he asked.

"I do not mount a guard on my stables, my lord," said Osbern. "Seeing you standing at that window, they knew that it was dangerous to come to the front door. That is why the message was delivered unseen to the rear of the house. You are up against a clever adversary here."

"Yes," conceded Ralph. "He is one step ahead of me."

"May I know the contents of the letter?"

When Ralph nodded, the reeve picked up the missive and carefully unrolled it. He saw the crumb of comfort at once.

"Your wife is still alive, my lord."

"But for how long?"

"Until this man has made his escape," said Osbern. "But he cannot do that if your men are breathing down his neck."

"No," said Ralph grimly. "They are clearly searching in the right area. Do I call them off and let this villain go?"

"What is the alternative?"

Ralph took the letter from him and read it once more.

"Two things are clear," he concluded. "Golde is alive and Philippe Berbizier himself is still inside the city. A cordon of steel has been thrown around it. There is no way that he will be able to get out of Canterbury."

The troop of soldiers trotted along the High Street and went over Eastbridge in ragged formation. The citizens were so used to the swaggering presence of Norman soldiers that they simply stepped out of their way and swore under their breaths. When they reached Westgate, the soldiers were allowed through at once by the armed guards. They swung left and headed toward the castle. Nobody stopped to notice that one of the men in helm and hauberk detached himself cleverly from his fellows and rode in a different direction.

Philippe Berbizier was soon ascending Harbledown Hill.

The lepers at the hospital of St. Nicholas were puzzled and alarmed at the sight which confronted them. Led by Prior

Henry and Gervase Bret, a dozen monks came riding up to the church with six men-at-arms in their wake. A deputation of that size could only betoken something of great importance and the lepers watched apprehensively from their huts. Brother Bartholomew and Brother Vitalis, who had taken over the running of the hospital, showed a proper deference to their prior and conducted him to the nave.

As soon as he stepped into the church, Henry felt the throbbing presence of evil and he identified its source just as Canon Hubert had done before him. Every monk was ordered into the church and the door was locked from inside. While the soldiers stood on guard outside and the lepers waited in trepidation, the service began. Prior Henry set about the task of reclaiming the house for God. Exorcism took place.

Gervase went in search of Alain and found him some distance away, perched on a tree stump as he fed crumbs from a hunk of bread to a bold robin. Alain's hood was down and his veil drawn back so that he could feel the play of the cool breeze on his face. Leprosy did not deter the bird. A source of food brought him within inches of Alain. When Gervase approached, the robin did not even look up from its meal.

Alain showed a degree of animation for once, standing up from the tree and raising a hand in greeting. When the leper went to pull up his hood, Gervase shook his head to indicate that it was not necessary. Alain did not have to hide his affliction.

"I hoped you would come," said the leper.

"Why?"

"I wanted to see you. I went down to the city but he stopped me at the gate and drove me away."

"Who did?"

"A soldier. One of the guards."

"A big search has been mounted for the killer."

"I gathered that."

"They are trying to pen him within the city."

"If he is there," said Alain.

"Nobody can be sure of that," said Gervase. "But why did you wish to see me, Alain?"

"I brought something to give you."

He took the piece of blue material from his sleeve and went to place it on the log beside the bread. Gervase moved in to take it directly from his hand, unafraid of the contact. He studied the material and felt its texture.

"I think it came from Bertha's attire," said Alain.

"Where did you find it?"

"A mile away. Caught on a twig."

"Would Bertha have had cause to be in that vicinity?"

"I do not know, Master Bret. She would not have been collecting herbs there, I am certain, because there were none. That torn material was in the orchard of a manor house."

"Who owns it?"

"I have no idea."

"Could you direct me there?"

"Yes." He looked at the blue threads. "You will need to match it against her kirtle. What happened to her attire?"

"It was given to her father."

"Will he let you see it?"

"If he is still alive."

Alain looked shaken. "He is ill?"

"Two men assaulted him at Fordwich and left him for dead. He lies abed. The doctor is not sure that Alwin the Sailor will survive the injuries."

Alain said nothing. He continued to stare at the tiny piece of blue material, reluctant to part with another keepsake and yet desperate to help Gervase trace the man who had murdered Bertha. Gervase examined the material again.

"Describe this manor house and orchard to me."

"It lies due north of here."

Alain gave rough directions and described everything that he could remember about his brief visit to the place. Gervase heard enough to warrant further investigation but first he had to establish whether the material had indeed been torn from Bertha's apparel. His gaze travelled in the direction of Canterbury.

"I believe that the killer is still in the city," he said. "Keep him in there long enough and we are bound to find him. One thing we can guarantee."

"What is that?"

"He will not slip past the guards. They are too alert and too numerous. Even at night, the security is intense. Nobody could possibly breach it."

"*He* did, Master Bret."

"Who?"

"The man I saw sneak past the hospital last night. He came from the city because he lives and works there. You know him yourself. You met him at Bertha's funeral."

"Did I?"

"He conducted the burial service."

"Reinbald the Priest?" said Gervase in amazement.

"Yes," confirmed the leper. "He was as close to me as you are. Even in the dark, I could not mistake him. What was he doing out at that time of night?"

Gervase could think of only one answer.

Reinbald the Priest spent an hour with Eadgyth and left her much comforted. The doctor's potion seemed to be combatting the baby's ear infection. When the child awoke, it did not instantly cry. The boy even permitted the priest to cradle him for a short while. When Reinbald quit the bed-chamber, he left mother and child in a less fretful state. Os-bern thanked him and showed him out.

Through the window of the solar, Ralph watched him leave. After first looking in on his wife, Osbern the Reeve joined his guest, feeling both reassured and disturbed. Ralph saw the confusion in his face.

"What is the matter?" he said.

"Reinbald was able to offer much solace to her."

"That is good news, surely?"

"Yes, my lord. But it comes with more awkward tidings."

"Awkward?"

"Eadgyth is asking for your wife."

"Has she not been told?"

"No, my lord," said the reeve, "and nor has Reinbald. He could not tell her what he did not know himself. Eadgyth is under enough stress at the moment. I did not wish to put her under more strain by drawing her into this latest crisis."

"Your memory is wondrous short, Osbert."

"Short?"

"Yes," said Ralph sharply. "You kept the truth about Bertha's murder from your wife in order to spare her more pain and what happened? Will you repeat this madness? She has a right to know. Golde has been a friend to her."

"That is why she would be so alarmed, my lord."

"How much more alarmed will she be if she finds out that she has been deceived yet again? Are you intent on driving a wedge between yourself and your wife?"

"No, my lord! I love her."

"Then stop treating her like a child."

Osbern nodded. "You are right," he said. "She ought to know. The truth is that I could not find the words to tell her."

"You will not need to," said Ralph. "I will."

"You, my lord?"

"Yes. Eadgyth must not be kept in the dark any longer. She may be able help me. At a time like this, I need a woman to talk to me about Golde." When Osbern stepped forward, he held up a hand. "No. I wish to be alone with her."

Ralph was in the bedchamber for some time. He broke the news gently and Eadgyth wept. She knew that something was amiss because Golde had not been to see her, but it had never crossed her mind that her friend might have been kidnapped. Instead of needing consolation herself, Eadgyth offered it freely to Ralph, telling him how kind and unselfish Golde had been toward her and praising her many good qualities. It was a salutary reminder to him of just how much he would lose if his wife did not come back to him.

While each was helping the other, a visitor called at the house and was admitted to the solar. Ralph took his leave of Eadgyth, rocked the baby in his crib, then stole out of the room and closed the door behind him. Two voices came up the staircase toward him and he froze in his tracks. With the door of the solar only slightly ajar, it was possible to hear a conversation quite clearly from the landing. Sound was funnelled up the staircase with extraordinary clarity.

Ralph suddenly had the revelation that he needed. He went quickly down the stairs and into the solar. Canon Hubert rushed across to greet him.

"Forgive my delay, my lord," he said breathlessly. "I came as soon as I heard. Archbishop Lanfranc and I were in conference this morning. It was only when the audience came to a close that Brother Simon was able to convey these frightful tidings."

"Thank you, Canon Hubert," said Ralph.

"Your men have called off their search, I hear."

"They were forced to."

"We are dealing with a Son of Satan here."

"And with his confederates," added Ralph. "No man could have done this without help from friends who live in the city. I think I know who one of them might be."

"Pursue him, my lord. Bring him to justice."

"In order to do that, I need your help."

"It is yours for the asking. The safe return of your dear wife is a priority. I would do anything to assist you."

"Anything?" said Ralph.

The familiar twinkle was back in his eye.

❧ Chapter Sixteen

THE PASSAGE OF time did not still Golde's apprehension. She was still held captive when the cathedral bell rang out for Sext and was horrified to realise that she had been bound and gagged for over five hours. Cramp was attacking her muscles and the gag was chafing her lips. One sign of mercy had been shown to her. Someone had removed her blindfold. Golde could still see nothing in the black void of the cellar but it was a small freedom. She was grateful.

He had frightened her. The man who came earlier had held up a candle to inspect her and made her feel like some dumb animal trussed up in a pen at market. His voice had been French and his manner politely gloating. Though he had not molested her in any way, Golde felt that he would not hesitate to do so when the mood took him. She guessed who he must be. From her fleeting contact with him, she knew that he would be an unpleasant person to meet in the best of circumstances. Since she was at his mercy, he was repulsive.

Yet his visits had given her some insight into her situation. She now knew why she was held and by whom. Golde was taken hostage as a means to disable Ralph Delchard. Her survival depended entirely on his cooperation with the men who had abducted her. That was why she saw the removal of the blindfold as a positive sign. It suggested that her husband had agreed to whatever terms they had demanded.

She knew him well enough to be certain that he would do everything within his power to rescue her. While appearing to obey the dictates of her captors, Ralph would be working out where she was and how he could get to her. Her main fear was that he simply would not find her in time. Those who held her seemed to have honoured their contract so far. What if they decided to break it out of malice? Her thoughts became ever more feverish.

The bolt slid back from the trap door and it was lifted up. A rectangle of light dazzled her eyes for a few seconds before disappearing. Two men had come down into the cellar and closed the trap door behind them. One held a candle but kept it well away from their faces so that she could not see them. The other man carried food and drink on a wooden tray. They bent over her.

"We've come to feed you, my lady," grunted one.

"Undo the gag," ordered the other.

"I expect a kiss for doing this."

The first man put his candle on the tray so that he could use both hands to untie the thick cloth which had been used to gag her. Holding her chin, he leaned over to plant a guzzling kiss on her lips but Golde reacted quickly. She bit him so hard that he jumped back with a howl of rage, then she let out a loud scream for help. The injured man slapped her viciously across the face and went to strike again.

"No!" shouted his companion. "He'll kill you."

"She bit me!"

"Put the gag back on."

"Look!" He touched his cheek. "My face is bleeding!"

"Shut her mouth again!"

"The vixen!"

When the man replaced the gag, he pulled it tighter than ever and took satisfaction from her groan of anguish. The side of her face was already on fire and the edges of her mouth were now ignited with pain as well. As a final act of torture, he put the blindfold back in place. Standing in front of her again, he wiped the blood from his own face.

"I'll get even for this!" he vowed.

"Come on," said his companion. "She's obviously not hungry." He sniggered. "Except for you."

"We'll be back, my lady."

"When this is all over, we'll both be back."

"Yes!"

"That was his promise. Keep her locked-up safe and sound here until it is all over. Then we both have her."

The man with the bleeding face grabbed her hair.

"I'm first!"

They went out of the cellar and slid the bolt back in the trap door. Golde shuddered violently. These men would never keep to any bargain with her husband. She was not their hostage. When the time came, she would be their victim.

Gervase Bret held the piece of material against the kirtle. It matched perfectly. He was puzzled. How had her apparel got snagged on a twig over a mile from the place where

Bertha had been found dead? What reason had she to be in the orchard of a private house?

He went upstairs to the stark bedroom where Alwin the Sailor still lay in a half-sleep of torment. The old woman got up from the stool and Gervase thanked her for allowing him to inspect Bertha's attire. When the neighbour went back downstairs, Gervase moved the stool closer to the bed and sat down so that his face was near to that of the injured man.

"Alwin?" he called. "Can you hear me, Alwin?"

"What do you want?"

"We are close to finding Philippe."

"He is mine!" he said, trying in vain to sit up. "Let me have him! I'll kill him!"

Gervase eased him back. "Rest, rest," he said. "If he is to be caught, we must have your help. We know that he is leaving next Wednesday. You found that out from Leofstand."

"Leofstand was his pilot!"

"Why not you, Alwin?"

"I refused to take him again."

"Did he not pay well enough?"

"All the money in France could not buy my boat."

"Why not?"

"It was the way he looked at Bertha."

"Just looked?"

"It was enough."

"Did you not warn her about him?"

"Of course. But she went behind my back."

Gervase remembered what another sailor had told Ralph Delchard to ask. "Tell me about Boulogne," he said.

Reaction was instant. Alwin gurgled noisily and rolled his head from side to side. He went into such a frantic paroxysm that Gervase feared the man was dying. Putting an arm around him, he held the patient until the tremors finally faded. The sailor made a supreme effort to control himself. For several minutes, he held a fierce debate inside his own mind and it produced some more convulsions. When he reached a decision, it imposed a weary calm upon him.

"I have to tell someone," he whispered. "I talked to the priest about it. Not Reinbald, he is too young to understand. Father Colswein. The old priest who died. He had been married himself. He knew the problems. I talked to him, and Helto learned something of it as well."

"Helto the Doctor?"

"He cured me, Master Bret."

"Of what?"

There was no point in keeping it buried deep inside him any longer. Alwin knew that his life was dwindling away. If his confession could in any way assist the capture of his daughter's killer, he was ready to make it. Gervase was as young as Reinbald but he had a maturity that the priest lacked. Also, he was a stranger. That made it easier.

"It was a long time ago," he began. "I sailed to Boulogne to pick up a cargo of wine. We were caught in a storm and had a bad crossing. I needed something to cheer me up. When we reached harbour, I went to an inn. Drink was taken. There was a woman there. An Egyptian. I thought she was beautiful."

"Did you stay the night with her?"

"Three nights—God forgive me!"

"Were you married at the time?"

"Yes."

"Had Bertha been born?"

"No," said Alwin. "We wanted children but none came at first. When I got back from Boulogne, it was impossible."

"Why?"

"The woman was diseased. I had to go to Helto."

"But he cured you?"

"In time. It was no easy matter."

"What happened then?"

"Bertha," he said, a wan smile appearing between the bandages. "Our own child. It was a miracle. I vowed to put the past behind me and lead a decent life from then on. But I made one big mistake."

"You confessed to your wife," guessed Gervase.

"I felt I had to, Master Bret." His voice grew faint. "It was a fatal error. My happiness ended there and then. My wife told her sister, Juliana, and she lashed me with her tongue every time we met. My sister-in-law made me pay dearly."

"What of Bertha?"

"When she was born, I was hardly allowed near her. I spent more time at sea, taking on longer voyages. Anything to occupy my mind and get me away from Juliana. One day, I went back to Boulogne. The Egyptian woman was still there." He rolled onto his back. "With my son."

"She had a child by you?"

"So she claimed, and the times certainly fitted."

"Did you meet him?"

"Oh, yes," said Alwin. "Whenever I went to Boulogne. The woman and I fell in together again, you see. I pretended that she and the boy were my real family." He gave a wry laugh. "Bertha was conceived in love and I could not be a proper father to her. My son was born out of lust yet he looked up to me. For a while."

"Why did he stop?"

"His mother and I quarrelled," said Alwin sadly. "The next time I was in Boulogne, I sought to make it up but she had left the city. They told me she had gone back to Egypt." He let out a long wheeze. "That was it. Years passed. I forgot them. Then my own wife was taken seriously ill. I promised her faithfully that I would bring Bertha up as a God-fearing Christian and I kept to that promise. If anything, I was too strict with her but I sought to protect her, Master Bret. That is a father's duty." He closed his eyes as he relived another tribulation. "Then came the letter."

"Letter?"

"From Boulogne. Leofstand brought it back."

"Was it from the woman?"

"Yes," he said. "A scrivener wrote it for her. She was as unlettered as me. They had come back to Boulogne but she was no longer able to look after our son. She begged me to help her. I could not refuse." He opened his eyes and fixed them on Gervase. "She loved me. She trusted me. She had named our son after me."

Gervase sat up with a start. He knew the rest.

"Alain!"

"The letter did not tell me what was wrong with him. I only found out when I reached Boulogne. He had caught the disease in Egypt. What future was there for him? I would have needed a heart of stone to turn my back on him."

"So you brought him back?"

"To the leper hospital of St. Nicholas."

"Did he know that you were his father?"

"No," said Alwin firmly. "That was the only condition on which I agreed to take him. His mother told him that I was just a friend. He never knew that I was his father. And Bertha never knew that he was her half-brother." His guilt made him wince. "I brought him over in my boat but we sailed up the river one evening when it was still light. Do you know what I did, Master Bret? I dropped anchor in midstream and waited. I waited until it was dark enough to sail into Fordwich when nobody would see us. I was ashamed of my own son! I brought him ashore in the night to hide his ugliness. I felt like a leper myself."

Gervase was moved by the story. Two separate strands of Alwin's life had become inextricably bound up together. He realised now why Alain and Bertha had been drawn together into a relationship that was deeper and more resonant than ordinary friendship. They shared the same father. Neither had brought him any real pleasure yet they found glimpses of joy in their time alone with each other. Bertha had gone to Harbledown in spite of strenuous objections from her father. She and Alain had an affinity which transcended everything else. They were blood kin.

"Father Colswein was right," mused Alwin.

"The old priest?"

"I know no Latin but he taught me one phrase that has stuck in mind like a spike. *Stipendium peccati mors est.*"

"The reward of sin is death," translated Gervase.

"My daughter murdered, my son a leper."

"Neither can be laid at your door."

"Both afflictions can."

"No, Alwin."

"I have known death in life," said the other. "And I have deserved it." He wheezed again. "There is nothing to keep me in this world save the wish to see that murderous villain caught. Philippe, with his knowing smile. When that is done, I will follow Bertha to a quieter place." One hand flickered in a gesture of great pathos. "Please, Master Bret. Avenge my daughter. And you will ease my son's mind."

Canon Hubert rode slowly along the busy street on his donkey. The animal was in a fractious mood and kept trying to turn down lanes and alleyways. He had to pull hard on its reins to control its wayward impulses. He swung right into

King Street and studied the houses carefully until he came to the one he wanted. It was a timber-framed dwelling of medium size in an excellent state of repair and with fresh thatch on its low roof. The neighbouring houses looked almost neglected by comparison.

Hauling his donkey to a halt, Canon Hubert dismounted and tethered the creature to an iron ring set in the wall of the house. He tapped meekly on the door, then put both hands inside the opposite sleeves. When the servant answered the door, all he saw was the inclined head of a hooded monk.

"I wish to speak with Helto the Doctor," said Hubert.

"He is not at home."

"I will wait within."

"He will not be back for a long time."

"However long, I will still wait. Stand aside."

"No," said the servant, barring the way. "I cannot let you in."

"Then I will let myself in!"

The hood was flipped back and Canon Hubert was transformed into Ralph Delchard. One hand came out to push the servant hard in the chest while the other appeared with a long dagger in it. Ralph darted into the house and shut the door behind him. The servant was sturdy and he launched himself at the newcomer but his visitor was far too skilled in the arts of combat.

Ralph chopped him across the throat with a forearm and brought a knee up into the man's stomach. All the fight was taken out of him. Before he could slump to the ground, Ralph caught him with one hand and heaved him hard against the wall. There was a thunderous crack as a skull met a thick oak beam. The servant dropped to the floor with a thud. Not even his master would be able to revive him for a while.

The commotion had alerted another man and he was a more dangerous opponent. When he came down to the stairs to investigate the noise, he was carrying a dagger himself. Ralph stepped into the parlour to give himself more room for manoeuvre. Encumbered by the cowl, he circled his man warily.

"Who are you?" growled the other.

"Canon Hubert," said Ralph. "I've come to shrive you."

"Then I confess I'll have to kill you!"

The man lunged at him with the dagger but Ralph parried him with ease. A second lunge was parried with equal adroitness. The man feinted and caught Ralph unawares. The dagger sliced through the arm of the cowl but made no contact with Ralph himself. His attacker did not know that. When Ralph mimed a wound and staggered back, the man was after him in a flash, only to find his own weapon slashed from his grasp by a downward stroke of Ralph's blade across his wrist. A kick sent the man to the ground where he lay howling, one hand trying to stem the flow of blood from his injured wrist.

Ralph was astride him with a dagger at his throat.

"Where is my wife?" he demanded.

"Who?"

"Golde. My wife. I know she is here."

"No!"

"Where is she?"

"Not here!" said the man. "You are mistaken. This is the house of Helto the Doctor."

"Are his patients always welcomed with a dagger?"

"You attacked first."

"Where *is* she?" yelled Ralph, using the point of his weapon to draw blood from the man's neck. "Speak or I'll cut your throat out."

"Stop!" pleaded the other, giving in. "I'll tell you."

Ralph grabbed his hair to bang his head on the floor. "Where?"

"Down the cellar. In the kitchen."

The man was too frightened to lie. Ralph pounded his head on the hard wood again, then got up. He searched the ground floor until he found the kitchen, then saw the trap door in the corner. Before he could slide back the bolt, he heard a rustling noise and turned to see his adversary coming at him with the dagger in his other hand.

Ralph's reaction was instinctive. He moved sharply to the left, parried the blow, swung in a circle and brought his own dagger around with deadly force to slide in between the man's ribs. After clinging to the cowl for a moment, the man slid to the ground with blood pouring out of the wound. Ralph retrieved his weapon and opened the trap door. It shed enough light for him to see her.

"Golde! What have they done to you!"

Unable to answer, she struggled from side to side.

He leaped down into the cellar and sliced through her bonds at once, clasping her in his arms and holding her to him. The sheer relief of being together again brought tears cascading down his face. Golde clutched at the blindfold then tore off the gag.

"Thank God you've come!" she sobbed. "They were going to kill me. It was terrifying."

He held her tight and they kissed away a long and frightening absence. Then he guided her gently up the stairs. It was only when they came up into full light that she saw what he was wearing. Her sudden laugh broke the tension.

"Where did you get that?" she asked.

"From Canon Hubert."

"He loaned it to you?"

"Cowl and donkey," said Ralph, grinning. "Not without

a lot of argument, mark you, but the disguise worked. If *he* can pass as a monk, then so can I."

"He?"

"Philippe Berbizier, my love. The man we are after."

"I think I met him."

The memory sent a shiver through her. Golde then noticed the dead man on the ground and let out a cry.

"Is that him?" she asked.

"No, my love. My guess is that he is one of the men who kidnapped you. The other is lying through there with a lump on his head."

"How did you know where to find me?"

"By talking to Eadgyth."

"*She* told you?"

"No, Golde. But when I stepped out of her room, I heard Canon Hubert speaking with Osbern in the solar. Their words were as clear as a bell. Someone on that staircase could spy on the whole house."

"But why should they?"

"To know what steps Gervase and I were taking."

"I do not follow, Ralph."

"How did Berbizier know you were in that house? How did he know what my movements were? Who helped him to outwit me at every turn? Helto."

"The doctor?"

"No wonder he called so often without need," said Ralph. "On his last visit, he even left your wimple in the stables with a letter for me. It had to be him. Nobody else came to Osbern's abode on a horse."

Golde began to understand. "Is that where we are now?"

"Yes, my love. In Helto's house."

"I have been in King Street all this time?"

"Not five minutes from us."

Still dazed by her ordeal, she looked slowly around. "Then where is the doctor himself?"

She gave herself completely. Lying between her thighs, Helto plunged and writhed until his breath was laboured and the perspiration was running down his naked back. He strove on until his passion was spent, then he sagged across her with a long sigh of contentment and fatigue. The girl held him tight until he was ready to roll off her. Without a word, she put on her apparel, then knelt beside the bed. Helto reached out to touch her cheek with an off-hand affection. When she left the room, he lay there to recover and to savour.

Wearing his white robe, he came silently into the chamber. He looked down at his disciple with a dark smile.

"Was she ready for you?"

"Yes," said Helto, still short of breath.

"And you were ready for her," said Berbizier. "As I promised. That is the essence of our sect, Helto. Choosing the right person, preparing her mind, opening her body to the joys of spiritual love. You have now shared in those joys."

"I have," agreed the other, sitting up to reach for his clothing. "Thank you, Philippe."

"You have earned the reward."

"I have tried to serve you loyally."

"Loyally and devotedly," said Berbizier, watching him dress. "Without you, none of this would have been possible. You have been my faithful intelligencer, working inside the city to provide everything that I need."

"Nothing is more important to me, Philippe."

"You found this place of safety for our temple. You helped to choose our neophytes. And—I will be eternally grateful to you for this, Helto—you carried my messages to that sweet, dear girl, Bertha." He gave a sigh of regret. "Such a pity that she could never be initiated into our circle. Bertha was too corrupted by Christianity. So many falsehoods locked inside that beautiful head of hers. If only she had let me open her eyes to the true light."

"Yes." The doctor grinned to himself. "I would have enjoyed teaching Bertha the precepts of our sect."

"No!" snapped the other. "Bertha was mine. All mine."

"Of course," said Helto quickly.

"Nobody else would have touched her. And now nobody else can." He became brisk. "Was everything in order when you left the house?"

"Yes, Philippe."

"Our little bird safely caged in the cellar?"

"They will never find her there."

"Then we can forget her until the morning. You may spend the night here, Helto." The doctor's face lit up. "It is another reward for your dedication."

"The new girl?"

"I have prepared her very carefully."

"She is mine all night, Philippe?" he asked eagerly.

"Yes," said Berbizier. "She is yours but both of you belong to me. Do not forget that. Come, my friend. They are waiting to begin the service. I will preach and there will be laying-on of hands. Beyond that, a long night beckons. With nobody to interrupt our spiritual pleasures."

"Are you quite sure that he will come?" said Ralph Delchard.

"No," admitted Gervase.

"Then what are we doing out here?"

"Obeying instinct, Ralph."

"My instinct is to be in bed with my wife at this hour of the night. Not hiding in the bushes on Harbledown Hill. There are all kinds of animals sniffing about in the dark. Not to mention the danger of snakes!"

"It is the snakes that we are after. Those that walk on two legs. Reinbald the Priest will lead us to them."

"If he deigns to leave the city."

"He will," said Gervase confidently. "He sneaked past the guards last night. Only the most urgent appointment could make him do that. I think he was going to a secret meeting of Philippe Berbizier's sect."

"A parish priest!"

"That is how heresy spreads, Ralph. From clergy to laity. Do not forget that Berbizier himself was once a priest. They subvert the Christian beliefs that they once embraced and taught."

The two men had been there since nightfall. It had taken Gervase a long time to persuade Ralph to join him on the expedition. Two of Ralph's men-at-arms had been left at the house in Burgate Street to protect Golde against any further attack and four others had been installed in Helto's house to arrest the doctor on his return. They were standing near the spot where Alain had been when Reinbald went past on the previous night. Evidently it was the priest's route. Gervase believed that he took it regularly.

"Have you forgotten your trip to Faversham?" he said.

"No man could forget the termagant Juliana."

"Was not Helto eager to be your guide?"

"Very eager. Even though he is a poor horseman."

"And did he not disappear in Faversham?"

"Only for an hour," said Ralph. "We found him at the church. He said that he had been to visit the priest."

"What if his name was Philippe Berbizier?"

Ralph pondered. "It is conceivable," he said at length.

"That might account for his readiness to visit Faversham. But it will not bring him out here tonight."

"Why not?"

"Berbizier is still in the city."

"No, Ralph."

"He is. Golde swears that she met him. Guards are waiting in numbers at every gate. How could Berbizier possibly get out of Canterbury?"

"How could Reinbald the Priest?"

A long whistle terminated their conversation and sent them crouching in the bushes. Six of Ralph's men-at-arms had been stationed at intervals on Harbledown Hill to keep watch for a lone figure leaving the city. The signal confirmed the approach of someone. Ralph and Gervase had to wait five minutes before the man came past. There was no doubting his identity. Reinbald the Priest was following a route he knew by heart. Descending the hill on the far side, he was so intent on reaching his destination that he never thought to look over his shoulder.

Ralph and Gervase tracked him on foot. The soldiers were not far behind, riding their own horses and leading two more by the reins. Reinbald was running now and the two friends had to break into a trot to keep him in sight. The priest suddenly veered off to the left down a narrow path between the trees. Ralph and Gervase paused. A lantern glimmered up ahead of them. Creeping nearer, they could make out the shape of a small cottage. Light showed through the cracks in the shutters. Gervase was excited by the discovery. The priest had indeed led them to Berbizier.

Revenge was uppermost in Ralph's mind. Heresy was no concern of his. Berbizier had ordered Golde's kidnap. That rankled even more than his other crimes. Ralph took charge with cold-eyed efficiency. Beckoning his men with a wave, he made them tether the horses, then fan out to approach the cottage in order to surround it. He and Gervase moved furtively toward the front of the building. When everyone was in position, Ralph went into action.

Tucking in his shoulder, Ralph heaved himself at the door with such force that it burst open on its hinges. He was through it at once, pulling out his sword and yelling at the top of his voice. Gervase and the others followed but they found no members of a heretical sect. Reinbald the Priest had his arms around a young woman, who was screaming in fear. The intruders gaped.

Reinbald made a nervous and shamefaced confession.

"Do not harm us, my lord. This is my wife."

Alain sat in the porch with his back against the church door. Unable to sleep in the cloying warmth of his hut, he had come out in search of a cooler spot to sit and to reflect. The commotion earlier in the day had been succeeded by a deep and restorative calm. Prior Henry and his congregation of monks had exorcised the church and driven out the spirit of evil. The leper hospital was at peace again.

He could never share in that peace. The loss of Bertha could not be repaired by a service conducted by the prior. Nothing could drive out the devil who was eating Alain's flesh from the inside and gnawing at his mind. Life was pain. Memory was his only balm. Bertha would continue to gather herbs to sweeten his moments alone.

The jingle of harness made him stand up. Eight riders were coming his way. They reined in close by and one of them jumped down and walked toward the wattle huts. Recognising Gervase from his profile and gait, Alain hailed him. Gervase trotted across to the church, relieved to find that he did not have to rouse the leper from his sleep.

"We need your help, Alain," he said.

"What could I possibly do?"

"Lead us to the orchard where you found that piece of material. It *was* torn from Bertha's apparel. I matched it to her kirtle. Bertha was there."

"Why?"

"Assist us and we may find out."

"In the dark?"

"It is not the orchard that interests us," explained Gervase, "but the house beyond. Will you take us there?"

"I have no reason."

"This is no casual request, Alain."

"I would rather stay here at the hospital."

"Bertha's killer is in that house."

The leper was stunned. "I'll take you at once, Master Bret," he volunteered. "But it is a mile or more and my pace is slow. You will have to be patient with me."

"Ride my horse."

"You do not *mind*?"

"Nor more will he, Alain," said Gervase. "We need to get there as soon as possible. Lead the way."

The men-at-arms backed away when they saw the leper coming and they were amazed when Gervase actually helped him up into the saddle. When they set off in single file, fear of infection kept the soldiers several yards behind their pathfinder. Ralph, too, had severe reservations about using a leper as their guide. Gervase was seated behind Ralph on his destrier, as they moved along the path at a steady trot.

"This is another wild-goose chase," hissed Ralph.

"Trust me, it is not," said Gervase.

"I do not want to lead an assault on another house to find that our only prisoners are a priest and his wife."

"Clerical marriage is forbidden. That is why Reinbald

had to keep it secret. The archbishop has insisted on a celibate clergy. If he knew the truth, he would throw poor Reinbald out of St. Mildred's and eject the priest who married them privily from his little church in Faversham. Besides," said Gervase, as a branch brushed the side of his face, "the raid was not in vain. We learned much."

"Yes," conceded Ralph. "We learned that Reinbald has a comely wife. No wonder he risked his neck to reach her."

"He told us of the man he saw at midnight, riding by a different way to the manor house ahead of us. Reinbald also told us who lives there."

"Mauger. One of the archbishop's knights."

"The sheriff's officers and the archbishop's men have searched every dwelling in the area except the ones that are above suspicion. Their own. Philippe Berbizier is completely safe while he is under Mauger's roof."

"But how did he get there? Golde was so certain that she met him at Helto's house. How on earth could the rogue get out of Canterbury?"

"Reinbald has given us the answer to that as well."

"I did not hear it."

"Who lives at the manor house?"

"Mauger. One of the archbishop's . . ." Ralph caught up with Gervase's faster mind. "Of course! Berbizier rode through the gates disguised as a soldier."

"A man who will lend him a house will just as readily supply him with a helm and hauberk. Even Reinbald the Priest would pass unnoticed in those."

Ralph chuckled. "I'll wager that he'd enjoy letting that pretty wife of his help him out of them."

Alain slowed to a halt at the edge of the orchard and they dismounted with the minimum of noise, tying their horses to low branches before setting off through the apple trees with a cautious urgency. Alain trailed after them at a more laboured pace. When the house came in sight, they could see the light through the shutters. They could also hear the horses neighing in the stables, suggesting a larger number of occupants than they had found at the cottage.

Ralph saw a problem at once. Two dogs were patrolling the courtyard, sniffing their way across its uneven surface until some sound in the darkness made them lift their heads. Unable to avoid the animals in order to reach the front door, Ralph decided to make use of them and he sent a hushed command along the line. His men spread out once more to approach from different angles.

When they were close enough, Gervase plucked an apple from the nearest tree and threw it just beyond the dogs. As it rolled across the courtyard and away from the house, they turned to race after it. Ralph and his men ran to take up their places near the front door. Gervase then flung two more apples from close range, hitting the same dog twice and making him bark loudly. As more fruit came hurtling out of the darkness at them, both dogs made such a clamorous noise that a servant came out to explore with a lantern.

One blow from Ralph knocked him senseless. He crept through the door with his men at his heels. They were in.

There were twelve of them in the circle. Philippe Berbizier stood in the centre, conducting a service with mocking echoes of the Latin Mass heard daily in every church and cathedral.

"*Introibo ad altare Dei,*" he chanted.

"*Ad Deum qui laetificat iuventutem meam,*" came the response.

"*Adiutorum nostrum in nomine Domini.*"

"*Qui fecit caelum te terram.*"

As the dialogue between celebrant and congregation

continued, he walked to the young girl who had just been admitted to the circle and who was trembling with holy joy. Placing his hands on her head, Berbizier blessed her and welcomed her into the sect. She dropped to her knees in an attitude of submission and kissed his bare feet. He looked down fondly at her and stroked her hair.

It was at this point that Ralph burst in with his men, all of them with drawn swords and clear orders. As the service broke up with screams and yells of protest, the soldiers formed a larger circle of their own to hold the group prisoner. Only Mauger himself, a stout man of middle height, tried to fight his way clear, but a swordpoint at his chest persuaded him to resume his seat.

Helto the Doctor tried to bluff his way out of the situation. Rising to his feet, he gave Ralph an oily smile.

"This is not quite what it seems, my lord."

"Silence!" snarled Ralph, felling him with a blow from his mailed fist. "I did not like what I found in your cellar, Helto. We will have more words about that before I have finished."

Helto cowered on the floor and looked up in alarm at Philippe Berbizier. The Frenchman remained calm and poised. Gervase came in to take stock of the situation. He had expected to find Mauger and Helto in the circle but not the three young women, the two priests and the Benedictine monk. The rest of the sect was made up of lay members who, judging from the quality of their attire, were men of some substance.

Ralph Delchard was only interested in the leader. He gave a command and his men herded everyone else into a corner so that their master could confront Berbizier. Showing no fear, the Frenchman strolled to the chair at the centre of the circle and lowered himself nonchalantly into it. He smiled helpfully.

"How may we help you, my lord?"

"By standing trial for two murders," said Ralph.

"Murders? I am a man of peace."

"Brother Martin did not die peacefully."

"He took his own life with poison. I watched him."

"What about Bertha?"

"She was bitten by a snake."

"I see him before me, trying to hide his fangs." He looked around with disgust. "So these are your followers, are they? Was Bertha dragged into this lunacy by you?"

"We are the true Church, my lord. Do not mock."

"Was she?" pressed Ralph.

"No," said Berbizier sadly. "She was too wedded to the errors of the Christian Church. Even I could not turn her from that false path. We were friends only—but intimate friends. Until she followed me here one evening to spy on our service. I chased her into the orchard and tried to reason with her."

"By throttling her to death."

"Bertha became hysterical. She would have betrayed us."

"You betrayed yourself."

"I am not ashamed of anything I did, my lord," said Berbizier, holding out both hands. "Come, tie my hands, if you wish. I am not armed, as you see. I will not resist."

When Ralph took a step toward him, Berbizier reacted with lightning speed, snatching the chair from beneath him and hurling it into his captor's face to send him staggering back. Gervase tried to intercept him as he raced for the door but Berbizier had pulled a dagger from his sleeve and slashed wildly at him. Rushing into the passage, he headed for the front door in the hope of escaping into the night on a horse. But someone was obstructing his exit.

"Out of my way!" roared Berbizier, brandishing his dagger.

The man in the doorway did not move. He simply lifted up the lantern which had been discarded by the fallen servant and held it close to a face which was exposed completely to view. Philippe Berbizier found himself staring into the rotting visage of a leper. He stopped in fear.

The delay gave Ralph the chance to catch him up, grab his shoulder and spin him round. Berbizier jabbed with his dagger but Ralph caught his wrist, twisted hard and sent the weapon clattering to the ground. Dropping his sword, he dived at the Frenchman and knocked him down. It was a fierce fight. Berbizier was strong and wiry, squirming from beneath his opponent, pushing his head back with a palm under the chin, then trying to gouge his eyes. They rolled over and over in the narrow passage, watched by Gervase at one end and Alain at the other.

Berbizier struggled hard but Ralph was too powerful. He was fired by the memory of what the man had done to Golde and to his two murder victims. Punching him until his resistance waned, Ralph got a grip on his throat and squeezed hard. Gervase had to pull his friend away before he killed the man. Philippe Berbizier had to be arrested and tried so that his heresy was made public and his fate turned into an example to all.

The Serpent of Harbledown had been caught at last.

❧ EPILOGUE

CEREMONIAL WAS VERY dear to Archbishop Lanfranc. It lent dignity to an occasion, it rendered it memorable and it raised the visibility of the Christian Church. He lost no opportunity to sanction a legitimate procession through the streets of Canterbury and would—if the event merited his presence—take part himself in his archiepiscopal robes and mitre. Ceremonial had another function. Lanfranc could use it as a huge, colourful curtain to draw across the squalor and misery from which every city inevitably suffered.

The procession that afternoon had a twin purpose. It was a celebration of the Church's triumph over heresy and it honoured the installation of Abbot Guy as the new father of St. Augustine's Abbey. Lanfranc abhorred delay. Though Guy had only arrived in the city that morning, his consecration as abbot followed the same afternoon. Having quelled rebellion at the abbey, Lanfranc was determined to close down the space in which it could flare up again.

Abbot Guy was more than happy to comply, believing that his obedientiaries should feel the smack of firm control at the earliest possible time.

A muscular young monk led the way, bearing a large cross at the end of a long heavy pole. Its shadow fell across all whom it passed and baptised them softly. Archbishop Lanfranc himself came next, moving slowly in his sacerdotal array and raising a tired hand to acknowledge the crowd with almost papal authority. Prior Henry was on his left, proud of his role in helping to combat heresy and gratified that Philippe Berbizier was now fettered in a dungeon. On the archbishop's right hand was Abbot Guy, a thin, shrewd, ascetic man with a reputation for strictness and a disdain of easy popularity.

Monks from Christ Church Priory formed the body of the procession, walking in pairs and raising their voices in a hymn of joy, their mellifluous chant blending with the peal of bells from the cathedral. The procession left the precinct and swung left up Burh Street, which was already lined by the curious populace. On through Burgate they went, at the leisurely pace of the great and the good. When they came to the abbey, they expected its doors to be flung open wide to welcome their new abbot.

Instead, they remained defiantly closed. Only one monk was waiting to greet the august assembly and he was no longer a member of the community. It was Gregory, the deposed prior and erstwhile leader of the dissenting brothers. He had been authorised to communicate a dread message.

"They are adamant, Your Grace. They refuse to obey."

Abbot Guy stiffened, Prior Henry turned puce and Archbishop Lanfranc fumed with controlled rage. Lest he be seen to be part of the resistance, Gregory gave a humble bow and, smiling inwardly at the general discomfiture, moved to join the end of the column as one of its dutiful members.

Lanfranc sent a monk to pound on the abbey door. It opened to reveal the entire community, standing shoulder to shoulder as they awaited the primate's response. It was loud and menacing. Lanfranc showed that he would brook no mutiny.

"He that will not obey his archbishop," he announced, "let him depart this place at once."

There was a momentary hesitation, then the monks filed out with a purposeful stride. They went past their new abbot without even a glance. The exodus continued until there were no more than a handful of monks inside the abbey. Old, weak, fearful or unable to defy their archbishop, they formed a poor congregation for such an important occasion.

Archbishop Lanfranc was not to be baulked.

"Come, Abbot Guy," he said. "You will be enthroned."

The scandal was still raging the following morning and it afforded Ralph Delchard endless amusement. He and Gervase Bret had arrived at the shire hall to recommence their work as commissioners. Even though it had shifted decisively away from their own arena, the battle between cathedral and abbey could not be ignored.

"By all, this is wonderful!" said Gervase. "Each new day brings a fresh delight. Two nights ago, we met an amorous priest with a forbidden wife. Yesterday, the monks of the abbey rebelled against the archbishop. And today, some of those same brave fellows are still barricaded inside St. Mildred's Church, saying that they would rather starve to death than accept Abbot Guy." He shook with mirth.

"When the Church can make me laugh so much, I almost begin to take it seriously."

"It is not really a subject for ridicule," said Gervase. "Have you any idea what will happen to those monks who still resist Archbishop Lanfranc?"

"Yes. They'll do what all the others did. Hunger is a cunning advocate. They will not find starvation quite so attractive a road when they have staggered a little way along it. I believe they will soon come out and kneel to the archbishop."

"And then?"

"He will scold them roundly and send them back."

"No, Ralph," said Gervase. "Those who have held out will never enter the abbey again. They will be dispersed to other monastic foundations with letters from the archbishop to explain that they are in disgrace. As for their leader, he is to be stripped, tied to the door of the abbey and flogged."

"Who told you all this?"

"Canon Hubert."

"Flogged in public?"

"Mercilessly. And then evicted from the Order."

Ralph was shocked. "Lanfranc has decided this?"

"Yes."

"But Hubert told us the man was a saint."

"Even saints can lose their temper at times."

"I am sorry for the leader of this revolt," said Ralph, "but I am heartened to know that there is steel in the good archbishop. If this is how he treats his own monks, imagine how much more ruthless he will be towards Philippe Berbizier and his accomplices. Flogging would be too light a sentence for him. I would happily be his executioner."

"Leave him to the rigour of the law and the condemnation of the Church," suggested Gervase. "We have done our share. Bertha's death is answered and her father can die in peace. Brother Martin's murder has been solved and the church of St. Nicholas is once again unpolluted."

"Golde's sufferings have been avenged as well. She is now free to help Eadgyth in a pressing task."

"Looking after the baby?"

"No, Gervase. Finding a new doctor."

Canon Hubert sailed in with Brother Simon. Both wore stern expressions and gave only muted greetings. It was evident that they were deeply embarrassed by Lanfranc's difficulties with perverse monks. Ralph spread a little early-morning unease.

"What is your view of clerical marriage, Hubert?" he said.

"It is expressly forbidden," said Hubert.

"Do you support that edict?"

"To the hilt. A priest should be pure and unsullied. Like myself and Brother Simon here."

"But what of a priest, for the sake of argument, who fell in love *before* Archbishop Lanfranc made his decree? Imagine his plight. He is betrothed at an early age and wants nothing more than to share his life, his work and his bed with his beloved. Then along comes this ruling from above and he learns that he is divorced before he is even married."

"He must renounce the girl."

"Supposing he is not willing?"

"His duty is simple. He has no choice."

"He can resign his ministry," noted Gervase.

"There is a third way," said Ralph mischievously. "What if he were to remain a priest but marry in secret?"

"An abomination!" exclaimed Brother Simon.

"He would not be able to serve God properly."

"But he would be able to serve his wife."

"My lord!" blustered Hubert.

"I merely put a case to you."

"If you know of such a one, he must be reported to the archbishop forthwith. Carnal knowledge is unbecoming in a man of God. Do you have a priest in mind?"

"No, Canon Hubert," said Gervase, jumping in quickly. "Ralph is teasing you. In any case, would Archbishop Lanfranc really have time for such a minor malefactor when he has so much else on his hands? Heresy in the city and dissension at the abbey will keep his mind occupied for some time."

"That is true, Gervase."

Osbern the Reeve appeared at the door to await orders. They took their seats and brought out documents from their satchels to set on the table before them. As Hubert put some charters in front of him, he noted the neat repair in the sleeve of his cowl.

"I am deeply grateful to your wife, my lord."

"Golde insisted on sewing up your sleeve herself. I got it slashed while trying to save her. Your cowl had many exciting adventures while I wore it."

"I am glad that it has been restored to me."

"Even though you may think it contaminated?"

"By what, my lord?"

"The very thing you spoke of just now. Marriage."

"I do not understand."

"When I rescued Golde, I did so as Canon Hubert. She was so relieved to see me that she embraced me warmly. A dagger is not the only thing which touched your cowl. It has felt the true warmth of marital passion."

Brother Simon was outraged and Canon Hubert began to pat himself all over as if he had a wasp inside his cowl. Ralph rocked with laughter. Having thoroughly upset the pair of them, he signalled to Osbern to bring in the first witness. Then he turned to nudge Gervase.

"Do not fear," he whispered. "I would never betray our wanton priest. Every man is entitled to keep one big secret."

Gervase thought of Alain at the leper hospital.

"Yes," he said. "Just one."